Country Passions

Rebecca Shaw

An Orion paperback

First published in Great Britain in 2004
by Orion
This paperback edition published in 2005
by Orion Books Ltd,
Orion House, 5 Upper St Martin's Lane,
London WC2H 9EA

An Hachette Livre company

A CIP catalogue record for this book is
available from the British Library.

Typeset at The Spartan Press Ltd,
Lymington, Hants

Printed and bound in Great Britain by
Clays Ltd, St Ives plc

The Orion Publishing Group's policy is to use papers that
are natural, renewable and recyclable products and
made from wood grown in sustainable forests. The logging
and manufacturing processes are expected to conform to
the environmental regulations of the country of origin.

www.orionbooks.co.uk

They climbed the narrow stairs, Oscar leading the way and Scott pushing her up step by step. Every footfall was an effort, and she clung to the handrail as though about to roll back down the stairs if she didn't.

Scott went into the bathroom to get her a drink of water while she undressed. He could hear Oscar saying, 'Mummy! Shoes off. Mummy! Please.'

But it was Scott who removed her shoes, Scott who undressed her with Oscar's help, Scott who tidied the bed for her and Scott who persuaded her to lie down. He pulled up the duvet, lifted Oscar up so he could give her a kiss and couldn't help smiling thinking of Zoe's words when the two of them kissed in front of Samson lying in pieces on the operating table. And now he'd undressed her, something he would have loved to do in the right circumstances, but it couldn't have been less romantic, their own son giving a hand. Would they never get things right?

'Doctor's on his way, Zo. Leave everything to me. I'll sort out things at the practice, don't fret.'

In acknowledgement of his generosity her hand came out from under the duvet and caressed his cheek, then she pulled the duvet right over her head to shut out the world. He thought to himself that she couldn't have looked more unattractive, tear-streaked and exhausted as she was, but the touch of her hand on his cheek was sheer bliss.

Educated at a co-educational Quaker boarding school, Rebecca Shaw went on to qualify as a teacher of deaf children. After her marriage, she spent the ensuing years enjoying bringing up her family. The departure of the last of her four children to university has given her the time and opportunity to write. *One Hot Country Summer*, published in hardback by Orion, is the latest novel in the Barleybridge series from Rebecca Shaw. In the Barleybridge series she has created an enchanting cast of characters, recreating the warmth and humour her readers have come to love and expect. Visit Rebecca Shaw's website at www.rebeccashaw.co.uk.

By Rebecca Shaw

LIST OF CHARACTERS AT BARLEYBRIDGE VETERINARY HOSPITAL

Mungo Price	Orthopaedic Surgeon and Senior Partner
Colin Walker	Partner – large and small animal
Zoe Savage	Partner – large animal
Daniel Franklin Brown	Partner – large animal
Graham Murgatroyd	Small animal
Valentine Dedic	Small animal
Rhodri Hughes	Small animal

NURSING STAFF
Sarah Cockroft (Sarah One)
Sarah MacMillan (Sarah Two)
Bunty Bird

RECEPTIONISTS
Joy Bastable (Practice Manager)
Stephie Budge
Annette Smith

Miriam Price	Mungo's wife
Duncan Bastable	Joy's husband
Letty Walker	Colin's wife
Rose Franklin Brown	Dan's wife
Megan Jones	Rhodri's wife
Nadia Dedic	Valentine's wife

Phil and Blossom Parsons of Applegate Farm and their foster son Hamish. Lord Askew, the local squire and stud owner. Mr Idris Jones of Beulah Bank Top, Megan's father. Miranda Costello, eccentric animal lover.

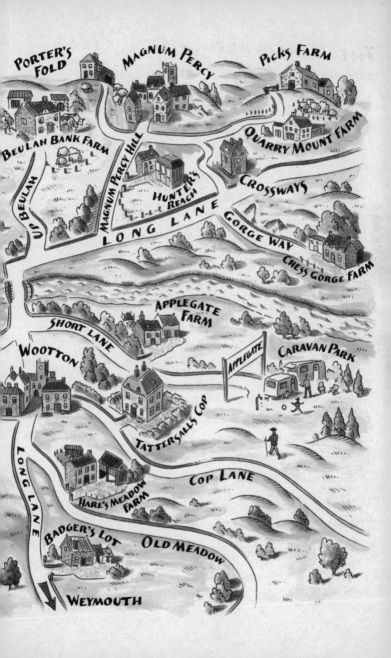

Chapter 1

Zoe slammed the back door shut and stalked across the car park to her car seething with temper. How dare Graham look at her with those lustful eyes? By what right? It was always the same when you had a child but no wedding ring on your finger; easy virtue was always the assumption. Well, believe me, Graham, this time you've backed the wrong horse. Zoe flung her visiting list onto the front passenger seat, climbed in and started the engine. She reversed furiously, went into first and almost ran down Dan as he went out to his car. Nothing less than he deserved. He always, *always* seemed to be waiting to pounce for some misdemeanour or other of hers. As she slowed before turning into the main road she recollected his reasons and shrugged. To hell with him. She glanced in her rear-view mirror and saw he was already waiting behind her. Right now he'd be saying to himself, 'Women drivers!' and criticizing her for not pulling away as sharply as he supposed he would in the circumstances.

As the traffic cleared momentarily, she swung away into the road, glad that Dan had turned left over the bridge and was not following her. Zoe loved driving. If only she could have a soft-top car then she'd have the roof down all year round, with the wind blowing her hair and invigorating her. But with drugs to be carried a vet's vehicle had to be secure.

1

Her first call was to Lord Askew's dairy herd. The daft old goat. But you had to admire him for sticking to his principles, even if they were as outdated as a horse and cart. Still, at least she didn't have to deal with him. She could leave all that to Dan with his instinctive equine talents. Zoe's face screwed up when she thought that as though she'd tasted something very sour. Huh!

The stable courtyard was built as beautifully as the main house. What taste the Georgians had! Such beauty. She parked as close to the archway into the farmyard as she could and went to find Chris, the head stock man, her spirits lifting as she smelled the warm, comforting smell of cows kept inside because of the severe weather. There was one thing about cows – they were always even-tempered. Never resentful or irritable, unless they were in pain, just patient and willing. She tried calling his name. Must be at breakfast. Since he would have been up since five or so she decided to leave him in peace and went to sit on the mounting block in the stableyard for a while.

It was cold, almost beyond belief, but there was a brilliant sun shining with the crisp smell of frost in the air and Zoe loved it. Small animals! Give her large animals any time. OK, sometimes her strength ran out when she was heaving an unwilling sheep, or battling with a difficult calving, but by craft and guile, learned with experience, she usually managed. In any case, it always boosted a man's ego if she had to ask for help.

Sound carried well in the sharp air and she heard his lordship coming back from his early ride long before she saw him. She'd half a mind to leap off the mounting block and escape him but the sheer cussedness that possessed her this morning made her stay.

He'd not lost a single stone of his massive weight. Still

2

the same florid face, the shoulders like giant hams, the big fleshy hands masterfully holding the reins, his thick legs tucked into his hugely shiny chestnut-coloured riding boots. Give him his due, he could ride. Impressive he was. His fine black horse, one of the biggest hunters she'd ever seen, took a very able rider to control him and was still lively even though he was sweating from his exercise. Professional politeness got her to her feet. 'Good morning, Lord Askew. Fine morning for a ride.'

Lord Askew swung down from the saddle, planted his great feet on the ground and said, 'Made all the better for seeing you, my dear. How are we this morning? In fine fettle, I see. What a pleasant sight; you match the morning! Happy New Year to you!'

'And to you, my lord.' Zoe remembered to say what she knew would please him. 'I see Lady Mary had considerable success at Olympia.'

'Indeed she did. Very proud of the gal I am. Not only Galaxy but Constellation too did well. Thank God that Dan of yours spotted Galaxy's problem.' The downturn of Zoe's mouth at the mention of Dan's expertise amused him. 'Breakfasted this morning?'

'No, I'm just waiting for Chris to finish his.'

Lord Askew's face lost its hail-fellow-well-met look. 'Call him out! It's what I pay him for.'

'I most certainly shan't. He'll have already been up at least three hours and he deserves to refuel. And for what I imagine you pay him for all the hours he puts in he's earned his break.'

Lord Askew, liking feisty women, said, 'Hmm. Well. You have breakfast with me then while you wait.' He ran an expert eye over Zoe and mentally licked his lips.

'Thanks all the same, but no. I've lots to do. Good

3

morning to you, my lord.' She deliberately turned her back on him and went through the archway because she'd heard Chris's boots slurping along, almost beating a tattoo as his boot heels bumped along the cobbled yard.

'Hi Chris! Lead me to the offending cow. I'm in a mood for instant diagnosis!'

'Glad about that because she has me foxed and not half. Happy New Year to you!'

'And to you.'

They went companionably through into the largest of the cow byres and became lost in veterinary discussions, which were meat and drink to them both. By the time Zoe left, Lord Askew was already back in the stableyard talking to Gavin, his head groom. Zoe waved to them both, calling out New Year greetings to Gavin, who sulkily acknowledged them. Obviously Gavin was getting torn to pieces over something. Lord Askew touched the peak of his cap to her and said nothing. How she'd hate to have him as her employer. Tied house, long hours and an attitude that said you owed Lord Askew something for the privilege of working for him. One day she'd have the most horrendous row with him, she knew she would. It was inevitable.

Beulah Bank Farm next and then along the cart track, which she used as a short cut to skirt past Magnum Percy to reach Pick's Farm. She enjoyed the drive to Beulah Bank, steep, twisting and very dangerous if it had snowed and afterwards frozen over. But today the icy patches would only be where the trees had prevented the sun shining on the road. Zoe decided to call into the Practice on the way with the samples she'd collected from the sick Guernsey at Lord Askew's and a quick coffee wouldn't go amiss.

4

She took them into the office to leave them with Joy. 'Here we are, samples to go off today, please.'

Joy glanced at the clock. 'It took a while there?'

'Well, Chris had gone for his breakfast so I had to wait.' Zoe leaned over the desk and asked quietly, 'You didn't hear from Duncan for Christmas?'

'How do you know I didn't?'

'Light's gone out of your face again, that's how I know. Thought you might hear, you know, festive season and all that.'

'Well, I didn't.' Joy fidgeted with a pen on her desk. 'Primarily it's all my fault, which doesn't help.'

'You mean Mungo?'

Joy stared at her and eventually nodded agreement.

'Duncan knows, obviously?'

The answer to Zoe's question was another nod from Joy.

'It could be described as banging your head against a brick wall. Mungo will never forsake Miriam for anyone, you know that, and still you persist. You must be mad. Absolutely mad. No man's worth that kind of devotion.'

'Some are.'

'I know Mungo's an absolute prize, a total charmer in fact, but there are limits.'

Somewhat tartly Joy asked, 'You know all about men, do you?'

'Not all, but a lot. Anyhow, it's you who's been left with *nothing*, no lover, no husband, so just think on that. Going for a coffee, it's blasted cold out there.'

Zoe turned on her heel and left as abruptly as she'd come. The coffee with plenty of sugar in it revived her flagging spirits and she was off to Beulah Bank in no time at all.

This was the best bit of veterinary practice, all the darting about from one farm to another, never knowing from one day to the next where you'd be going, what problems you'd have to solve, who you'd be chatting to about the best subject in the world.

Beulah Bank Farm nestled in the foothills, sheltered from the wind by the high point of the moor above Barleybridge. Zoe always had the same thought as she arrived in the farmyard. If she had to choose somewhere else to live and she had the money she'd live here. The views from the back of the house were spectacular. She saw Megan waving to her from the kitchen window and waved back. She didn't go in but shouted through the window that she'd find Josh first and then come in for a word when she'd finished.

She found Josh sitting in a stable with the lad. They had a fan heater going, the electric light on and the lad was dealing a hand of cards onto the old trunk they used for a table.

'Hi, Zoe.' Josh pulled up a box for her to sit on.

'What's this, then? Here am I, slaving my guts out in all this cold weather, and you two are as snug as two bugs in a rug, playing cards.'

The lad winked.

Josh laughed. 'He's beating me. Would you believe it? Beating me.' He punched the lad on his arm.

Zoe, who had a soft spot for the lad, said jokingly, 'Well, it's not your brains is it, lad? It's your sheer native cunning.'

'Won two pounds off him this Christmas, I have.'

'Good lad. Just what I like to hear. Well, come on then, Josh, let's be having you. Rhodri said one of your ewes was in distress. Said something about her being special.'

6

They turned off the fan heater, put on their warm coats and stumped off with her to a sheep pen at the far side of the barn. 'She's early, been straining since first light. I've had a feel round and I don't like it. It's beyond me. I don't want anything to happen to her. She's Megan's pet sheep Myfanwy.'

'I'll have a look.' Zoe believed in hands on and didn't always bother with the elbow-length plastic gloves and . . . 'My word, you don't think it could be quads, do you? There's an almighty jumble in here.' She was silent for a moment and then said, 'There's an awful lot of legs. OK, old girl, OK. Zoe's doing her best. Has she had a multiple birth before?'

'Megan says she's had twins twice before, but then that's common nowadays. Bloody hell! You don't really think it might be quads?'

The lad's eyes grew large with interest. 'Is that four? I'd best boil a kettle like they do in films.'

Josh muttered, 'It's not a baby she's having, it's a lamb, you daft beggar.'

'I know. I know. But it's Megan's, shouldn't we do something special?'

Zoe, still feeling about inside the ewe, said, 'You can bring me a big bucket of hot water and a bar of soap, please. I'll need that.'

'Right!' The lad got up off his knees and dashed away, bent on doing the right thing. 'Bucket of hot water and a bar of soap. Bucket of hot water and a bar of soap.'

He came back with some towels too and the news that Megan was coming when she'd put the baby in his cradle.

Zoe was still knee-deep in straw, trying as best she could to disentangle however many there were inside Myfanwy. 'I've nearly got one of them. How's the mother looking?'

'Down in the mouth. Straining all the time.'

'Don't I know it. She's making it difficult.'

Zoe gave a heave, the nose and front feet of a lamb appeared, and then out on the straw popped one of the smallest lambs she'd ever seen, bleating though and struggling. Megan arrived at that moment and said, 'It's small.'

'Exactly. Can it go in your warming oven, Megan, just for an hour while I sort out the rest? Needs a bit of TLC. Not too happy about it. The lad'll give it a clean with some straw for you.'

'Quads or triplets, do you think? That must be why it's so small. Here we are, young lady.' Megan scooped up the lamb in one of the towels she'd sent in with the lad and, snuggling it inside her jacket, went back to the house.

Zoe managed to extricate another lamb, bigger and stronger than the first, and then the third. The fourth slipped out easily. She sat back in the straw. 'Well, there's a first time for everything and this is my first set of quads. Wonderful! I'll give Myfanwy a booster and some antibiotic as a precaution, she's had a rough time. Give those lambs a good rub with the towel, lad, she's too weary to bother just yet. I'll do the injections and then we'll see if she'll let them feed.'

Josh was beside himself with delight. 'It's a first for me too. Brilliant. I can't believe it. Though a lamb in the house will be a lot of work for Megan with the baby, too.'

'Leave that to me. I'll get Old Man Jones on with feeding it. He needs to earn his living somehow.'

'You'll not. He's an awkward cuss, he is. The less I have to do with him the better.'

'Just you wait and see.'

Josh grunted, 'I'll wait a long time.'

'You won't. See, look, she's letting them suckle. Great,

they're real doers, this lot.' The lambs' little tails were waggling excitedly as they drew down their very first food from their mother's udder. 'If I was a sentimentalist I'd say, "Don't they look sweet?".' Zoe rubbed her hands and arms vigorously with the soap, rinsed them clean in the bucket and dried them off on her sweater.

'I'll leave you here and go see Old Man Jones.'

Josh shouted after her, 'Bet you a pound.'

'You've lost already,' came Zoe's voice on the wind.

In the sheep pen Josh and the lad knelt in the straw together, admiring the lambs and marvelling at the mother's loving attention. 'Wonder how little Tom Thumb's doing?' asked the lad.

'Tomasina more like. He was a she.'

'Oh! That's what we want, isn't it? Girls?'

Josh had to smile at the innocence of his double entendre. That was what both of them wanted but were unlikely to get.

Zoe tapped on the back door of the farmhouse and opened it shouting, 'It's me! How are we doing in the oven department?'

Leaving her boots outside the door, she padded into the kitchen and couldn't help smiling to herself. The pound was hers, no doubt about it. 'Good morning, Mr Jones. How is she?'

As far as he was able, in that he was crippled with arthritis, Megan's father turned to look at her. He was sitting in a chair by the cooker with the newborn lamb on his lap, trying to get it to suck from a baby's feeding bottle. 'Not so good. She's no strength to suck.'

'I'll watch for a moment.'

Mr Jones was right. She was eager but couldn't muster any energy for the life-giving milk.

'I've got just the thing in my car.'

Zoe returned carrying a syringe, which she used for dosing various noxious liquids such as worming potions. 'This is brand new, never been used, and I can't think of a better use for it at the moment than feeding this little scrap.'

She drew some of the milk into the syringe and handed it to Mr Jones. By dribbling the milk in drop by drop through the syringe so there was no effort on the lamb's part except swallowing, he managed to get some milk into her. Zoe's approving tone when she said, 'Your kind of patience is just what she needs,' gave Old Man Jones the impetus to volunteer to take over feeding.

He took his eyes from the lamb for a moment and said, 'Normally I would have thought it a waste of valuable time keeping a lamb like this alive, better to finish it here and now, but being one of quads and one of Myfanwy's I think we'll have a go.' He glanced towards the door to check that Megan wasn't within hearing distance and whispered, 'Megan needs a boost. Very low at the moment.'

'Ah! Right, I see. Post baby, you mean?'

Mr Jones nodded. 'Rough time at the birth, and she's not really recovered. So we've got to succeed. Can you put her back in the oven for me?'

Zoe took the fragile lamb from him and briefly hugged it, enjoying the homely smell of it and the weight of it in her arms; it reminded her of Oscar when he was newborn. 'There we are, young lady. You hang in there, for Megan. Right.' She placed the lamb on the blanket in the bottom of the oven and left the door ajar. Zoe was so moved by this lamb hovering between life and death she almost kissed it before she let go of it, but that kind of slushy behaviour to an animal was against her nature so she didn't. 'All I can say is thank heavens for an Aga. They do have their uses. Be seeing you, Mr Jones. Any probs give me a bell. Anytime. For some reason I've taken a shine to this lamb, seeing as she's one of my first quadruplets ever. What a start to the New Year.'

'We'll give it a damn good try. Many thanks and good morning to you, Zoe. Happy New Year.'

'And to you. And to Megan, of course.'

'Of course.'

Zoe took the cart track to Pick's Farm, leaving Magnum Percy undisturbed, and joined the tarmac road to the farm thinking about her lunch. At least today this was her last call, except for emergencies, so she'd treat herself to lunch in Barleybridge, do some vital shopping and go home.

She arrived home three hours later to be greeted by her mother in complaining mode.

'Zoe! Where have you been? I'm at my wits' end. Oscar's done nothing but race about all morning and it's been too cold for me to take him for a walk.'

'Didn't you take him to nursery?'

'No.' Her mother avoided looking at her so Zoe knew she'd not taken him on purpose.

'Why not?'

'Because . . .'

'Yes?'

'Because I couldn't be bothered.'

'So don't complain at me that's he's driven you crackers.' She walked into the sitting room and was aghast at what she saw. There were toys everywhere, apparently flung out of the toy cupboard then discarded, some of them without even being played with. There wasn't anything which annoyed her more. 'This room would have stayed tidy if only you'd taken him. Look at it. Just look at it.'

Hands on hips, her mother, with that icy tone Zoe knew only too well, said, 'Well, he's your son, you tidy it.'

A thought occurred to Zoe. 'Where is he?'

'I've no idea. I went out to the bin—'

'And left the door open, of course.'

'I was only out a moment and he'd disappeared.'

'How long ago was that?'

Her mother glanced at the clock. 'Ten minutes.'

'Half an hour more like! God! Mother, you need your brains examining.'

Zoe ran at a furious pace into every room in the house, which didn't take long. 'He's not in the house. Anywhere. Had he a coat on?'

'Of course not, he was in the house.'

'What then? The clothes I put out before I left?'

'Well, he didn't want his jumper on so he just had a T-shirt. Said it was his tickly one and he didn't like it. I hadn't the energy to insist.'

Zoe shrugged her coat back on again and rushed outside into the lane calling, calling, 'Oscar! Oscar! Oscar!' Eventually she spotted him coming out of a neighbour's gate.

'Mummy! Not in. All gone out.' He ran to her, arms outstretched. In her relief Zoe clasped him to her and swung him round and round.

'You're a naughty boy, do you know that? A very naughty boy. Granny's cross.'

'Mummy cross?'

Zoe nuzzled her face into the softness of Oscar's neck. 'Not cross, but very worried. Boys your age should never run off without someone with them. Don't do it again. Ever. OK?'

Oscar's thumb was in his mouth and his blond head snuggled onto her shoulder.

'Hungry?'

Oscar nodded.

'Then while I make lunch, you go say sorry to Granny. Right?'

Oscar nodded.

'Really sorry. She's very upset.'

Zoe carried him back up the lane to her house, closed the garden gate with the special catch she'd had fitted to keep him safe, though why she did that when he'd apparently already learned to undo it she had no idea, and then stood looking up at her house.

Twelve years she'd been qualified and what had she to show for it? A dream of a country cottage, which though small was very lovely, a son whom she adored when she remembered, a mother who endeavoured on a daily basis to drive her out of her mind, a partnership bought with Dad's money, which meant a good job which she loved . . . but that was it.

Zoe hitched Oscar's weight onto her other hip and marched up the path, determined not to row with her mother if she could possibly help it. The sitting room hadn't been touched, the lunch not even started even though it was two o'clock and Oscar wouldn't have eaten since she'd given him his breakfast at half past seven, and her mother was stretched out in an easy chair with a G and T in her hand. Zoe's temper rose inside her like bile.

'I work damned hard to keep a roof over your head. I feed you, pay all the bills, shop for you, pay for your car, your pension is your own, what more can I do? All you're asked to do is look after Oscar. Taking him to nursery isn't that onerous, is it? You know, turn the key in the ignition, take off the handbrake and go. I bought the car, I pay for the petrol, what's hard about that? It must be easier than this.' Zoe waved her arm at the chaos in her sitting room.

Joan Savage took a sip of gin before she replied, 'I don't approve of nursery at his age. He shouldn't need to go. You should have married his father.' She paused and then added spitefully, 'Whoever *he* was.'

Zoe stood Oscar down saying to him, 'Lunch in five minutes, go play for a minute.'

'Hungry. Cri'ps? Biccy?'

'In a minute.' She leaned over her mother and with her mouth close to her ear she said, 'I've told you before, don't mention his father in his presence. I won't have it.'

'I haven't mentioned him because I don't know who he is. So how can I?'

Zoe looked at Oscar, at the blond hair, his fair skin and his big blue eyes, so unlike herself, but the familiar pang she usually felt was missing. Maybe at long last she'd got over him. Then Oscar smiled at her. 'Juice?' he said and before she knew it, his smile had re-awakened the memories of his father.

Chapter 2

While Zoe was spending what remained of her afternoon off taking Oscar out for a walk through the woods and paddling in a stream, cracking the ice at the edges with their boot heels, Joy was experiencing a seriously bad afternoon. Two clients on the small animal side arrived believing they had made appointments, which proved not to have been entered in the schedules, and as both Graham and Valentine had full lists it meant squeezing the unexpected clients in between other appointments. Nothing annoyed her more than this happening and she swore that before nightfall she would have found the guilty party and had a severe word. Either Stephie or Annette was at fault.

But worse was yet to come.

Dan had been out since early morning driving from one farm to another on severely icy roads. He was using his own car because the Land Rover was in for a badly needed servicing. He was cautiously climbing the hill from Chess Gorge Farm where he'd been seeing to one of their ponies and on the steep climb up towards the main road at Crossways, Dan saw a farm lorry approaching him. He drew in close to the hedgerow to leave plenty of space for it, then, too late realized it was beginning to go out of control. Unable to take any action to avoid it, he watched with horror as the lorry skidded on the ice towards him.

The noise of crunching metal was terrifying, and the impact of his forehead on the windscreen and then the crushing of him by his own distorted dashboard and his smashed car door, momentarily knocked him unconscious.

When he came to there was silence.

Broken in moments by the lorry driver appearing at his smashed door, numb with shock.

The chap tried to open it but he couldn't and so shouted through the shattered glass, 'All right?'

'No.'

'Well, then.'

'I can't get out, my legs are trapped.'

'Door won't open.'

'Then could you kindly get me some help? Like an ambulance, or the fire brigade to cut me out.'

The lorry driver shrugged. 'Got no phone. Nearest is at the Dog and Partridge. My lorry won't move.'

'Use my mobile.' It was on the seat beside him and Dan, despite the pain of which he was suddenly becoming aware, reached for it and handed it to the chap through the broken glass.

Solicitously the driver observed, 'Mind, be careful, you don't want a scratch with broken glass. Glass cuts deep.'

Rather sarcastically Dan said, 'That's the least of my problems. Go on then nine, nine, nine.'

'Ah! Right.'

When they arrived, the ambulance medics found Dan sweating and grey from the pain.

'Keep absolutely still. You'll need cutting out.'

The remainder of his rescue went by through a haze of searing pain and then unconsciousness.

In a lucid moment he phoned Rose and told her his news but nothing at all about the severity of the crash. 'No, no, darling, I'm absolutely fine, just taking me to hospital for a check-up, don't worry please. Barleybridge A&E. That's right. No need to come to the hospital, I'll be OK.' Then he fainted dead away. His last conscious effort was to switch off his phone.

When Joy heard the police saying they were taking him to hospital as soon as he'd been extricated from the car she felt sick at the thought of how close Dan must have been to being killed. Having to be cut out of his car! Heavens above. Then to her shame she selfishly thought, Hell! Now what? How would they manage? With them all working at full stretch, and Dan obviously going to be out of action for a while they were almost completely stuffed as far as farm work was concerned, except for Zoe and Colin.

Rose needed to know. Joy rang her number, planning, while she waited for Rose to answer, how tactfully she could best phrase her news.

'Rose Franklin Brown speaking. Oh, it's you, Joy. It's all right, they rang me first. Don't worry. I'm going to the hospital right now. My help's looking after Jonathan. No! Please. Just let me go. I'll ring with any news. No, no, he's conscious, I've spoken to him. Thanks for ringing. Yes, yes, I will. Bye for now.'

Rose squeezed herself as best she could behind the wheel of her Volvo, took a deep breath to calm her nerves, fastened her safety belt and set off, hands gripping the steering wheel with fierce determination. Rose's one thought was how badly had Dan been hurt. In her head she could hear the almost superhuman effort Dan had made in order to be able to speak reassuringly to her, but she knew in her heart of hearts that matters were serious. You didn't have a big farm lorry score down the side of your car and emerge uninjured. She paused at that stupid roundabout which no one liked, went what she considered to be the wrong way round it and ended up in the hospital car park, parking quite by chance in exactly the same space as when she'd brought Letty to the hospital that time and Letty had proved to be pregnant. Well, that was good news *then*, maybe *she'd* have good news *now*.

They'd taken Dan down for a brain scan when she arrived in A&E so Rose sat patiently waiting his return. They'd given her the news about Dan quite cheerfully but Rose could sense there was an awful lot they weren't telling her. Dan! Dan! I love you. So much. Please don't let go. Stay here for me. For Jonathan. For this little one. Rose placed a soothing hand on her bump and briefly communicated with this new one like she did every day during her pregnancy. Two months to go. Dan! Dan! She couldn't stop his name running through her head. It was all she could think to say. Dan! Dan! Begging him to stay alive.

A lone woman left the department, weeping inconsolably. For a single second Rose thought that might be herself in a moment, in an hour, tomorrow. No! No! She'd no one she could call who could comfort her like Dan could. No one at all. Oh God! Please. He hadn't the best of good looks, he could be tetchy, he didn't suffer fools gladly and sometimes his squeaky clean morals infuriated her, but he had such presence, such an aura of strength. A pillar of strength, that was Dan. And a very loving man. Where he loved he gave his heart and soul, everything that was him, unconditionally. Daniel Jonathan Franklin Brown, don't you dare leave me.

Rose was so immersed in her pain that she didn't realize that Letty had arrived, until she plumped down beside her and took her hand. 'I've come. Colin told me what had happened.'

'Oh! You shouldn't have. What about the baby?'

'My sister's staying with me at the moment. She's delighted for the chance to be in charge. Have you any news?'

'They've taken him for a brain scan. He hit his forehead with an almighty blow on the windscreen, you see.'

'Well, I'll stay. My sister will look after Colin. Nothing she likes better than a man to look after. Thinks I don't feed him enough.' Letty smiled. She still gripped Rose's hand and didn't look like letting go.

'There's no need to stay, you know. You can't do anything.'

'I know, but you can't be alone, not right now. I've never forgotten how grateful I was to you for that day, you know when you brought me here and I heard our wonderful news. So now it's my turn to wait with you.' Letty smiled encouragingly, releasing Rose's hand and adding, 'I need something to drink. How about you?'

Rose nodded.

They brought Dan back just as soon as Letty went to find a coffee machine.

They took her in to see him.

They said his brain scan had proved fine. He must have a skull made from concrete to take a blow like that and his brain to be unaffected. They told her both his legs were broken where he'd been trapped by the dashboard collapsing, so he was in a lot of pain. They were taking him down to theatre as soon as maybe to fix them. She mustn't worry, he was sedated. Perhaps he wouldn't know she was there.

Rose stood beside the bed, staring down at Dan. His

19

forehead was badly swollen and coloured a strange black and purple and it overhung his eyes, which were also blackened. In her mind arose the picture of him striding away from her when she'd told him she didn't want her unfaithful husband any more. As if Dan could ever be unfaithful to her, or she to him. Oh, God! Her heart broke at the memory of her gross lack of trust.

She felt him squeeze her hand. 'Dan? It's Rose.'

'I know. Love you. I'll soon be up . . . and about.'

'I know you will. They won't keep you tied to a hospital bed for long.'

Dan's eyes opened and he half smiled and then drifted away again. His hand fell away from hers so she found a chair and sat down, exhausted by witnessing Dan's pain.

Before she knew it Letty had come in with the nursing staff. 'They're taking him down to theatre now, Rose. It'll be a long time, so I've promised them I'll take you home and make you a meal. You need to rest, being as you are.'

Rose only half heard what she said because she was bending over the bed kissing Dan. 'My darling, take care. Love you.' She thought she felt him squeeze her hand again and she clung to that feeling the whole interminable evening.

Finally, at almost midnight, the hospital rang to say they'd fixed his legs, he was beginning to come round and they were very satisfied with what they'd done. 'Be a new man in a few weeks, Mrs Brown, as if it's never happened. He's a strong chap so he's withstood the operation very well indeed.'

'I'm coming to see him.'

'You're welcome to come, but we'd rather he had a chance to sleep. Best cure in the world. So you get a good night's sleep too and come in tomorrow. Goodnight.'

Rose put down the phone and reported to Letty. 'They aren't hiding something from me, are they? Maybe I'd better go, whatever they say.'

Something of the old Letty, the Letty that had dominated Colin's every thought and action for years, came back. 'Absolutely not. They're thinking of you with a baby and another on the way. No point in sitting all night looking at a man asleep. Bed is what you need. Anyway, you must take care of yourself. We don't want Dan upset by you having the baby too early. That wouldn't do at all. Set him back weeks, that would. I'm ringing Colin to ask him to pop over with my night things so I can stay here.'

Rose stood up, intending to protest.

'No! I won't listen to a word. You'll do as you are told.' Letty pushed her gently back into her chair and bustled out to phone Colin, turning at the door to say, 'If Jonathan wakes, I'll see to him – if he'll let me. After all, I'm used to babies now, aren't I?' She gave Rose such a lovely proud smile that Rose had to smile back. It was amazing what one small six-pound scrap of humanity called John had done for Letty.

Rose's help arrived by eight the next morning, but by then she was up, showered and dressed and was breakfasting with Jonathan and Letty, having already rung the hospital and been told Dan had had a good night, was conscious and looking forward to seeing her.

'Toast, Rose?'

'No, thanks.' Rose saw Letty's disapproving look and changed her mind. 'I know, I know. I've got to keep up my strength. I'm dreading seeing him in case I fall about weeping.'

'You won't, for his sake.'

'I guess you're right. I hope not. You go home, Letty.

My help will care for Jonathan for me. Little John needs to see his mum.'

A dreamy look came over Letty's face. 'He's so beautiful. Just like Colin was at his age, judging by his baby photos. So amenable to everything. No trouble at all.' Letty popped the last piece of her toast in her mouth and said, 'I'll see you off to the hospital, then I'll leave. If you need me for anything at all, you've only got to ring me. Right?'

That morning at the Practice they were inundated with phone calls from clients, who, having heard about Dan, were anxious for progress reports. Joy, Stephie and Annette steeled themselves for a busy day.

'Look, girls, it's only to be expected that they'll all want to know, though how they've found out in such a short space of time I'll never know. It isn't twenty-four hours since the accident so I know there isn't much to tell, but tell it and remember to thank them and say you'll pass their good wishes on to him. Make a list on the computer of the calls and we'll print it out and send it to him tomorrow or the day after. OK?'

Annette said, 'Let's go round with the hat and buy him flowers from everyone or something just to let him know we're thinking of him. Agreed, Joy?'

'Absolutely. Yes. You do that. Meanwhile I'm going to sort the farm calls for today. Routine calls are abandoned, otherwise Zoe and Colin won't cope.'

'So what is the message? About Dan?' Stephie asked.

'Two broken legs. Rather nasty breaks though. But in good spirits. OK?'

Stephie commented, 'It'll take more than two broken legs to get Dan down.'

Joy nodded. 'You're right. It's Rose I'm worried about. Pregnant again, and all that anxiety. She loves him so.'

'He loves her. Wish I had a man who loved me like that. Talk about Romeo and Juliet. They're completely dotty about each other.' The three of them laughed when Annette said that.

'To work, the pair of you, and let me get on.' Joy disappeared into her office.

Zoe came in at that moment. 'What's the latest on his lordship?'

Stephie raised an eyebrow at her. 'On Dan, you mean?'

'Who else?'

'He's got two broken legs. They operated last night and they were nasty breaks.'

'Ouch! That's him out of action for at least three months then. Poor chap.'

'No routine calls, just emergencies, Joy says.'

'I see. My list.' Zoe dug in her pockets and brought out a five-pound note. 'That's for flowers or whatever. Right. List? List? Come on.'

Annette handed it to her and watched while she studied it. 'Is it all right?'

'Oh, yes. Busy day. I'll be in touch. Just Colin and me today then and for the foreseeable future?'

'Well, yes, unless we get a locum.'

'Come on, Annette, you know Mungo doesn't like paying out locum charges. They come extremely expensive, you know, well, he thinks it's expensive, but if you're in a hole you have to pay to get out of it.'

'Exactly, Zoe. Bring back Scott, I say, whatever it costs.' Stephie laughed as she said this. With hand on her heart and her eyes sparkling, she added, 'Oh for a sight of his gorgeous blue eyes. And those pecs, absolutely fabulous. And that unbelievable tan! Wow!' She gripped the edge of the desk and pretended to fan herself.

23

Zoe leaned over the reception desk and quietly, but viciously, snarled, 'Over my dead body. He's best left where he is, in the outback, thousands of miles away.'

She left behind a stunned silence.

During the morning Zoe added another call to her list. She still had on her mind the little lamb at Beulah Bank Farm, so she made it convenient to call to see how she prospered.

Knocking on the back door of the farmhouse and opening it at the same time, she called out, 'It's Zoe. Called to see my favourite lamb.'

Megan called out from the kitchen, 'She's doing well. Come and take a look.'

The lamb, now forty-eight hours old, was cosily tucked down in a cardboard box placed close to the warmth of the Aga. She got to her feet when Zoe walked in and performed a kind of hop, skip and a jump towards her, unconsciously making a very pretty picture.

'My word! You look much better than when I saw you last. Megan, you've done wonders with her.'

'Not me. Da's done all the work. Up all hours. Thrilled to bits, he is. Josh is out lambing at the moment, but he keeps popping in for a look just in case Da isn't doing things properly.'

Zoe didn't answer for a moment because she was busy petting the lamb. Then she looked up and said, 'This young lady should join the others, she's strong enough now. We might just get Myfanway to take her on, but time's running out for that. Been away from her too long. I'll go see Josh.'

Josh was in the lambing barn attending another ewe that was giving birth. Beside him on the straw lay a dead lamb. 'Bad do here, Zoe. They're both dead. Well, certainly one

24

is. Think this one is too.' Josh brought out another dead lamb. 'Yes. No point in trying to revive it. Can't understand this. I'm so disappointed. Can't bear to lose a single lamb. Always seems such a failure on my part. I'm glad it's the lad's day off, he takes it so badly when they're dead. He's asked for a funeral service in the past.'

'I've an idea. Hold on, don't let her go.'

Zoe ran down the yard to the farmhouse, kicked off her boots and raced into the kitchen. 'Megan! I might have got a foster mother for this little one. All right if I have a go? Or would you prefer to keep her?'

'I'd be glad for Tomasina to have a mother. Take her. Go on. See if it works.'

Zoe snatched the lamb up under her arm, dashed out, struggled to pull on her boots and then headed for the barn.

'Look, Josh, this is what we'll try.'

Josh sat back on his heels to listen, as Zoe told him what she wanted him to do. 'Put your hand inside the ewe and get some of her discharge on to it. That's it, now rub your hands together and smear it all over this little one, go on, all over Tomasina, especially her face and head. Now bring her round to the front of the ewe, as though you've just delivered her and let the ewe have a chance to smell her. That's it. Yes!' Quickly Zoe moved the two dead lambs away from their mother's sight.

Josh and Zoe waited breathlessly to see if their ruse would work. At first there was hesitation on the part of the foster mother and then more interest and then contact was made with the little lamb and she began nuzzling it as though it was her own. The lamb bleated joyously.

'See! See!' Zoe was beside herself with delight. 'Now, first hurdle over, let's see if it goes instinctively to suckle.'

25

The two of them knelt silently in the straw, watching and waiting for the miracle. Josh had his fingers crossed on both hands. Zoe, not being superstitious, merely watched with her heart in her mouth. One satisfied ewe. One happy lamb. All's right with the world. Instinct overruled forty-eight hours in the house and the lamb started searching for the ewe's udder. When its little tail began waggling with pleasure, Zoe knew she'd succeeded. 'Brilliant. What a sight. Just look at it. Just look!'

'Never seen that done before, but it works! Lot better than skinning a dead lamb and using that. It's saved Megan a lot of work.'

'Indeed! That's made my day that has, absolutely made my day. Keep an eye on them both for the next twenty-four hours, just in case there's a blip. I'm off to tell Megan. Shake hands on a job well done.' So they did, triumph in their eyes at the successful outcome of their trick.

Zoe raced back to the house to tell Megan the good news. 'Megan! I think your Tomasina has found a new mother. Josh will tell you all about it. He's a good chap, is Josh. Worth his weight in gold. Must go, should have been at Porter's Fold an hour ago. Your da will miss her.'

Megan said, 'To be truthful he was finding it all a bit much, with his arthritis, you know. I think he'll be glad. How's Dan?'

'Both legs broken, had the operation, be a long while before he's fit for work again, so we're hard pressed as you can imagine. Must fly.' She looked at Megan and added, 'Your Rhodri is so proud at being a dad, you know. He tells all the clients about how wonderful you are at being a mother.'

Megan blushed. 'Does he indeed? It doesn't always feel wonderful.'

'No, but enjoy. Before you know it, your seven-week-old Owen will be a seventeen-year-old Owen asking for a car.'

Megan shuddered. 'Oh, don't. I can't begin to imagine that!'

'Believe me, Oscar will soon be two and it doesn't seem a week since I brought him home from hospital. Be seeing you.'

'Zoe, before you go, give Dan our love if you go in to see him. He's well loved by everyone, not just Rose.'

'Right. Yes.'

Rashly, considering the weather, Zoe chose to go across country to Porter's Fold. She was halfway there, bumping steadily over the rough frozen ground, when round the bend came a broken-down, battered, fit-for-the-knacker's-yard saloon car at a foolhardy rate of knots. She swerved to avoid it, as did the broken-down car to avoid her, and after some swift manoeuvring they both slid to a halt alongside each other. Zoe whizzed down her driver's window and shouted, 'You blithering idiot! You absolute nincompoop! What the hell do you think you're doing driving like that?'

The other driver's window slid slowly open with the owner winding furiously. 'You stupid cow! Me a nincompoop? Me?'

'Yes, you. No one uses this track except for me and then you come charging round the bend like a damned idiot.'

'And good morning to you. I'm Gab Bridges.'

For a moment Zoe couldn't think why she knew the name. 'Well, I'm Zoe Savage from the Barleybridge Veterinary Practice.'

Gab Bridges got out after a battle with the door,

pretending to examine his battered old car for damage. 'No harm done anyway. Are you OK?'

'You wouldn't notice if I had damaged your car, it's completely smashed up already. It won't do much for your image with all the girls.' She could have bitten her tongue out as soon as she'd said that. She was almost inviting him to flirt with her. And predictably he did.

'No problem with girls, they queue up to go out with me. Ready to join the queue?' Then he gave her a wicked grin, which didn't affect Zoe but she could see it would melt most girls' hearts. He had a long, athletic body with broad shoulders, a fine face full of character and, oddly for an outdoors man, wonderfully slender, expressive hands. It didn't require much perception on her part to see how attractive he was to the opposite sex.

He turned his head so she got the full-on view of his grin and she saw for the first time the red scar, which ran from below his right eye and disappeared under his hair line. Of course. He'd tried to shoot himself over Megan. This was he, Josh's brother.

'I'm joining no queue, thank you very much for the offer though. I'm running late for Porter's Fold, must go.'

'Just come from there.'

'I didn't know you worked for him.'

'Occasional work that's all, a bit of this and a bit of that. No regular job.'

'Why ever not? A big strapping chap like you. You'd be a godsend.' Could she never say anything at all without it being an open invitation for him to flirt with her?

'Oh, I am.' Gab gave her another of his ladykiller grins and got back in his car. 'Wish I'd hung on a bit longer, give a lot for a view of your backside bent over with your arm up a ewe. Be seeing yer!'

28

Zoe had to confess to being charmed by him. Then she recollected he was like it with all women, whatever their age or good looks, and drove to Porter's Fold, hoping Connie might give her some lunch or at the least one of her balm cakes filled with her homemade cheese. After all, she needed something to take her mind off Gab Bridges.

By the end of that day Zoe had done seven visits to farms, a lot in one day, achieved only by thorough devotion to duty. She didn't get her balm cake at Porter's Fold because Connie was having one of her rare days out shopping in Barleybridge, so she'd had no lunch at all when she finally arrived home at six o'clock. Tired and starving hungry, she was in no mood for her mother's complaints when she got in.

'Just got a call to make to the Practice and I'll be with you.'

'Work first as usual.'

Matter-of-factly, Zoe answered, 'Can't help it. It's what puts food in your mouth.'

'Any news of Dan? The lovely man that he is.'

Picking up the phone, Zoe said, 'Holding his own, I think they would say. Hello, Zoe here. Done all my calls. Will you switch the phone through? Please.'

Joan sighed. 'Not on call again?'

'What else can we do? Can't really see Dan getting up out of bed with two broken legs to go out on call, can you? Colin's done the last two nights, so now I'm covering for Dan. OK?'

'OK.' Joan said this with as much resignation in her voice as she could. 'Why can't you get a nine to five job like other people?'

'Because unfortunately animals can't tell the time.'

'Neither can farmers. Why they have to ring you at six

in the morning I do not know. Don't they realize other people might be asleep?'

'Because that's when they go out to see to their animals, especially when it's a milking herd, so that's when they find they've got problems. Now, shut up, Mother, I've had no lunch. I've worked continuously without a break and I need food. Where's Oscar?'

'Having tea with the Whitworths.'

Zoe turned on her mother, allowing all her exhaustion from her day's work to boil over. 'You know I don't like him going to the Whitworths. That man is a cruel, sadistic beast and I'm terrified of Oscar doing some innocent little thing and that chap's temper erupting. Do you never listen to anything I say?'

'I listen all the time. Every day, day in day out. I'm tired of it. It's too much expecting me to look after Oscar. Too much. It really is. I can never do anything right, well, according to you I can't.' Joan Savage allowed her self-pity full rein. 'I slave here all day, with no one to talk to, all by myself. It's so lonely. And Oscar doesn't help. He can't play five minutes by himself, not five minutes, without it being Granny this and Granny that. And your long hours don't help.'

'After you've taken him to nursery you could always go into Barleybridge for a while. There's nothing to stop you. Hairdresser's, coffee mornings, visit friends, whatever. I don't mind. I pay for him to be at the nursery from eight until six, but you never leave him that long. There's always some silly excuse to take him late or pick him up early. It's a waste of good money.'

'I'm only thinking about him. I don't like him being looked after by strangers, it's not right. Just wish you'd married someone nice like Dan, you'd never have to earn your living ever again. Just think of that.'

'And if I did – which I wouldn't because no man as nice as Dan would want someone like me, I couldn't give him the devotion he gets from Rose – and never had to earn my living ever again, where would that put you? You couldn't expect a husband of mine to support you like I do, could you? In any case, I love my work. It's my raison d'être, believe me.'

'Raison d'être, my foot.'

Their voices had been rising louder and louder each time they spoke and when Zoe answered her mother's scornful remark she was almost screaming. 'Shut up! Shut up! Just because you no longer have any reason of any kind for living doesn't mean I haven't. Nothing, I repeat *nothing*, will stop me from doing my job.'

'Much as I love him, you could have had an abortion, then this problem wouldn't have arisen.'

Zoe froze. She'd come so close to doing that very thing, but something, she knew not what, had held her back from that final step. What an easy way out that would have been, to cleanse herself for ever of him who had brought Oscar about. But would she have cleansed herself? Or would he have stayed with her in the background through the years, colouring her every thought and action? The guilt of infanticide – was that the right word? – reminding her she'd murdered his child. Just something of his to have and to hold. Looking down at her mother, puffing away on her cigarette, G and T in hand, Zoe knew once more for certain, abortion would not have been an option. She'd done the right thing about Oscar, so she'd have to put up with her mother never doing the right thing for him. Her mother's eternal complaints though, were becoming intolerable. Zoe shrugged, too weary to continue arguing. 'I need food, is it ready?'

31

'In half an hour, it's in the oven.'

'I'll have a shower, I must stink with what I've done today.'

'That's another thing, your job isn't even ladylike. It's a man's job. Cats and dogs would be easier.'

'I'm not interested in small animal work. I've never done it, and I don't intend to. Be down in fifteen minutes. Are the Whitworths bringing Oscar back?'

Her mother nodded.

Zoe went up the stairs two at a time, furious with herself for having allowed her mother to ignite her temper again. As the hot water poured down over her body Zoe began to relax. Into her mind came that exchange of opinions with Gab Bridges. He had the same sexual magnetism as Oscar's father . . . Though he must be a mite unstable to try shooting himself over Megan. Still, he had a lot going for him. As she soaped herself Zoe thought about their need for a locum. It was almost impossible for her and Colin to keep up the relentless on-call schedule between the two of them. Dan had only been in hospital four nights and the strain was already beginning to tell.

As it happened Joy and Stephie were discussing locums at the very same moment as they were tidying up and putting the finishing touches to a long day.

'Joy?'

'Yes.'

'Do you think we shall need a locum? After all, Colin and Zoe can't go on for ever on call every other night and weekends too, it'll kill them.'

'I know. It's very worrying. I've spoken to Mungo about it, but he was thinking about his next operation and didn't really give his mind to it.'

'Just a pity Scott isn't here, he'd be all right now with Kate at college.'

Joy glanced oddly at her. 'Yes, he would. I don't ever want Kate to meet him again, he was a bad influence on her.'

'She never let on, did she, what we already knew?'

'No, she didn't, but it must have hurt her very badly when he left so suddenly.'

'Let's face it, he was a bit of a sod where women were concerned.'

'He didn't put you on red alert though, did he?'

'Only because I knew he wouldn't give me a second glance. Not attractive enough.'

'Oh, Stephie, that's sad. You mustn't think like that about yourself. But still, you've got Adam now.'

'That's true, and he and I are just right for each other.'

'Good. I'm glad. I shall speak to Mungo on the phone tonight. Something has to be done.'

When Joy had finished her lonely meal in her quiet house with only Duncan's two cats for company, she fed them both, cleared up the kitchen and settled herself in an armchair with the phone, ready to do battle with Mungo. She ignored the fact that she always sat in Duncan's favourite armchair in the evenings now. She'd been doing that since a week after he'd left. It gave her comfort and seemed to bring him nearer. Truth to tell, she'd begun missing him. Was it seven months since he'd gone? Seven days had been the longest he'd been away before. Joy knew, but wouldn't admit to it, that she longed for him to be home. The lock of hair that fell over his forehead, she'd give anything for the opportunity to push it back off his face. Where the devil was he?

She dialled Mungo's number. 'Mungo? It's Joy. Have you got a minute?'

'I have, yes.'

'I'm ringing about Dan . . .'

Joy recognized the anxiety in his voice as he interrupted her. 'He's not worse, is he?'

'Worse? Oh, no. I'm ringing about getting a locum. Let's face it, Dan is going to be out of action for weeks, if not months, and Colin and Zoe can't carry on with just the two of them. Worse still, what about the equine side? He's getting that built up so beautifully. All his good work is going to go down the pan if we're not careful.'

'I know. I know. So damned expensive though.'

'We are insured for vets being put out of action while on duty. Surely that would go some way to paying for the extra salary?'

'I know, I know.'

'It's no good saying "I know, I know". What are you going to do about it? It's different managing when some-one's on holiday – we know that's only a couple of weeks. This is serious.' Joy listened for Mungo's reply and didn't get one. 'Are you hearing me?'

'Yes. Yes. I am.'

'I'll organize it all, you'll have nothing to do except agree. Anyone with two legs, a good head on their shoulders, a capacity to work all hours, good rapport with the gee-gees and an MRCVS will fit the bill. That's not much to ask, is it? Well, it is, but there must be someone.'

'You're right. Of course, we can't manage. Yes. Go ahead.'

'Good, thanks. To start Monday if I can get someone. There's no one in the Practice flat at the moment. If they need accommodation they can have that?'

'Yes. You'd better ask Colin and Zoe, they are part-ners.'

'Don't fret. They'll agree, gladly. Believe me.'

'OK. Joy. Night-night.'

She'd forgotten he'd always said that when there was just the two of them starting up his practice and she was his veterinary nurse. It had always been 'Night-night' at the end of the day. But her heart strings didn't twang quite as much as they'd used to do, and Duncan's smiling face suddenly popped into her mind. Had she been chasing shadows all these years? Had she never given Duncan even half a chance? Come home, Duncan, come home.

Tomorrow she'd organize a locum vet. She knew a couple of reliable agencies. Yes. That's what she'd do, if it took her all day on the phone. There was no alternative. She had to find someone.

Chapter 3

By Friday neither of the agencies had come up with a suitable locum, and Joy was at her wits' end. She rang them every day as soon as they opened. But now it was Monday and again, today, she drew a blank. Zoe had come in at eight as usual but she was looking distinctly weary.

'Zoe! You got called out last night? I can see.'

'Absolutely. I was up at midnight for two lambings at River Farm, and up again at five this morning and I've all weekend to face. Have you got anyone yet?'

Woefully Joy shook her head.

'Oh God! Something will have to be done. I can't keep this pace up.'

'I'm doing my best. My very best. I'm trying another agency right this minute, but I'm starting to run out of options.'

Zoe slumped down on a chair and rubbed her face to freshen herself up. 'Well, I will do it. I knew before I qualified, so I can't complain.'

'I have tried persuading the other three to do a bit to relieve you but it's no good. Rhodri positively blenched when I suggested it. Complains he's forgotten more than he ever knew about farm work. As for Valentine! Well. Least said. And Graham quite bluntly said no way, and that if he had to do it, it was a resignation job. So get your list,

36

do your best and if there's a chance of a couple of hours off, take it. I've stopped all routine calls for the foreseeable future.'

'Right.' Zoe dragged herself up from the chair and left Joy's office just as Mungo came bouncing in.

'Morning, Zoe. I may have solved our problem.'

'Oh, good! I don't care if they have two heads so long as they can do the job.'

Mungo laughed. He went in Joy's office and firmly shut the door. 'Right. Your favourite vet has solved our staffing problem.'

Joy stopped dialling, replaced the receiver and looked up at him. 'You have?'

'Friday evening we got a phone call from someone who fits the bill. Miriam answered and I heard her shrieking with surprise and delight.'

'Really?'

'Yes.' Mungo sat down, rested his elbows on Joy's desk and said, 'You know him, and all the farmers' wives will be delighted.'

'They will?' A terrible suspicion entered Joy's mind. 'Go on.'

'He knows the area too.'

'I see. I do sincerely hope it isn't that fool who helped us out and we never knew where he was all day? I spent hours tracking him down.'

Mungo looked puzzled for a moment then waved a dismissive hand. 'Oh, no. Not him. Even Miriam had no time for him, and she can find something good in the devil himself.'

'Go on then.'

'He's been staying with us all weekend.'

'He has? Well, go on then, who is it?'

37

He teased her by not answering directly. 'We've spent most of the weekend laughing. He's done us a power of good.' He grinned at some remembered story.

Joy, growing impatient, banged her fist on the desk. 'Get to the point.'

Mungo hesitated and then told her. 'Scott Spencer.'

Joy shot to her feet. 'Scott Spencer? Scott Spencer? Over my dead body!'

'But I thought—'

'You didn't think, Mungo. After what he did to us, disappearing overnight without the slightest warning, I swore, and so did you at the time may I remind you, we'd never employ another of our itinerant brothers from the Commonwealth. You swore it.'

'I know I did. But that was then. This is different.'

'It is? How?'

'He knows it's only until Dan recovers.'

'Sorry. I don't care if I have to send *you* out on call, but I am *not* having Scott back here again. He created mayhem in Barleybridge.'

Mungo stood up and, leaning his hands on her desk, said quietly, 'But he didn't create mayhem veterinary wise, did he? Everyone thought he was the tops. Which he was. Which he is. It was only the damn fool women who couldn't keep their hormones under control who suffered.'

'He's not down here, is he? Talking to everybody?'

'Of course not, he's upstairs in bed still. I had to wait to see what you thought.'

'Well, you have and I say no.'

Rather acidly Mungo asked, 'The agency's come up trumps, has it?'

Joy hated having to confess to not having found someone. She hesitated and thought about Zoe this morning and how weary she was. She was tough though, and she did have her mother to cope when she wasn't at home. No, she'd survive.

'The answer is still no. Despite his charm. He wreaked havoc when he was here, and thoroughly upset me.'

'I'll ask Zoe and Colin then. They're the ones faced with all Dan's work, not you, and if they say yes, then I'm sorry, Joy, yes it will be.'

'How dare you go over my head!'

'I dare.'

'I'm Practice Manager here.'

'I'm senior partner and I can't have the staff going to pieces when there's an obvious opportunity to solve our problems. It's not our clients' fault that we can't cover the work. So it's up to us to solve the problem quick smart, or we shall be losing them. The three of us went to see Dan yesterday and he agrees it will be a brilliant idea to have Scott while he's laid up, one reason being that he's overcome with worry about how we'll manage. So that's two partners out of four agreeing with my decision. I reckon Scott's a godsend. Now. I have a client at nine but the first free minute I have I'm phoning Colin and Zoe, and if they've any sense they'll jump at the chance.'

'So you're overriding my wishes?'

'Yes, I am. For the good of the Practice and to stop Dan's recovery being held back by worry. He's a conscientious man and if employing Scott relieves his mind then employ him we shall.'

Mungo spun out of the office and left Joy seething. Her hands were trembling, she was hyperventilating and she felt sick. Confrontations with Mungo always upset her, and this one had been worse than usual. But Scott! Oh, God, no. She was not having him working at the Practice. Definitely not. In fact, she'd give her notice in if he did.

This was one hill she wasn't prepared to climb. Twenty years of devoted service she'd given to Mungo's Practice and if this was to be the end, well, so be it. She was a good manager and there was always work for people like her. There was quick tap at her door and there stood Miriam.

Ah! thought Joy. Here come the support troops. 'If you've come to persuade me to agree to Scott working for us again then I'm sorry, the answer is no.'

'I wouldn't dream of interfering in practice politics, Joy. Certainly not. I've merely come to tell you about our weekend.'

'Mmm.'

'As a friend.' The chair everyone appeared glad to sit on this morning was now occupied by Miriam. 'He stayed with us, and we've had an hilarious time. Can I tell you why he's here?'

'All right. But I've lots to do.' Joy shuffled some papers about and tried to look disinterested, but she couldn't be rude to Miriam. She owed her too much.

'His mother died three days after he got back, while she was having heart surgery. So he did go home because of her. He stayed with his pa on the ranch, thinking he ought to make a go of it for his pa's sake, but he found himself bored out of his mind. So after a lot of soul-searching he decided to come back to England. Rang us when he'd had a few days in London and I couldn't do any other than invite him to stay. Frankly, at the back of my mind I was thinking he might be able to help us out of this hole we're in. Which he'd be delighted to do.'

'I see. You know the trouble he caused when he was here. Poor Bunty for a start. The baby she lost was his, you know.'

Miriam nodded.

'And Kate. He broke her heart.'

'I know he did.' Miriam smiled to herself. 'He's still an absolute charmer.'

'He's downright unreliable as well. That's why I don't want him.'

Miriam stood up. 'His mother was seriously ill; that was the only reason he left so abruptly.'

'He left abruptly because he was in deep water with Kate and it was the best way to get out of it. Commitment is not his style.'

'OK, I hear what you say, but it's up to the other partners.'

'If he comes here, I shall give in my notice.'

Miriam folded her arms and looked very disappointed. 'Now that verges on the ridiculous.'

'Miriam!'

'Sorry, but it does. I'm disappointed in you. Got to take Perkins out. I shall tell Scott not to come in to see everybody till it's been decided.'

'You mean you're on Mungo's side about this?'

Miriam paused in the doorway looking tremendously sad. 'On this, yes, I am. We have to think of the clients. Their needs must come first, despite any petty disagreements amongst ourselves. Sorry. I hate falling out.'

Joy began to protest. 'Petty! You use the word petty? I am not . . . petty . . .'

But Miriam had gone. Joy leaned back in her chair feeling defeated. Damn and blast. Just damn and blast. Now she'd no one on her side. No one at all. She wished Duncan were here. With his clinical detachment from the human race he'd have an answer for her. He'd see the situation for what it was. Solvable. Engage Scott and let the women look after themselves, he'd say. But it wasn't just that, it was the shock of him leaving, literally over-night, with a letter on her doormat informing her of what he'd done, and that was one thing she hated, unreliable staff. No. She was determined to take a stand over this. Scott in. Joy out. She wouldn't even give notice.

Blithely unaware of Joy's decision, Mungo contacted Colin as he said he would and Colin delightedly agreed. 'Getting a bit long in the tooth for alternate nights on call. Be glad of his help and I'm sure Zoe will be too.'

But contacting Zoe proved more difficult. Her mobile phone must be out of range and though he tried several of the farms on her list, she'd either just been or was expected but late. Taking his cue from Colin, Mungo decided yes, she would be grateful, and he'd act on it straight away. So between clients, he'd been up to the flat to find Scott gracefully munching his breakfast toast. There was no doubt about it, he was an attractive devil. The sun-bleached glints in his fair hair, his startling blue eyes, his tan and his in-your-face sexual magnetism were a spec-tacular combination. No wonder . . .

Mungo cleared his throat. 'Now, Scott. I've spoken to Colin and he agrees. I tried to catch Zoe but can't make contact. However, seeing as three out of four partners agree, I've decided to take you on, could be three or even four months until Dan is on his feet again, so we'll shake hands on it. On the understanding that you stay absolutely as long as you are required. No hopping on the first bus that goes by. Right?'

Scott stood up, all six feet three of him and vigorously shook Mungo's hand. 'Right. Good on yer, mate. Thanks. When shall I start?'

'Tomorrow morning? Use Dan's Land Rover. It'll be

42

quite like old times for you. You can have the Practice flat like I said. Miriam says she'll get it ready for you, so stay with us another couple of nights and then you can move in. Must press on, got a client in five minutes. Help yourself to showers and things. Just make yourself at home.' He made to leave, but came back and said, 'You're a godsend.'

Then he went into Joy's office to tell her the news, confident that she would agree. She always had agreed with his decisions, so he couldn't see why things should be any different today.

'Well, Joy, there you are. I've got things sorted so there's no more need to worry. Scott's starting tomorrow morning and he's promised he won't leave us in the lurch like he did the last time. So that's one problem out of the way.'

'OK.' Joy stood up, took off her reading glasses, found the case for them and put them in it. She then began selecting her own bits and pieces from the top of her desk: her pens and the fancy jar she kept them in; the ruler she used when doing the rosters; a vase, at the moment flowerless. Then, with Mungo watching, she opened a drawer and began sorting through it for more of her belongings.

'Excuse me, but you are making all the signs of clearing your desk.'

'If you're leaving, that's what you do.'

'Now? You're leaving now?'

Joy nodded.

'What are you thinking of, woman? All I've done is find us a locum and a good one at that.'

'I know and I suppose I should be grateful, but I'm not staying.' Joy took off her uniform overall, and carefully laid it on her chair. Then she dumped the flowers from the

43

vase on top of her filing cabinet into the wastebasket, found a carrier bag for her things and looking at Mungo, who was standing there watching her, feeling stunned, she said slowly and carefully, 'Watch my lips. You have gone over my head for the last time. I told you I didn't want Scott back but, full of your own importance, as usual, you rode roughshod over my decision. Well, I'm going, and I'm not even going to say sorry either.' She unhooked her coat from its peg and laid it over her arm.

Mungo shouted, 'What the hell do you think you're doing? You must have gone mad. Completely mad. There is absolutely no need for this.'

'Oh, yes, there is.'

Then the tone of Mungo's voice dropped into that icy calm, which Joy knew full well meant he was terribly angry, but this time she didn't care one jot. 'Joy. I have never done anything ever with the intention of distressing you, and you know full well that is the truth, but at the moment you are making me so angry. What a petty thing to be doing. It's beneath you. I've always thought of you as a woman of great composure and control and here you are behaving like a thirteen-year-old, with all her hormones on red alert.' He took in a deep breath after he'd said this, and waited for her reply.

'How dare you speak to me like that, treating me like a child. You are insulting. I said I didn't want him and I don't. I can't be any plainer than that.'

'You're being damned bloody-minded.'

'Am I? And you're not?'

Mungo snapped out, 'No, I damn well am not. I'm behaving very reasonably. It's you who's behaving like a bloody idiot.' Met with silence he eventually changed tack and tried cajoling instead. 'Now, come along, Joy. We've always worked together so well. Remember the old days when it was just the two of us? Long hours, but what fun. Don't do this. I can't manage without you.' Then he played his final card. 'Think of Miriam, she'll be so upset. Please don't disappoint her.' He stepped towards her, intending to gently take the carrier bag from her and relieve her of the coat folded over her arm.

But Joy forestalled him and moved so the desk was between them. His tender persuasion could no longer work its magic on her. 'Don't try sweet-talking me. The time for that is long past. You're not used to people not doing as you wish, are you? How the blazes Miriam has put up with you all these years I'll never know. You're so self-opinionated, so damned sure of yourself. It's about time someone told you a few home truths and I'm just the person. Out of my way.'

'I won't have this.'

'Well, Mungo, you've got it, like it or not. Am I glad to be leaving this place! I can't get away quickly enough.' Joy stormed off, struggled out through the back door and left the wind to bang it shut.

It was Annette who finally made contact with Zoe. She'd been sitting fast asleep in her car for the last hour and was just waking up and checking her mobile when Annette's call came through. 'We've been trying to contact you, are you all right?'

Zoe stretched and yawned. 'Yes, I've been asleep. Switched off my mobile. Thought I'd just have five minutes. Oh, God! Look at the time. You wanted me?'

'Just to say your troubles are over.'

'They are?' Still dazed with sleep, Zoe couldn't think what troubles she had that needed Annette to solve them.

'Yes, we've got a locum.'

'Oh! Right. That's a relief.'

'Yes. It's someone called Scott, he worked for us for a few months before my time.'

'Fine. I'll get sorted and carry on. Bye.'

Zoe shook herself awake, checked her face in the mirror and decided that sleeping during the morning was not a good thing looks wise, but who cared? She hadn't been able to help it; it would have been dangerous to have continued driving. She got out of the car and stood breathing in the cold, no, freezing air to freshen her brains. Which it did with startlingly quick results. She hurriedly got back in the car, turned on the ignition, checked it was safe to pull away and only then realized what Annette had said. I must have imagined it. She didn't say Scott, did she? *She did. Hell.*

She arrived at Lord Askew's in turmoil. There was no one in the stableyard so she parked her car and went through into the cowyard to find Chris to give him the results of the tests she'd had done on the Guernsey.

'Chris! Oh, there you are. I've got the tests back and they're all fine. They've found nothing. So we're back to square one with poor old Ruby. Let's go take another look and rack our brains again. How's she been?' They went together into the byre where his cows were spending the winter.

When they finally emerged with more samples for a further range of tests, Lord Askew and four of his sons were standing talking in the middle of the stableyard.

'Morning, my lord. Nice fresh morning. Good morning, gentlemen.'

They all touched the nebs of their caps to acknowledge her greeting.

'Good morning, Zoe. Are you going to be with us on Saturday?'

'When?'

'Now you must know what's happening on Saturday.'

Zoe joined the group and smiled her most beguiling smile. 'No, I don't. Should I?'

The sons laughed kindly but Lord Askew said abruptly, 'The protest march. *Our* protest march, m'dear.'

'To where?'

'Bristol. About the licensing and what not for hunts. We're going to show those damned MPs that they know nothing about the countryside at all. We'll give you a lift if you're willing to come.'

Zoe faced Lord Askew and, looking him in the eye, delivered a broadside. 'If you do give me a lift, I shall be rooting for the other side.'

Lord Askew was startled. When he'd absorbed what she'd said he blustered, 'Other side? But I thought you were a country gal. Surely. You being a vet.'

'Me being a vet makes it as I can't be in favour of hunting. Cruelty and all that.'

'Cruelty! What about our chickens being left with their throats torn out just for the fun of it. They're a menace. We've got to keep the numbers down. Shooting 'em risks only maiming 'em so they crawl away to die in agony and that's worse, it's no solution. Being eaten by maggots before they're dead. Come on. That *is* cruelty.'

'When I was in my teens, quite by chance I saw, actually saw from a few yards away, hounds tearing a fox apart. I heard its screams, saw the terror, smelled the blood, saw the manic killer instinct in the eyes of the hounds. Seeing that made a devastating impression on me. That same week my father died, which drove the sight of that killing deep into my soul.'

There was a silence when she finished speaking, broken

47

by Lord Askew patting her arm in sympathy. 'I'm sorry, m'dear. Very sorry about that. Nevertheless, we country folk have rights.'

'Rights? Just because you own acre upon acre of land does not mean you are free to do as you like. You have a responsibility to this land to care for it during your lifetime, that's what. An example to set. Sorry. But I shan't be coming.'

'I've never heard such sentimental claptrap in my life. It's rubbish.' His huge clenched fist banged against the palm of his hand. 'Of course the land is mine and if I want to hunt foxes on it I shall. I don't come and dictate to you about what you do with your garden. It's yours and I've no right to interfere, and neither have the government a right to interfere with what I do in my garden or you do in yours . . . 'cept mine's bigger than yours.' His florid face grew purple with agitation.

One of the boys said, 'Steady, father. Steady.'

Zoe had to smile. 'You're right, of course. But I'm sorry, it's not for me this protesting business. Having said that, my opinion about fox-hunting in no way affects my ability to treat your cows, nor do I allow my professional integrity to be affected by my personal stance about cruelty. I suppose all you boys follow your father's opinion on this matter?'

One by one they agreed they did.

'I thought at least one of you might object to the cruelty.'

The taller of the four said, 'We don't agree it's cruel. So don't badger us with your cock-eyed opinions. We're all off to support a centuries-old tradition of the countryside. Full stop.'

Zoe shrugged, smiled round at the four sons and then at

Lord Askew. 'You won't fall out with me, will you? Still friends?' She tried her hardest to look appealing, but saw a nasty glint come into Lord Askew's eye.

'You're here again, I see. Not solved Ruby's problem?'

'Not yet. I've taken more samples, let's hope this time we're on the right track.'

'You'd better be. All money, you know. Money. You vets consult the telephone directory when it comes to billing me. The cost of keeping up this place is astronomical . . . however, that's my business. Where's that Aussie who used to come? He'd have had it solved in no time at all.'

'You're in luck, he's come back. I'll call him in for a second opinion, if you like.'

'Good idea. And if you change your mind about the protest march let me know and we'll squeeze you in. It's a six a.m. start.' He raised his cap to her and crossed the yard. The four boys watched him go, grinned at her, touched their caps, one of them winked and they all followed their father.

Zoe laid her samples carefully on the seat beside her and watched the Askew sons disappearing towards the house. Money. That's what it was. It all came down to money. Those sons of his all had good jobs in one field or another mostly because of who they were, not whether they merited it or not. They should have been put down at birth. Then she remembered she'd offered to bring Scott in for a second opinion. She'd only said that because his lordship was obviously going to say that women vets were no good and, thinking he'd object to another vet having to be paid for, she'd come out with the first thing that had come into her head. Damn and blast everything and everybody this morning. She was at the end of her tether.

Because she wanted the samples off to the laboratory that day Zoe made a point of calling in at the Practice on her way to her next call. It was lunchtime so she decided she'd have a bite to eat before picking up the strands again. She went in through the back door and took the samples into Joy's office: no Joy. She frowned, sure in her own mind that it was not Joy's day off. She went into reception to find her.

'Joy, is she at lunch?'

Annette shook her head, leaned forward and whispered so the waiting clients couldn't hear, 'No. Actually, she's left.'

'You mean, as in coming back after lunch, I assume?'

'No, as in for ever.'

'For ever? Pull the other one.' Zoe looked sceptical.

'No, she has, honestly.'

'But she's been here for years. What's happened?'

Annette leaned even further over the reception counter and whispered, 'Had a row with Mungo when he told her he was employing Scott Spencer as locum and she's cleared her desk and gone. Terrible row they had. Unbelievable. Mungo *swore*.' Annette's eyes widened considerably as she added, 'I mean really swore. Joy was livid.'

Zoe was flabbergasted. For Mungo to swear the row must have been earth-moving. Swearing was banned so far as he was concerned. 'Well, well. It's a strange world.'

'She said he'd gone over her head. She told him she'd resigned because she wasn't having Scott. Then Mungo turned on the charm, like he can, and she, well, she exploded.'

'I bet. Who's going to post the samples then?'

'Miriam is. She's stepping in temporarily till Joy comes back, Mungo said.'

'He's sure about that, is he?'

'Says Joy needed a few days off and she'd be back. Confident he was. Very.'

Zoe speculated for a moment and said, 'I wouldn't be too sure about that.'

'What are we going to do without her?'

'Don't know. I'll get lunch and then I'll be off. Keep me informed!'

Annette tapped the side of her nose and nodded, thought about Joy and how she relied on her, and hoped she wouldn't be long making up her mind to return to work. Had she seen Joy at that moment she would have had her doubts that she'd ever see her again.

After storming out of the building, full to the brim with anger and disappointment, Joy had walked across the car park to get in her car, changed her mind, dumped her lifetime vital belongings in the boot and set off up Beulah Bank Top. She had no coat on and only the soft flat shoes she wore at work. Not even a scarf with her, but she didn't care, she was so angry she didn't feel the cold. She began the climb up the winding path leading to the Bank Top. Joy didn't care if she died. She'd lost everything. As Zoe had so kindly reminded her a few days ago, she'd no husband, no lover and now, to add to the misery, no job. Her job in the veterinary world was *her*. It was her very soul. But she'd no regrets, she told herself defiantly.

She climbed on, fiercely determined, up and up. She was getting out of breath, after all, exercise had never been her forte, she left all that to Duncan. He used to laugh saying, 'The only exercise you get is turning the knob on the washing machine.' He was right too, exercise was something she was always going to do next week and never did.

The landscape was wild now. The grass withered and almost petrified looking, great tufts of it sticking up where the sheep didn't care to graze it, the stones bigger, more like full size rocks. The path narrower, the wind stronger and colder, her heart beating faster, almost pounding. Heavens above, she couldn't even take a walk but the odds were piled against her. She'd now got so high up the hills that she knew this must be where Duncan had used to walk. He'd told her of the places where he'd rest, used by the sheep in extreme weather, small secret hiding places to keep them out of the worst of it. She found a hollow like the ones he'd described to her and gratefully sank down into it. If she shuffled a little lower, the top of her head would be out of the cruel wind. Sheep obviously knew a thing or two.

Crouched there, Joy surveyed the world. If she tried very hard, was that a glint of the sea she caught right away on the horizon? She blinked her eyes and looked again. Yes, she was sure it was. Nearer she could clearly follow the route of the river threading its way through the town. Barleybridge. Until today there wasn't a single place in the entire world she'd ever wanted to live but here. It satisfied all her needs. Now there was nothing left. Absolutely nothing left. Almost unnoticed, stinging rain smacked onto her upturned face, joining the tears that were pouring down her cold cheeks. She yearned heart and soul for Duncan.

Chapter 4

'Miriam! *She* gave in her notice. Well, not her notice, she simply resigned, there and then. I didn't sack her. Damn the blasted woman.'

'Darling! That's hardly fair.'

'Fair? It isn't her up in the night lambing and whatever and then doing a full day's work next day because we've not got our full complement of vets. It's Zoe and Colin and our clients who are suffering. She's had almost a whole week to find someone and she hasn't. I come up with a solution and bang! She goes berserk. Nothing short of berserk.' Mungo knocked back the rest of his whisky. 'She admits he's an excellent vet. Actually admits it, but still doesn't want him. Anybody would think it was her he'd put in the club.'

'Mungo! That was OTT.'

'Well, I'm not responsible for the sexual yearnings of our staff. If they can't resist Scott's charms, well, hard cheese.'

'You know, my darling, if anyone should be glad she's left it should be me.'

Mungo, hearing this, came sharply into focus. 'Why should you be glad she's left? I thought you were friends. What's she said to upset you?'

'She's said nothing.'

'Well?' Mungo poured himself another whisky, topped it up with water and sat back, prepared to be enlightened.

'I've known all along that she loves you, and that she married Duncan knowing that.'

Mungo sat upright in his chair, carefully placed his whisky glass on the table beside the decanter and said very slowly, 'Did Duncan tell you that?'

'No. I just knew.'

Mungo studied his hands to give himself time, not being quite able to take this astonishing piece of news on board. 'How long have you known?'

'Since the first day I met her. I watched her face when you said I was your new wife and she looked as if she'd been stabbed.'

'But it was on our wedding day I introduced you, at the old practice.'

Miriam nodded.

'All this time and you've never said.'

'I know.'

'I never . . . you know . . . said anything to . . .'

'I know. You simply didn't know.'

'Well, I did, actually.'

It was Miriam's turn to be surprised.

'Duncan told me that night we were deciding whether we liked Dan enough to employ him. I made him promise he wouldn't tell you.'

'I see. Well, he didn't. I know it's maddening that Joy has given her notice in but she is in turmoil at the moment. Things are just not going right for her. In fact, I think I'll go round there and see how she is.'

Mungo wagged a finger at her. 'Now just a minute—'

'Not only is Duncan missing but she's lost her job and, what's even worse for her possibly, she's lost you.

54

That steaming row you've had will not have helped at all.'

Truculently he answered, 'She deserved it.'

'It's only eight o'clock. I'll drive up to their house and see.'

'You won't. I shall drive you. You've had a long day doing a job you're not familiar with. I'll drive.'

'You're not coming inside.'

'No, perhaps not. I'll take the *Veterinary Times* with me and sit in the car. OK?'

With relief Miriam nodded agreement. 'OK. She may not even want to see *me*.'

'We'll take the chance.'

They arrived outside Joy's house to find it in darkness. Getting no reply at the front door, Mungo lent Miriam his torch and she went round the back to see if the kitchen light was on.

It wasn't. The cat flap sprung open and Copper came out. He twisted and turned around her legs in welcome and then began mewing. Miriam bent down to stroke him. 'Oh, my love, you do seem sad. Has she not come back?'

There was nothing Miriam could do about Copper because she hadn't got a key for Joy's house. 'She'll be back soon. Promise.'

Making her way round to the front of the house again, Miriam heard more pathetic mewing. She shone the torch around trying to see where it was coming from, tracing the sounds to a lavender bush down the side of the house. She shone it closer and saw to her horror Duncan's other cat, Tiger, laid beneath it, looking helpless and afraid. 'Oh, God! It's Tiger. What have you done to yourself?' She shouted, 'Mungo! Mungo! Will you come?'

Mungo got out of the car calling, 'Shine the torch, I can't see where you are.'

She flashed the torch about so's he'd find her. 'I'm here, down the side of the house. It's Tiger. She's injured. Or sick or something. Look!'

Mungo knelt down beside the lavender bush and by the light of Miriam's torch he examined Tiger. 'She looks as though she's been mauled. There's no broken limbs that I can tell, but she's got a huge gash right down her side. I'll have to take her with me and attend to her. My God, whatever can it have been?'

'Even if Joy's in bed asleep I'm ringing the doorbell again. She'd never forgive me if we didn't.' But ringing and hammering on the door was to no avail. There was apparently no one in.

Very, very, carefully, to cause Tiger the least amount of pain, Mungo lifted her into his car, lying her down well supported and covered by his car rug. 'She's in deep shock. The poor thing. Come on, let's get home with her.'

With a painful tremor in her voice Miriam asked, 'Mungo, you don't think Joy's done something foolish, do you?'

'Foolish? What kind of foolish?'

'Like . . . done away with herself. It's not like her isn't this.'

'I think she's had that kind of a day, Miriam. My first priority is to get this cat attended to. If Joy loses Tiger it will only make matters even worse for her. After all, she is Duncan's cat.'

Back at the surgery together they set up a drip for Tiger. 'Can't operate till she's revived a little. See that gash? It's quite bad, but nothing compared to the shock she's in. There's another one on her other side as though something big has had her in its mouth.'

'A big dog perhaps?'

'I've an idea maybe her ribs are cracked. Can't tell by touch, but I can't imagine she's been gashed open like this without the pressure causing at least cracked ribs. But I'll X-ray her when she's come round a bit. There we are, my beauty. You'll feel better in a while. Duncan would be distraught if he were here.'

'I love Duncan and I can understand why he's had enough and gone walkabout, but it's about time he came home. Joy really needs him. At the very least he'd make her see sense.'

'I'm sorry for her, but she isn't being sensible about this.'

'She's way beyond being sensible about anything. One good thing might come out of this. She might realize how much she loves Duncan.'

Mungo leaned over Tiger to kiss Miriam. 'I'll say this once more and then we shan't mention it again: I never encouraged Joy. All she's ever been is a well regarded, greatly valued colleague. It's you who's stolen my heart.'

'She's my dearest friend. And I'm worried sick.'

'I know. I know. Tomorrow we'll do something serious about her. I'm leaving Tiger for a while and then I might well operate tonight before we go to bed. I've a full list tomorrow and won't be able to find the time then. Would you help me? Don't want to call one of the girls out.'

'I'll try for Tiger's sake. We've got to save her.'

It was two o'clock before Mungo and Miriam got to bed. Tiger survived the operation but only just; the ragged gashes on both flanks needed careful, intricate stitching. Miriam was tremendously moved by Mungo's skill. Watching his elegant hands skilfully bringing together the sides of the gash, she was truly humbled.

As Mungo straightened up when the last stitch was tied

off, Miriam said, 'My darling, you're impressive at work. Impressive. What a wonderful job you've done. Once the stitches have gone it will hardly be noticeable.'

'Thank you. Right. Let's get her stowed away in a cage. I'll carry her, you come with the drip.'

Miriam couldn't resist bending down and kissing Tiger. 'Goodnight. Keep fighting. OK. See you in the morning. Is it warm enough in here for her?'

'It is. The heating's on all night. Now bed for you. And me. Let's wait and see what tomorrow brings.'

Tomorrow brought the good news that Tiger had survived the night and was looking positively perky in the circumstances. Tomorrow also brought Scott on stream for a day's work. He burst into reception at exactly five minutes past eight, full of get up and go. 'G'day, Stephie.'

Forgetting the engagement ring on her finger, Stephie flung her arms round him and kissed him. 'Welcome back, Scott. Am I glad to see you.'

'Think I'll go out and come back in again if that's the reception I'm going to get!' He gave Stephie the full Scott Spencer treatment of kiss, squeeze and big hug, which normally brought most girls to heel – his heel. As Scott gripped her hands he felt the engagement ring and gave it a thorough inspection. He staggered across to the reception desk and gripping tight hold he groaned loudly and mopped his forehead, sobbing, 'She's found someone else while I've been away and all this time I thought she was saving herself for me. I thought I was the man in her life.'

It occurred to Stephie that Scott had been very scathing about her Adam when he was in Barleybridge before, so she decided not to tell him who her fiancé was.

'Come on, Scott. For heaven's sakes, we're not all

worshipping at your feet, you know. You've never had the slightest interest in me. Be honest.'

Scott sprang upright, agreed he hadn't while giving her the benefit of a big grin, and asked for his list. She gave it to him and studied him as he read it. There was no doubt Scott had changed. He might be playing the fool as he'd always done but there was something different about him. He'd kind of grown up. Even his clothes were different: tweed jacket, though still the same Australian wide-brimmed hat without the corks, restrained tie, and believe it or not, brown leather slip-on shoes, and not those whacking great Timberland boots he'd used to wear. Sober to say the least.

'I might never have been away. I can't believe it. The same old names. Amazing!'

'Life goes on.'

Scott smiled at her and for a moment his charm began to work. 'Of course.'

'Go on, get cracking. They'll all be so glad to see you.'

'*Au revoir*, my beauty. See you anon.' Scott reeled off down the back corridor, opened the back door and shouted, 'You're not expecting this poor old Aussie to go out in this, are you? Stone the crows! It's bloody perishin'!'

Stephie heard the door slam shut and laughed. Hell! He was so sexy, it was unbelievable. Whoever it was who finally got his ring on her finger, she'd have to be one heck of a woman, and a good runner to boot even to catch up with him in the first place. Between answering the tele-phone and noting down clients who'd arrived for their appointments, Stephie kept remembering the feel of his arms around her and the sharp, sandalwood smell of him kissing her, and came to the conclusion that her Adam would never compare, but then she couldn't live with all that overt sexy charm, so she'd have to be content with what she'd got.

Uppermost in her mind was the fact that Miriam, who should have been on duty instead of Joy, had cried off coming in early because she was so worried about Joy.

'You see, Stephie, we rang and rang the doorbell and knocked and shouted but there was no reply at all. No lights. Nothing. So I'm doing a quick run over to her house just to check. Be as quick as possible. Bye!'

Miriam didn't take her car right into Joy's drive but parked it round the corner of the lane where it couldn't be seen from the house. She thought that if Joy realized who was at the door she might well not respond to the bell.

But she did, and the sight of this sad, fraught-looking Joy peering round the half-open door, still in her dressing gown and very obviously suffering from a serious hangover, scared Miriam to death.

'Joy! My dear!' She opened wide her arms to hug her, but Joy darted back so she couldn't.

'Miriam!'

'Can I come in?'

'If you want.'

Joy staggered off to the kitchen, leaving Miriam to follow if she wished.

'We came last night, but you didn't answer.'

'Dead to the world, I'm afraid.'

'Ah! Right. I've come to tell you about Tiger.'

From where she was sitting at the kitchen table with her head in her hands, Joy asked why.

'Last night we found her under your lavender bush, you know the one I adore and wish was mine, and she was crying, and very poorly. She'd been in a fight.'

'Oh!'

'So we couldn't leave her. Mungo operated on her last night.'

'Right.'

Miriam found it uphill work trying to explain. She could have been describing a morning in a launderette for all the reaction she was getting. 'She looked as though she'd been mauled by a dog. Gashes along her flanks. Perhaps we should have asked your permission but it was rather urgent. She's doing well this morning. Mungo's pleased with her.'

'Glad he's pleased with something.'

'Black coffee?'

'No.'

'Come on, Joy. This isn't like you.'

'No, it isn't. Will you bring her back when she's ready?'

'Well, of course we will. But aren't you—'

'Don't think I'm coming back, because I'm not.'

'In that case I'd better be off because I'm covering for you.'

'Oh, dear. How sad!'

'I may as well say this: Scott's started back this morning.'

'Oh! Well then, so long as the Practice is OK.'

Miriam couldn't miss the sarcasm in her voice. 'It's our livelihood. Yours and mine.'

'Not any more. I've resigned.'

'I know you have, but I'm absolutely sure we'd all welcome you back.'

'Don't hold your breath.'

Miriam walked towards the kitchen door. 'If you change your mind, just come back. OK? Be seeing you. I'll ring with news about Tiger. I'm still your friend whatever happens. Bye for now.'

'Bye.' Joy didn't even turn to watch this dear friend of

hers leave, but continued sitting with her head in her hands. When the door shut and Miriam was safely out of hearing, Joy let her tears roll down her cheeks unheeded. Between her sobs she repeated time and again, 'Duncan, please, come home. Please. Just come home.'

Duncan, chilled to the marrow in the unheated hovel where he was living, was listening to the Atlantic waves crashing on the shore with their monotonous regularity and was making up his mind whether or not to return home. He'd had enough of deprivation, this hairshirt lark and the isolation. When, before, he'd longed for solitude in some godforsaken place he'd passionately envied all those people who'd chosen such a life. Now he'd got what he'd wanted it had gone sour, very sour, and the comfort of his open fire, his cats curled beside his feet and a glass of brandy warming in his hands seemed extraordinarily appealing. But still he shied away from including Joy in the vision of home he'd conjured up in his mind . . .

Chapter 5

Visiting Dan in hospital every day was distressing Rose more than she had ever imagined it could. She longed for his love and support, for the warmth of him in bed beside her, for his smiling face over the breakfast table, for the way he loved Jonathan and her and showed it without reservation. She tried hard to make sure she had news which would interest him, but eventually there didn't seem any point in telling him anything at all, because his response was so slight. When her stepfather Lloyd came over to England without warning a few days after Dan's accident she almost fell into his arms with delight.

'Pa! How wonderful. You should have rung and let me know.'

He hugged her and kissed her, hugged Jonathan and kissed him too. 'Been far too long since I saw you. I can scarcely recognize this young man. My, how he's grown. Come to your step-grandpa, young man. See! He remembers me! He truly does. I'm sure he gets to look more like me the older he gets. Now, my girl, you're not looking your best. Tell me about Dan.' Lloyd settled down on the sofa, lifted Jonathan onto his lap and gave him a parcel to open. 'Well. I'm waiting, Rose. How is he?'

'Physically he's doing fine, but his spirits are very low. I dread going to see him. I mean, I want to go, but he's so depressed. You see, he's not used to being confined, is he? They've kept him in because his blood pressure has been dancing all over the place, and also because he won't make the slightest effort to use his crutches. Hobbles out to the loo and that's it. Mention physio and he point blank refuses even to get out of bed. He hates the restrictions, the noise and the bustle, and he can be very snappy. Belligerent almost. The nurses say he is quite difficult some days, but they claim it's only to be expected from a man in his kind of active occupation. But it's not Dan, is it?'

'Have you been to see him today?'

Rose nodded. 'I go every day. Each morning, my cleaner comes in to look after Jonathan while I go. I'd love to go for the whole day, but he won't allow that.'

'So I should think. Too much for you. Is it the hospital where you had Jonathan?'

'Yes.'

'Then I shall go see him tonight. Give him a surprise. I'll get him sorted. He's pining, I expect.'

'Pining? What for?'

Lloyd was amazed she didn't realize why. 'I should imagine he's pining to be with you and this young man.'

'Do you think that's it?'

'Of course. The man adores you. It's obvious even to a blind man.'

Suddenly Rose burst into tears. Jonathan slithered down from Lloyd's lap and ran across to her. 'Mummy, Mummy.'

Lloyd stood up. 'Cup of tea called for. I'll get it.' He left Rose to weep alone. Knowing her he guessed it was probably the first time she'd cried since Dan's accident. He loitered in the kitchen, giving her time to get herself together. He grieved over her tears within himself and wondered how he was going to solve things for her. There was nothing on earth he wouldn't attempt for her sake. Never having had a child of his own, Rose was the closest to his heart anyone on earth had ever come. And that included her mother.

'Now, my dear, when you've drunk this we'll take Jonathan for a little walk in his buggy, shall we? Just down the lane and back to get a bit of fresh air. I need it after being in that plane for an age. Then I'll go to the take-away in the village for us and then I'll be off to the hospital while you get Jonathan to bed. Don't worry about putting sheets on the bed for me, I'll do that when I get back.'

Rose began to protest.

'No, my dear! No objecting. It's my plan and we're sticking to it. Drink your tea, though it beats me what good it does a living soul. You've lived here too long, you know, you're getting English habits!' But he smiled as he said it and allowed his eyes to rest on her beauty. Could there be a more beautiful girl in the whole world than his Rose? Not only did she have physical grace but her facial features were exquisite and what was best her beauty also came from within, a sweet glow, which radiated her whole being.

'So do we know what this baby is?'

Rose gave him a watery smile and shook her head. 'No, we decided we'd wait and see.'

'Well, if this one's a boy they'll make a real duo. Dan will be so very proud.'

Rose agreed. 'So will I. I don't care boy or girl, so long as the baby's OK.'

'Exactly. Exactly. Quite right. Shall we go?'

Lloyd arrived at the hospital full of plans. He'd brook no interference. He was getting Dan home where he knew he needed to be. Fretting would only hamper his progress so it was up to him to fight for what was right.

He found Dan fast asleep and therefore unaware that he was about to be swept up in the tornado that was Lloyd, who'd had a shock when he looked at Dan. All the vigour appeared to have drained away and he'd lost weight. In fact, Lloyd had never seen him so thin, and his forehead was still multi-coloured from the impact he'd had with the windscreen, which didn't improve his looks. He strode straight to the ward desk and addressed the nurse sitting there.

'Good evening. My son-in-law is a patient in this ward. His name is Daniel Franklin Brown and he has two broken legs due to a traffic accident. Everyone calls me Lloyd. And you are?'

She showed him her badge.

'Ah! I see. Sister Melody. Nice name. How's he doin'?'

'Not too well. He's refused his physio again this morning. We're wanting him to use crutches, you see, get about a bit, circulation and all that, but he won't have it. His blood pressure is see-sawing about too. He's picky about his food and doesn't want to eat. Claims he's lying in bed and doesn't need it. Which is rubbish. He's a very difficult man.'

'Kind of switched off, has he?'

Sister Melody nodded. 'Depressed, I'm afraid. It gets some people like that, you know. Shock and things.'

'Mmm. I'll have a word.' Lloyd marched back to Dan's bedside to find him on the brink of waking up. 'Good evening, Dan.'

Dan came to with a start. 'Good heavens! Lloyd! What a surprise.'

'Couldn't have you laid up here and me not seeing how things stood.'

'Is Rose's mother with you?'

'Certainly not. No. I'm here on my own.'

'Have you seen Rose?'

'I have.' He pulled up a chair and prepared to over-egg the pudding a little. 'I'm not very impressed with her, Dan. She's pining, you know.'

'I thought she didn't seem too good this morning.'

'Getting very upset and it won't do. Be better when you get home. Any chance of it in the near future?'

Dan shook his head, 'No, there isn't. I'm a permanent fixture here, I think. I'm still getting severe headaches, they give me painkillers and they make me sleep and sleep.'

'I see. I'm worried about the baby coming early, you know, with all the upset.'

Dan fell back on his pillows, looking both helpless and defeated.

Change of subject needed, thought Lloyd. 'Has anyone from the practice been in to see you?'

'A continuous stream. Someone comes every day.'

'That's good. And very kind of them. And all these cards stuck above the bed? From clients?'

'Yes, and from the staff.'

'They'd look good in the cottage on the wall near those French windows that look out on the garden. I could take down a couple of the pictures and they'd fit real nice there.'

'Yes.'

'Given you crutches, have they?'

'Yes.'

'Oh well, then you could manage. Pity the bedrooms are upstairs. Otherwise . . .' Lloyd got to his feet and began measuring the length of the bed, then its width.

'What are you doing, Lloyd?'

Other visitors began taking a great interest in Lloyd's activities.

'Just thinking, I bet we could get a bed down those stairs of yours, even though there's a bend.' From the corner of his eye he could see that Dan was beginning to take notice. 'But, of course, you can't, can you, the state you're in?'

'They'd never let me out.'

'They will if I have a word.'

'But Rose wouldn't be able to cope. No, it's not fair to her, she's got less than six weeks to go. It's better if I stay here.'

'She wouldn't have to cope. I'd employ nurses and therapists, believe me, round the clock if necessary. If I've learned anything at all in business it's that nothing is impossible.'

Lloyd saw a light come back into Dan's face. 'I'm dreading weeks in hospital.'

'Dread no longer. There's no need for you to be here. It's all up to you. I'll make it work. Believe me. I will. How about it?' He took Dan's hand in his and gave it a squeeze. 'We'll organize it a.s.a.p. Give me a chance to get a bed down the stairs. What do you say?'

'I don't know.'

'Just think, you'd have Rose all day and little Jonathan. Now that's worth something, isn't it? Nothing ventured—'

'You're on.'

The two of them clasped hands, as though acknowledging a victory at the end of a race.

Sister Melody came up to them and said, 'I've been watching the two of you. What are you cooking up?'

'We're wondering about Dan coming home. It's a big struggle for my daughter to get here every day, her being so far gone, as they say.'

The nurse pointed to her desk, 'A word if you please.' The way she spoke gave Lloyd no alternative. His hackles rose but if he was to get his way . . . He humbly followed her.

Having seated herself comfortably, she indicated the chair she expected Lloyd to sit on. 'No, there is no way he can go home, whatever the facilities, unless he is to some extent mobile. Can we say that as soon as he is reasonably agile with his crutches then he can go. Give him an incentive to get up off his backside and make the effort, mmm?'

'Ah! Right. Yes. I see. Good thinking.'

'How is he placed at home? Stairs wise and such?'

They discussed the whys and wherefores at length until eventually Lloyd had persuaded her. 'OK, then. Tomorrow, first thing, I'm moving a bed downstairs for him. They've got a downstairs bathroom, so that's no problem. I'll pay for nurses to attend every day if that's best, physios, whatever you recommend. I just want him home. He's not himself at all and I don't think however much care he gets in here,' Lloyd remembered he was trying to get his own way, 'and I'm sure it's excellent care with someone like you in charge, that he'll improve away from his home.'

'You've still got to put the idea to Sister Frost, she's on tomorrow. And his doctors, of course.'

'No problem. With your support I'm sure we'll get him home.'

Sister Melody grinned from ear to ear. 'If ever you were

condemned to death you'd talk your way out of it; the judge would just crumble.'

Lloyd laughed. 'That's my girl! I'll say goodnight to Dan and be back tomorrow.'

He strode back to Dan's bedside, smiling to himself. 'Now, Dan, I've extracted a promise from Sister there, that once they can see you've got the crutch business sorted out and you're fairly nimble, we can have you home. Which is wise, of course, so up on your feet tomorrow and let's have you swinging down the ward when I come in. OK, pal?'

There was a fluster at the sister's desk, and a few sharp words exchanged, and when they turned to look it was Zoe come to visit.

'Two minutes, I promise. Cross my heart.'

'Very well, but it's way past visiting time now. My patients should be settling down for the night. I shall time you.' Sister Melody wagged her finger at Zoe and checked her watch.

Zoe escaped to Dan's bed, plonked a bag of fruit and a car magazine on his locker and held out her hand to Lloyd. 'I don't think we've had the pleasure? I'm Zoe Savage, Barleybridge Practice.'

She and Lloyd shook hands. 'Hi! Nice to meet you. I'm Lloyd Kominski, Dan's father-in-law. I'm just going. Remember our agreement, Dan. To the end of the ward and back tomorrow first thing. I'll get the bed organized at the cottage. Sleep well.'

Zoe sank gratefully into the chair beside the bed and said, 'Well, now, Dan, the dragon at the desk says two minutes. How long are you stuck in this mausoleum?'

'On the understanding that once I get a bit mobile I shall be going home. Lloyd's flown specially from the USA just to get me up and about, he wants me out of here.'

'Nothing quite like getting home, is there? Are you still in pain?'

'I ache all over but actual pain, no. Just sickened by it all.' He turned away from her and she thought this wasn't the pushy, vigorous Dan she'd always known.

'Brought the car magazine because quite by chance I saw your car being hauled off to the police compound. Just be thankful you've survived. What a mess! You must have someone batting on your side.' She'd got him looking at her now. 'That Lloyd seems on the dynamic side?'

'He is. There's no sitting about when he's around. He's up there at the front leading the troops.'

'Glad you're OK anyway.' Zoe paused for a moment and then said, 'Nothing new at the Practice . . . apart from Scott.'

'Seems a good chap. Came to see me on Sunday with Miriam and Mungo. He's certainly relieved my mind.'

'Excellent vet is Scott.'

'So I hear. Just glad he turned up when he did. Heaven sent.'

'You know Joy's resigned?'

'Joy's resigned? Never!'

Zoe told him the story as she'd heard it, glad to be able to distract him from his depression. 'Of course, what she needs is Duncan home. He'd make her see sense.'

'I wonder where the blazes he's gone?'

'Don't know, but it's not fair to stay out of touch. At the very least he could put her mind at rest.'

'He should, you're right. And Oscar, how is he?'

'The "blip" as I used to call him?'

Dan managed a smile. 'I remember.'

'He's doing fine. Full of life, like little boys are.'

'I'm glad.'

'The dragon's making signals. I'd better go.' Zoe hesitated for a moment and then leaned over the bed and placed a kiss on his cheek. 'Hurry up and get better. We all miss you.'

'Thanks. I'll try. Goodnight and thank you for coming. Thanks for the magazine and the fruit, too.'

Imitating Lloyd's New York accent, Zoe said, 'And remember, to the end of the ward and back, first thing tomorrow.' She turned to go but came back to say, 'Sorry we got off on the wrong foot when you first came. I've learned to value you since then.'

Dan watched her thanking the sister for letting her see him, thinking how much less prickly she'd become.

But she hadn't, not really. She'd lost her edge because she was bone tired and desperate to be tucked up in bed enjoying a long sleep. Which was where she was going the moment she got home. How she hated hospitals! Giving birth to Oscar in this hospital had been the most horrendous experience of her life. Finals, working on pig farms, in stables, lambing in some godforsaken place in the midst of a seriously severe winter had been a cake-walk by comparison. She looked at her hands on the steering wheel, not artistic hands but quite adequate, and thought about how red and swollen they'd been for the whole of the three weeks she'd been working alongside the shepherd, and how she'd cried with the unimaginable fatigue and the cold and being convinced her hands would never get back to how they used to be.

No. The arrival of Oscar and having to try so hard to love him had truly been the worst thing that had happened to her. She did love him. Some days more than others. Some days she could well do without him and most especially without the obligation he'd put her under with her mother. They'd never got on when she was at home. She and her. Never. And never would. It would all have been better if there'd been a houseful of children, then her mother would have been too busy to dwell on her, Zoe's, shortcomings. Having to ask her to come to live in the cottage to care for Oscar because of her difficult hours had been the greatest of humiliations.

Zoe turned into her drive, switched off the engine and braced herself for the inquisition. As she opened the car door she could hear the Whitworths having yet another of their marital disputes, and was thankful she wasn't married. She shuddered at the thought of being on the receiving end of his kind of macho brutality. Though Rose and Dan made it work. But then Rose was Rose and who wouldn't make a go of it with her? She, Zoe Savage, couldn't hold a candle to her.

Zoe was greeted by the sound of Oscar crying hysterically upstairs.

'What's the matter, Mother?'

'I've been upstairs twice and I can't make head nor tail of him. I'm glad you've come.'

Zoe raced up the stairs to find Oscar in a sweat, shaking and incoherent.

'What is it, darling? Come on, then.' She lifted him out of his cot, sat herself down in the big easy chair by the window and hugged him close. 'There, there, tell Mummy what the matter is.'

Gradually his fear began to subside and he stuttered, 'Big man. Frightened Oscar. Shouting.'

'That was just a dream, you know. There's no big man here. Not at all. No. Never.'

'Big snake in my cot.'

'Well, believe me, Mummy doesn't have big snakes in

73

the house. Honest. So it definitely was all a dream. A nasty dream.'

Oscar nodded his agreement, but continued to sob against her shoulder.

'I say, shall I get hotty teddy for you? Yes?'

Oscar agreed. 'Yes, hotty teddy.'

'Right, well, you get back into your cot and I'll fetch him.'

But this made him cling tighter. 'No. No.'

'Well, you come downstairs with me then while I warm him up.'

She put the bag from hotty teddy's tummy into the microwave and heated it up for two minutes. 'Go sit on Granny's lap while I get you some warm milk.' Without asking his permission, she carried him through to the sitting room and put him on Joan's lap. Oscar stiffened and screamed louder than ever. Zoe quickly took him off her knee, soothed him again and did the balancing act of warming milk for him while holding him close.

'Right, back up to bed.'

She eventually put him back in his cot, snuggled up close to hotty teddy and with cuddly blanket close to his cheek. He gave her a beaming smile and settled down to sleep again.

When she got downstairs, Joan's first words were, 'He's got you right under his thumb, has that child. He knows exactly how to play your tune. You've spoiled him. That's what.'

'He'd had a nightmare, brought on I've no doubt by the warring Whitworths, my bedroom being the nearest to their house. They were out on the path screaming at each other when I came home. He was terrified.'

'You never had nightmares.'

'No. But he *does*. All he needs is reassurance. Thanks for looking after him while I went to see Dan. Poor chap needs cheering up.'

'If that's your idea of sarcasm I'm not impressed.'

Zoe puzzled for a moment. 'But I meant it. I am grateful. I wanted to go. No chance during the day.'

'When's your next day off?'

'Saturday and Sunday, now we've got Scott.'

'Well, I've got friends coming to tea on Saturday.'

'That's nice. In that case, Oscar and I will clear off, out of the way. OK?'

Joan beamed her satisfaction. 'Good. That's very thoughtful.'

'I'm going to bed. Anything you want before I go?'

'I'll have a G and T please, dear.'

'How many will that make tonight?' Arms akimbo Zoe waited for her reply. It didn't matter if her mother lied about it, because she always took a fresh glass each time she had one, not liking refills, so all Zoe had to do was count the glasses waiting to go in the dishwasher.

'Only my second.'

There was only one other glass in the sink, which hadn't been there when she'd filled the dishwasher before she went to the hospital. So perhaps her mother was getting things under control at last. But even so, was her mother a fit person to be caring for such a young active child? Was she never to have peace of mind? And now she had to add Scott to her list of problems. She'd managed two days without seeing him, but avoiding him for ever wouldn't be possible. One day he'd be there and so would she and wham! She'd have to put on a front. Zoe turned over in bed, pulled the duvet even higher up and snuggled down for sleep. She heard Oscar in his cot beside her bed shuffling about and opened her eyes to check he was still covered up, closed them again and began drifting off to sleep.

In the event, she carried off her first meeting with Scott rather well.

The reception area was full of waiting clients and there was Scott making a late arrival and there was she coming in for a word with Mungo about a farm client who expected her to call this morning to examine their pigs, which kept dying for no apparent reason, but they'd not paid their account for three months now. Scott saw her and his face lit up. 'Zoe!' he shouted and before she knew it she was swept up in his arms and getting the full Scott Spencer treatment.

The clients cheered to a man.

'What's she done to get a kiss like that?'

'He didn't give me a kiss like that.'

'By heck! That'll get her engine started!'

'I bet she's real glad you're back, Scott.'

Scott released her, grinning. He bowed to the assembled admirers.

Zoe put her spinning heart back in its rightful place and minded not to let his kisses weaken her resolve.

'Hi, Scott. Glad to have you back. Couldn't keep up the one-off one-on regime for much longer and neither could Colin. Glad to be back?'

'I certainly am. Your knight in shining armour to the rescue, eh!'

'Absolutely. I'm hoping to catch Mungo before his first appointment. Sorry! Be seeing you.'

Mungo's decision was that she should see the pigs, and suss out the situation about payment. They weren't a charity, but all the same, the animals mustn't suffer.

So Zoe escaped through the back door, thinking Scott had gone, but he hadn't. He was standing beside Dan's Land Rover reading through his visit list.

'Hi! Sorry about your mother, by the way.'

Scott looked up at her. 'Getting over it, thanks. Time for a drink tonight? Fox and Grapes, for old times' sake?'

Zoe nodded. 'OK. Can't stay long though. Mother gets in a spin if I'm late.'

'Got your mum living with you now?'

'That's right. Needs the company, you know how it is. Oh! Sorry, didn't think.'

'That's OK. See you then.'

He hoisted himself into the driving seat and pulled away immediately. Something of Dan's mad driving must have transmitted itself through the steering wheel because he rushed out of the car park like crazy, but when she got to the exit he was stuck across both lanes of the road trying to turn right but couldn't because the traffic was so heavy. Eventually the gridlock resolved itself and he swung away, leaving Zoe to turn left with comparative ease.

Quarry Mount Farm, though fairly close to other farms, always felt to be totally isolated. There was something about the way the road to it dipped away from the main road running up to Pick's Farm, and the trees growing around it, which desperately needed some intelligent husbandry to clear them out and give light to young trees struggling for existence. The floor of the woods was littered with fallen trees from the big storm way back in the eighties, so the hint of desolation and desertion gave a feeling of a haunted wood. The house itself where the Goodwoods lived was little more than a woodsman's cottage making do as a farmhouse, and the farm buildings had an air of being temporary, that someone one day would be constructing permanent buildings, but the day had not yet arrived.

Zoe parked on a piece of land roughly cleared for the purpose. What always gave her a shock was the appearance of Mrs Goodwood. Being at least six feet tall she dwarfed Zoe. Her hair was blacker than black, were that possible, her eyes darkest brown and piercing, her eyebrows bushy, her jaw square and her mouth long and full, at odds with the rest of her hollow-cheeked face. She had a uniform for the farm, which never changed, summer and winter. A minimum of two men's sweaters, a pair of dungarees in need of a wash, massive, steel-capped wellington boots and a man's cap, too small, crammed on her head. Tucked in the neck of her sweaters there was inevitably a neat silk scarf that did change with the seasons. Today, being winter, it would be a fiery red.

Shutting the farmhouse door behind her, Mrs Goodwood shouted in that deep voice of hers, 'Good morning to you, Zoe. And how are you, my dear?'

'Very well thank you and you?'

'Fine. Fine. Weather chilly for this time of year.'

'It certainly is.'

'Won't get any better until late March.'

'I'm looking forward to spring.'

'So am I.'

Having gone through her usual greeting ritual, Mrs Goodwood led the way to the field where she kept her pigs. As far as the eye could see the field was dotted with corrugated-iron pig shelters. It was a vast field, the last level area before the land shelved deeply down into the Chess Valley, accommodating a positive battalion of pigs of all shapes and sizes, all busy rooting and growing big for the market. In the crisp morning air they were a glad sight.

The two of them walked steadily round the field, stopping now and then to look at first one group and then another, observing their antics, studying them for the slightest hint of illness. Some came up to them curious, litters of small pigs gambolled away in a flurry. Others stood and stared.

'Well, they all seem very happy and energetic. There's a feeling of well-being wherever you look. Surprising.'

'Then, you see, out of the blue I'll have a batch of them drooping. I can't understand it. It's money, you know, them going dead on me.'

Zoe looked Mrs Goodwood in the eye. 'I'm glad you mentioned money. I've spoken to Mungo this morning. We're not prepared to allow animals to suffer but—'

Shocked and offended, Mrs Goodwood said, 'You're not asking me for money, are you? Not at a time like this.'

'Well, yes, I am. You owe three months now. As Mungo frequently says, we are not a charity. You can't expect expertise and not have to pay for it.'

'What expertise? You haven't solved anything yet.'

Zoe had to admit to herself she hadn't. 'Look, the next time you have a group taken ill, ring us. Don't keep hoping they won't die. Ring immediately and I'll try to organize it so that two of us come out and take a look together. It's the spasmodic nature of it I can't get to grips with. Nothing and then deaths. There must be something I'm missing.'

Mrs Goodwood agreed. 'Right. I'll do that. Come into the house. I've got something for you.'

She led the way out of the field, secured the gate with an intricate arrangement of tying ropes and fixing catches, and headed for the house.

The moment she entered the front door of the farm-house Zoe felt she was on a filmset for a horror movie. Thankfully there weren't any cobwebs, but there was strange heavy furniture, which loomed over the room, spooky engravings heavily framed in black, a cauldron hanging above the flames in the vast open inglenook of inglenooks, massive logs awaiting their funeral pyre stack-ed beside it obviously dragged in from the surrounding woods, and small windows, all of which made for a strange, gloomy atmosphere that sent shivers down Zoe's spine.

'Here, look, in the kitchen.'

On the ancient oak table, set in the middle of the kitchen floor, was a beautiful cake, round and fruity, the top decorated with toasted almonds standing shoulder to shoulder.

'That's for you.'

'I couldn't possibly accept—'

'You must. It's yours. My speciality.'

'That's most kind.'

Mrs Goodwood dived into a kind of pantry and emerged, bottom first, triumphantly waving a Harrods' carrier bag. 'My Cecil loves this recipe. Says it's my finest.' She wrapped the cake in greaseproof paper and popped it delicately into the carrier. 'There, my dear. Yours.'

'Thank you. I shan't be depriving Mr Goodwood, shall I?'

'No, certainly not.'

Zoe thought there must be a Mr Goodwood some-where, but where? She obviously didn't care for all those pigs by herself, there wouldn't be enough hours in a day, so where was he?

'Promise to let me know as soon as you notice them

drooping, won't you? At the very least it might give us a clue if we watch their behaviour when they're actually ill.'

'I will.'

'Thank you for the cake, be seeing you.'

As Zoe drove up out of the valley she realized it was still possible to smell that all-pervading pig aroma. She didn't find it obnoxious herself, but to more sensitive people living in the area it could be a definite drawback. She'd ask Scott tonight if he had any clues. Give them something to talk about.

Scott was such a tonic. He had her laughing before she'd downed even a quarter of her wine. 'It's true, believe me.'

'Well, I find it hard to believe. I thought all Aussies were very manly.'

'There's an element creeping in about getting in touch with your feminine side. It's all very disturbing.' He grinned at her. 'How are you, Zoe?'

'Me? I'm fine. What's it like coming back?'

Scott shrugged and took another long drink of his lager. 'At least the beer's cold now.'

'True. That's a bonus.'

Scott was silent for a moment and then asked very tentatively, 'Kate, how is she? Have you heard from her?'

'At veterinary college and according to a lecturer Mungo knows, proving an excellent student.'

'I'm glad she got in.'

'So were we.'

'Great girl.' He looked beyond Zoe's shoulder, lost in thought.

Somewhat sceptically Zoe snapped at him. 'Well, there's one thing your mother's illness gave you, a good excuse to disappear, quicko.'

Scott came back from wherever he'd been and said, 'I wouldn't have been any good for her. No good at all.'

'You don't think so?'

'I know so.'

'So who would you be good for? Not Bunty. She's married, by the way, to Sergeant Bird.'

Briefly Scott looked guilty. 'Good, I'm glad. What she needed, security.'

'You still haven't answered my question.'

Scott straightened his beer mat, read the advertisement printed round the edge and then, putting his glass down on it, said, 'I'd be good for no one.'

'What has happened to the great Australian stud I used to know?'

A wicked grin lit up his face. 'I'm still the stud, but I'm not husband material.'

'Don't you get lonely leading such an irresponsible life?'

'No, it's fun. Don't you get lonely?'

Dangerous ground here. 'No. I've always got Mother to nag me. I don't need a husband, too.'

'I see. Another drink?'

'No, thanks.'

'Time for a meal? They do a damn good steak here.'

'My meal will be ready right now and I'm heading for a first-class nag, being late.'

'Ah! No possibility that I might—?'

'Certainly not, my mother needs a week's notice if someone's coming for dinner. Thanks for the drink. Be seeing you. Must go.'

On her way home Zoe deliberately called in to see Rose. She'd give her mother something to nag her about when she got in.

'Rose! Are you in the middle of things? If so I'll buzz off home. Can't stay long because of Oscar.'

82

'No, come in. Lloyd's gone to the supermarket for me so I'm sorting the freezer to make space. He doesn't know when to stop shopping, it's the result of being married to my mother for so long; she shops like there's no tomorrow. Jonathan's in the sitting room so we'll sit in there.'

'Hi, Jonathan! How are you?'

He smiled up at her but was too engrossed in the toy farmyard he was playing with to bother to speak.

Rose lowered herself into a chair. 'Things must be easier for you now you've got Scott. He's a lovely chap. He called the other night.'

'Yes. He is. A womanizer though. Got no commitment at all. Free lover on tap if needed. So watch it!'

Rose had to smile. 'I don't think he'd be fancying me at the moment, do you?'

'Anyone's fair game to Scott. Boosts his frail ego. Did I say frail?' Zoe rolled her eyes. 'How long is it now till the baby?'

'Four and a half weeks.' Satisfaction seemed to ooze from Rose as she spoke.

'You enjoy married life, don't you?'

'Married to Dan, yes. Except he's so depressed at the moment. But yes, he's great.'

'Ah! That's the rub, there aren't many Dans about.'

'True. But I believe there's someone for everyone, somewhere, and when you find it don't let it go. I came very close to losing Dan, but retrieved him in the nick of time by flying the Atlantic to plead my cause.'

Zoe recollected the surprise arrival of Rose after her transatlantic dash. 'Oh! Yes, of course you did.'

'So I've learned you mustn't miss out on love because of this and because of that reason. Take it while it's offered with both hands and work to keep it.'

83

They chatted a while longer until they heard Lloyd coming back with the shopping, and then Zoe took her chance and left. What lucky people Rose and Dan were.

Chapter 6

Duncan's cat Tiger was making good progress and Mungo was feeling very pleased. Another couple of days and he felt sure that Tiger could be taken home. But when the day arrived, Joy asked if someone could take her home for her as she wasn't up to driving at the moment. So Miriam asked Annette if she would mind taking Tiger. Just before Annette was ready for leaving in her car to oblige Joy, a client came rushing in carrying a cat basket.

'Please! Can you help? It's Cherub.'

'Why, Miss Chillingsworth, whatever is the matter?'

'Oh, Mrs Price. She's in a terrible state. Can someone look at her, please? Now. Right away. I'm sure she's dying.'

'Sit yourself down. I'll check with Graham, he'll perhaps have a free minute. Sit down, before you fall down.'

'I'm terrified.' But Miss Chillingsworth sat down. She'd been such a long time on the bus and she was sure that . . .

Miriam came back to her. 'His client is just leaving so he can see you immediately. Come along.' With Miriam's hand under her elbow Miss Chillingsworth dashed into Graham's consulting room.

'Good morning, Miss Chillingsworth. Now, what can we do for Cherub today?'

'She's been in the most terrible fight. Who with I don't

know, but she spent last night out of the house and I found her by the back door this morning, not an hour ago. Oh, Mr Murgatroyd, please help.'

While she'd been speaking, Graham had been gently opening the door to the cat basket and feeling around inside. 'Was she unconscious when you found her?'

'Well, yes. Oh dear! I'll have to sit down again.' Miss Chillingsworth plunged down onto a chair only just in time. 'My heart's beating so fast.'

Graham gently drew Cherub out of the basket onto the examination table and his heart sank. Her flank had a great jagged tear right from her shoulder to the base of her tail. She also had what Graham thought would prove to be fractures of at least two of her legs. She was in a state of deep shock. He put his stethoscope to her chest and listened to her heart, and he didn't like what he heard. This cat was so precious to Miss Chillingsworth he could scarcely bring himself to tell her what he thought he should do.

'Now, Miss Chillingsworth, you and I have been through a lot together over the years, haven't we?' She nodded. 'I've always been truthful, haven't I? Not pulled any punches.' Miss Chillingsworth nodded again. 'With your old Cherub and this new Cherub?'

She could read his message in his eyes. 'I – I know what you're trying to say.'

'Well, yes, I am. If you want me to try to save her I will, but we can't operate at the moment. The anaesthetic would, well, let's say she couldn't withstand it because she's in such deep shock. If you wish, I'll put her on a drip and see how she goes, but I'm not holding out much hope.'

'We have to give her a chance. Please.' In her anxiety Miss Chillingsworth was sitting at the very edge of her chair, her hands twisting and writhing where they lay on her lap.

Graham hesitated, trying to decide if Cherub was truly the hopeless case he was convinced she was. He shook his head but then looked at Miss Chillingsworth and made his decision for her sake. 'Very well, we'll give her a chance but . . . you've to promise me that you'll face the fact we may not be successful. Go sit in the waiting room and I'll put her on a drip and you can see her in the intensive care room before you leave, so you'll see for yourself we're doing our best.'

It was Miriam who took Miss Chillingsworth in to see Cherub later. 'I'll be brave, Mrs Price, I shan't make a scene.'

'You go right ahead and make a scene if you wish. I've never had a pet injured like she's injured but I'm sure you've every right.'

The two of them stood looking at Cherub, cradled on the woolly blanket with the drip feed anchored to her. Motionless. In fact, quite close to death.

Miss Chillingsworth poked a finger through the bars and could just touch a back leg. 'She's all I have, you see. All I have.'

'I can imagine. They're such a comfort, aren't they, animals? She's so prettily marked too, isn't she?'

'Oh, yes. Very pretty.'

As Miriam gazed at Cherub it occurred to her that the jagged tear down her side was worse than the one Tiger had sustained but exactly the same configuration. Was it possible they'd both been attacked by the same dog?

Her eyes full of tears, Miss Chillingsworth said softly, 'I love her so. Can I stay till the clinic closes? Just in case, you know.'

'Of course you may. No reason why not. We'll keep you supplied with tea.'

So Miss Chillingsworth sat through the long day waiting, waiting. Miriam provided her with a hearty packed lunch, which she scarcely touched, and with cups of tea until eventually at half past five she decided to go home.

'I'll go. You've been most kind. Mr Murgatroyd says there is a little more hope seeing as she's lasted all day. So I'll keep praying. I'll be back in the morning.'

'Very well. Wrap up tight. They say it will be even colder tomorrow.' Miriam watched her leaving and wished, how she wished, that Cherub would survive.

Before she went upstairs to make their evening meal Miriam had a word with Graham.

'You know Joy? Well, of course you do. Her cat Tiger, did you see her?'

'Not close up.'

'Well, she had exactly the same wounds as poor old Cherub. Ask Mungo to have a look at her, but I'm pretty certain. It seems odd, doesn't it? However, you ask Mungo. Are you going to be able to operate tonight?'

'Just going to take another look. If she's up to it, would Mungo help?'

'Ask him. He's nothing on tonight.'

In the event they both decided that they would X-ray her before they left that night and leave the operation until tomorrow. Mungo gravely shook his head. 'She's still in deep shock. I tell you what, we'll both come in early tomorrow and if she's survived the night we'll operate before my clinic and yours begins.'

'My day off tomorrow, but for Cherub's sake I'll come in. I can't stand the thought of her dying. And what's worse, I can't stand the thought of Miss Chillingsworth having to mourn her.' Graham stroked Cherub's head and added softly, 'Do you hear that, Cherub? You've to hang in there. No giving in. Right?' He looked up at Mungo, embarrassed. 'Apologies for sounding all kinds of a fool, but . . .' He shrugged and Mungo smiled.

'Look, as it happens, Sarah One is sleeping here tonight because I've got two valuable dogs needing attention, they've both had major operations today, so she can keep an eye on Cherub too. Just keep your fingers crossed. I think Miriam's right about Tiger and Cherub. They both have identical wounds, except Cherub is in a more desperate state. It's all very odd. See you seven a.m. sharp unless you hear from Sarah that Cherub hasn't lasted the night.'

Graham's phone rang at half past six the following morning. He rolled over, fumbled for his glasses, found his phone and answered, 'Graham here.' His heart sank when he heard it was Sarah One speaking. 'It's me. About Cherub.'

'Yes?'

'Just to say that Cherub is still with us. No probs during the night and she seems a bit better now. So the operation can go ahead.'

'Thanks.' Graham swung his legs out of bed.

'Shall I stay and assist?'

'That would be great. Absolutely. I'm having a quick shower and then I'll be there. Does Mungo know?'

'Yes. He rang down a few minutes ago.'

'Right. See you.'

'OK. I'll get organized.'

Mungo and Graham set about the operation with intense enthusiasm, each knowing the other's strengths and looking forward to working together.

Mungo studied the X-rays intensely, saying as he did so, 'Complicated, you know, Graham. Look here at the fracture line. It'll need a pin. Very delicate job, she's such a small cat. This is a challenge, by Jove.'

'I'm glad you're here.'

Mungo studied the X-rays for a while longer and then asked Sarah One to anaesthetize Cherub.

They worked on Cherub for almost two hours. And finally declared themselves satisfied with what they'd done.

'So glad it was the two of us, Mungo. Hell, but it was touch and go there.'

'I'm surprised she didn't have internal injuries because whatever it was that had hold of her was much bigger than her. See that hole there? It must have been a damn big animal to have a molar that size.'

'Right, Sarah, stow her away. Then off you go home to bed. Thanks for your help.'

Mungo took off his operating gown and went into reception to see if Miss Chillingsworth had arrived. Of course she had. She'd been there since eight o'clock sharp, waiting and praying.

When Mungo walked in she got to her feet, her hands clasped to her chest. 'Oh, Mr Price! They said you were . . . is she . . . all right?'

Mungo clasped her hands in his. 'Whatever you've been doing all night, keep on doing it. We've just finished operating, and though she's a long way to go yet and I'm making no promises, understand, things are going our way.'

'If you've assisted Mr Murgatroyd with the operation then I know she'll be fine. I've great faith in you both.'

'Thank you. We can't work miracles, but we do try. We don't usually allow clients in the back, but would you like

90

to take a peep? She hasn't come round from the anaesthetic yet, but she won't be long, and then you've to promise me you'll go home and get a meal and a sleep, because I expect you've hardly slept all night.'

Bunty was in the intensive care room, about to check on the two dogs in there, but when she saw Miss Chillingsworth come in she quietly slipped out and left her alone.

Dazed from lack of sleep, Miss Chillingsworth stood in front of Cherub's cage and wept. Partly with relief and partly because she couldn't bear seeing Cherub with her two front legs stiff and straight, wrapped in bright blue dressings, and a drip attached to her. She was horrified by the great bald patch right down her side where they'd shaved her fur so as to stitch the gash. Miss Chillingsworth shuddered at the sight of the intricate stitching needed to close it. Graham and Mungo. So compassionate. So very clever. Then she felt guilty. Should she have let them put Cherub to sleep rather than her have to go through all this? But she had to be given her chance to live. Heaven alone knew what it would all cost. But she didn't care, Cherub was worth every penny.

There came a tap on the door. It was Bunty. 'May I carry on?'

'Of course, my dear, of course. You're all so clever and kind. I do appreciate you all.'

As she was leaving, Miss Chillingsworth went to reception and said to Miriam, 'Mrs Price, you will ring if anything untoward . . . you know . . . with Cherub?'

'Of course. We've great hopes. But it is early days yet.'

'I might come back this afternoon.'

'That's fine. If you feel more comfortable close to her then be our guest.'

'Thank you, my dear. Is Joy ill? I haven't seen her.'

'No, she's having a few days off.'

'She deserves it, she works so hard. Give her my love when you speak to her.'

Miriam nodded and smiled. The phone rang and gave her a good excuse not to take the matter of Joy any further. When she had a few minutes to spare Miriam went into Joy's office to ring her for news of Tiger. The telephone rang several times and Miriam was just about to give up when Joy picked up her receiver and said, 'Joy Bastable here.'

'It's me, Miriam. How is Tiger today?'

'Curled up in front of the fire in her bed fast asleep. Everything healing nicely by the looks of it.'

'We've been wondering . . . Miss Chillingsworth's Cherub is in and she has almost identical wounds. Mungo and Graham have operated on her and we're all keeping our fingers crossed. You haven't heard anybody talking about a stray dog causing them trouble, have you?'

'No.'

Miriam thought Joy might expand but she didn't. 'How are you, Joy?'

'Fine. Thanks.'

'Miss Chillingsworth sends her love. How are you about coming back?'

'I've said, haven't I?'

'Yes, but I rather hoped—'

The phone clicked off and Miriam was left holding her receiver feeling thoroughly dejected. If Joy really meant it then they would have to get a new manager. She, Miriam Price, was only good as a stopgap and she was dreading doing the monthly rota and tackling the salaries at the end of the month. Something would have to be done, quick smart.

Duncan! Come home! Soon!

The weather was bitterly cold so lunchtime found all three of the Practice farm vets inside, getting warm in front of an electric fire turned full on, eating their lunch. Colin arrived first with the lunch Letty had made for him. He was boiling the kettle for his packet soup, while discussing life and such with Zoe, when in came Scott, clutching a lunch bag from the delicatessen in Barleybridge.

'Hi! Strewth! It's cold. I must be mad to have come back to England in the middle of winter. Snow on Beulah Bank Top, roads like glass. Total madness!' He extracted a fat club sandwich from his bag and sank his teeth into it.

Colin asked, 'That flat of yours is warm though, isn't it? Miriam had a new boiler put in last year.'

'It saves my life. I have it as hot as I can get it all the time and sit with my back to a radiator. Bliss!'

'It won't be bliss when Mungo sees your gas bill!' Colin said.

'Don't worry. I shall offer to pay it. Worth every penny. Make me a coffee, Colin, while you're at it. Black, no sugar. Zoe! How's things? I don't see much of you. Keeping busy?'

'Very. I've a problem I need to share with someone, though.'

'I specialize in solving intimate personal problems. Dinner tonight and we'll discuss it.' Scott winked at her.

'You idiot. It's Ruby.'

'Ruby? Is this some sizzling local talent who has mistakenly avoided me?'

Patiently Zoe explained. 'Ruby is one of Lord Askew's Guernseys.'

Scott's face fell. 'Oh! Well, never mind. What's her problem?'

'If I knew that I wouldn't be asking, would I? I'll have a coffee as well, Colin, please. I've taken several blood samples and nothing. Zilch. Everything as clean as a whistle apart from a touch of anaemia, but she's low on milk yield and listless. Any ideas? Thanks for this, Colin.' Zoe placed her coffee on the table beside her, glanced up and met Scott's eyes. For a brief moment she saw a spark of interest in her flare in his eyes and then he quickly looked away. 'I have said to Lord Askew that I might get a second opinion in and for once in his life he said yes. He was so full of his protest march I think he agreed before he realized what he was saying.'

Colin was too busy trying to drink his boiling hot soup to answer, so it was Scott who asked, 'What protest march?'

'The march is over with now but he's heading up the protest over banning hunting. Very keen. He even offered me a seat in his coach if I wanted to go, but I declined.'

'Which side are you on?'

'I think they should ban it. When I told him that he was livid.'

'If it keeps the foxes down and gives loads of people a good morning out in the country what harm is it doing? Harms no one.'

'Except the foxes.'

'For Christ's sake, Zoe. They're vermin, not some cuddly toy.'

'Does that mean they have to suffer?'

'Suffer? They're dead in a second once the dogs get to them. Quicker than a badly aimed bullet. Now that is agony, dying slowly by degrees. Or for that matter, what dignity is there is being gassed in your den?'

'But being chased like that till they're exhausted?'

'But that's a fox's life. The biggest problem as I see it is

94

the loss of all the jobs connected with the hunt. Though there are far worse things in the world to worry about than taking a stance over a few foxes. Like starving kids all over Africa. Or child prostitution.'

Zoe got to her feet. 'We'll never agree. Never. I can't do a thing about abused children halfway across the world but I can do something about fox-hunting right here on my own doorstep.'

Scott decided to change his approach. 'We'll agree to differ on that, then. Do you want a second opinion on Ruby? I've a slot this very afternoon.'

Colin having finished his soup and roll, postponed starting on a piece of incredibly tempting looking almond tart and said, 'He's on a hiding to nothing is Lord Askew. The greens will win this argument. Then we'll have the job of putting down all the foxhounds, because they can't be rehabilitated. I hate putting down a perfectly fit animal. In fact, I might say I will not be involved. Against my veterinary principles et cetera.'

Both Scott and Zoe looked hard at Colin. He so rarely took a stand on anything or volunteered an opinion on any matter.

Colin, seeing their surprise, felt he should explain himself. 'Since getting our son, John, I've taken to studying my principles because of how I might affect him as he grows up. I wouldn't want him to know I was willing to put down a healthy animal just because of a government order banning their reason for living, wouldn't want him to look on me as a murderer. Which I would be if I put down a foxhound. If they're incurably sick, then yes. But healthy, no. Big responsibility, having children. They colour how you think on just about everything.' He took a large, satisfying bite of his almond tart.

Scott conceded the point. 'Yes, I can see that. Having a child to consider must alter your perspective. Over just about everything, I expect.'

Zoe said nothing. She washed out her mug, threw the remains of her lunch in the wastebin and said, 'I'm off now. Busy afternoon.' She left.

Scott got to his feet calling out, 'Lord Askew's?' but he was too late, she'd already gone. But he caught her on her mobile and asked her about her promise to have dinner with him that night.

'I didn't promise, as well you know.'

'Well, make a change from your mother nagging you? Eh? How about it? I'll nag you instead. I can be quite good at it if I put my mind to it. I'm in need of company anyway. Lonely in my flat.'

Zoe considered and thought, why ever not? It would be a test of how strong-minded she had become. 'Very well. Fox and Grapes at seven?'

'You're on. Be seeing you!'

Zoe got Oscar ready for bed so all her mother had to do was attend to his toilet needs and pop him under the covers.

She found a warm red top she hadn't worn in an age, chose a pair of black trousers and wore a silver pendant Miriam had bought her for Christmas. With her hair up and a new ornament in it to hold it all under control she felt well armed for her evening out. Was she being a fool, having a meal with him? She remembered his look that afternoon when briefly she'd seen some of his old fascination come to the surface. Well, she was old enough and wise enough now not to be taken in by his charm.

Downstairs Joan raised an eyebrow when she saw the

effort she'd put into getting ready. 'So. It's someone important, is it?'

'Heavens above, Mother, it's only Scott.'

'I've never met him, have I?'

'No. Goodnight, little one. Be a good boy for Granny.' She kissed Oscar and when his face began to crumple she made a hurried departure. 'Nighty-nighty. See you in the morning.'

The roads were still icy, making her wheels crunch as she came out of the drive and onto the main road. Zoe turned up the heat in the car, which suddenly made her think of Scott with his back to his radiator trying to keep warm. She had to smile. He was actually as tough as old boots, just liked to think he was a tender plant for effect.

The car park at the Fox and Grapes was only half full. Unusual but she supposed the bad weather had kept the punters at home. She found a space right next to Scott's Land Rover, put on the handbrake and picked up her bag – she'd insist on going Dutch tonight. No obligations. No way, José.

He was seated right beside the huge log fire in the main dining room, lager in hand, chatting to, of all people, Mrs Goodwood and Phil Parsons.

Scott, with a delighted smile on his face, got to his feet when he saw her walking across. 'You've come. You know Francesca? And I don't need to introduce Phil, do I?'

'Hello, how are you? Still cold, isn't it?'

Mrs Goodwood gave her a melancholy grimace. 'Hanging on by a thread, I am, that's what. This weather's killing me, outside most of the day. Not had any more drooping, by the way. You'll hear though when I do.'

Scott's ears perked up. 'Drooping?'

'Just a problem, Mrs Good . . . Francesca has with her pigs. I'm calling you in, Scott, the next time it happens. See if you can solve it.'

'Oh! Right. Drink?'

'Yes, please. My usual.'

Scott looked embarrassed. 'Yours is a . . .'

Mrs Goodwood roared with laughter. 'He can't remember, Zoe. Oh dear!'

Phil, just about to take a long haul on his glass of ale, chortled, 'That's marked yer card, Scott. Not very flattering, that.'

'Whisky and water, please.'

'Of course. Sorry. Ice?'

'Certainly not.'

At that moment a little man arrived and joined them beside the fire. He was small and very thin, a positively unnoticeable kind of person, with very sloping shoulders and a sloping kind of face to match, rather like a Basset Hound. He gave the impression of never having smiled in the whole of his life.

Mrs Goodwood inclined her head towards him. 'My other half, Cecil. This is Zoe, the vet.' Zoe guessed he didn't come up even as far as Mrs Goodwood's shoulder. What a curious couple they made.

Cecil nodded.

'You've got some fine pigs, Mr Goodwood, all organic, I understand. The organic business is certainly taking off.'

While Zoe waited for a reply, Scott came back with her whisky, gave it to her and sat himself back down again. There were no introductions so Zoe had to assume that Cecil and Scott had already been introduced. Phil Parsons obviously knew Cecil, for they just gave each other a nod and Cecil added a wink when he saw Francesca wasn't looking. Phil tapped his top pocket. Clearly a message had passed between the two of them but everyone pretended not to notice. A heavy silence fell and Zoe could see that Scott was becoming agitated by it.

Zoe saved the day for him, though it would have been fun to watch his embarrassment a little longer. 'Scott, would you mind if we ate? I'm desperately hungry.'

Scott stood up, glad to have been rescued from an embarrassing interlude, though he couldn't understand why he was at such a loss for words. 'Of course. Would you excuse us, please? They'll be running out of food if we don't hurry.'

'Of course, off you go. Cecil and I are leaving in a minute, we've already eaten.'

As Zoe turned to go with Scott and Francesca was collecting her coat from the back of her seat, she caught sight of Cecil handing Phil a bundle of notes. So, what was that about? She heard Cecil whisper, 'Won by four lengths!' and Phil winked his thanks and nodded his head in Francesca's direction as though saying, 'Don't let her know.'

Zoe smiled to herself and said, 'Night, Phil. No doubt we shall meet in the not too distant future.'

'No doubt about that. Enjoy, as they say in America.'

'No Blossom tonight?'

'No, she's staying with Hamish, he's got a touch of the flu.'

'Give her my regards, then. Goodnight.'

Scott had reserved a table by the other big open fire in the smaller dining room.

'Thought I'd better.' He pulled out her chair for her and saw her nicely seated. 'Look at the menu and then I'll go and order. Table number thirteen. Oh help! I didn't realize that.'

'You're not superstitious, are you?'

'No, but I thought you might be.'

'Well, I'm not.' Zoe studied the menu, aware that Scott was watching her.

Very softly he said, 'You look stunning tonight.'

She ignored him completely. 'I'll have an eight-ounce steak, no fancy sauce, with a portion of French fries – I wonder why chips have become French, maybe they always have been – and grilled tomatoes, with a side salad. Please.'

'Right. Suits me. I'll get that twice. Drink? Wine? Whisky?'

'Wine. Red would be best, wouldn't it?'

Zoe watched the reaction of the girl taking the food orders. The moment she saw Scott coming towards her the girl beamed with excitement. She laughed, she giggled, she sparkled and gave a very good performance of someone absolutely captivated with this prize specimen of manhood. And no wonder. Scott, as they used to say, was a fine figure of a man. Lean and bronzed and filled to the brim with sex appeal. He just couldn't resist making her like him. That was the child in him, she supposed, always seeking approval. But it was justified.

He came back to sit at their table, grinning all over his face.

'Scott Spencer, you can't resist getting everyone eating out of your hand, can you?'

'Why shouldn't I make everyone's life a little brighter? Isn't that what one is supposed to do? Spread a little sunshine? "Jesus wants me for a sunbeam" . . . Can't remember the rest of it.'

'You don't mean to say you went to Sunday School?'

'I did.'

'You really are the most surprising person. Just when I think I've got you sussed, you come out with something and I know I haven't.'

'Complex person me.' He raised his glass to her. 'I give you a toast.'

'Yes? To what?'

'To renewing old friendships.'

'I don't know about that.'

'What do you mean? I thought you and I were friends.'

'You had a rather wider circle of "friends" than I realized when you were here before.'

'I make friends wherever I go.'

Zoe counted his friends off on her fingers. 'Kate. Bunty. To name just two.'

'Ah!'

'It was your baby Bunty lost. Did you know?'

Scott nodded. 'I wasn't proud of that.'

'That was bad news. Showed a careless disregard that did. How about Kate? Was she a "friend" or—'

Scott broke in indignantly. 'I treated Kate with the greatest of respect.'

'Glad to hear it. She was far too young for you anyway. The age gap was what, fourteen, fifteen years? I felt very angry about that.'

'Why should it bother you?'

Zoe took care to be chewing a large mouthful of food to give herself time to think of an answer. 'It didn't, not really. Looking back on it, though, you were grossly in the wrong. You'll have to be more careful of other people's feelings and the damage you are doing, albeit unintention-ally. She never let on how heartbroken she was when you left so hurriedly. Brave face, and all the rest.'

Scott looked doleful. 'You're right. I should have been.'

He concentrated on his steak and then said right out of the blue, 'Can we carry on where we left off?'

'Absolutely not.'

'Zoe!'

'I said absolutely not. You are not having me as yet another trophy notched on your bedpost. I am definitely off limits as far as you're concerned. In any case, we didn't leave off because we never really got going, now did we? You went off after Bunty.' She offered her wine glass to him and he refilled it.

'Ah! I thought we had.'

'You've a poor memory then.'

Scott reached across the table and touched her hand. 'You've a very special place in my heart, Zoe.'

'You've had too much wine on an empty stomach.'

'I mean it. Bunty . . . well . . .' He shrugged. 'She was panting for it. What can a fellow do?'

'Keep his trousers zipped?' Zoe had to laugh at the expression on his face. 'I mean it. Poor Bunty, you broke her heart.'

'Well, she's safe now because I don't go in for irate husbands. Only single girls who are fancy free.'

'That's me!' Oh Lord, Zoe thought, I've given him the perfect opening. But he didn't take it so they ate in silence for a while. 'Remember Gab Bridges, the eldest of the Bridges boys?'

Scott nodded.

'Well, he tried to shoot himself just over a year back.'

'Did he?'

'All over Rhodri's wife.'

'Who did Rhodri marry then?'

'Megan Jones.'

'The stunning redhead. I remember her. Beulah Bank

Top. Fancy that, there must be more than meets the eye in Rhodri Hughes. How is he? Gab, I mean?'

'Perfectly well, except for the scar down the side of his face and into his hair. He's still rated as the local Lothario, and I can see why. The local girls go mad over him. Bees round a honeypot, as Dan Brown would say.'

'You're still interested then?'

'In Gab Bridges? No, I am not.'

'I meant in men.'

'Do you realize that our entire conversation has been about sex? In one way or another?'

'What else is there?'

They finished their main course at the same time.

Scott raised an eyebrow. 'Pudding?'

'Yes, please. This cold weather is giving me an appetite. I could eat a horse, so I could manage a pudding very nicely indeed.'

'Good on yer. I can recommend their banana split.'

'Fine, that'll do me.'

'Same here.'

Zoe found the presentation of the split incredibly tempting and the constant pleasure of the different flavours hitting her palate a sheer delight. She looked up to watch Scott's reaction and saw him running his tongue over the bowl of his spoon to draw a raspberry into his mouth. Steady, girl, just go steady, she thought. The raspberry disappeared and she watched his obvious physical appreciation of its sharpness as he processed it. Scott caught her eye and she blushed. Now she was behaving like a schoolgirl. She busied herself with her own enjoyment and didn't look up at him again, so his slow smile remained his secret.

Partway through his banana split he asked very softly, in

a voice loaded with double entendre, 'Zoe, shall we have coffee at my place or yours?'

She looked him straight in the eye. 'Neither. I'm going home when we've finished. I'll have a café latte right here.'

'Oh! OK. I see. So will I.'

'You order the coffee, seeing as you have such a rapport with the waitress, and we'll go halves with the bill.' She'd anticipated a fight over the bill, expecting that his over-developed male ego would make him insist on picking up the tab. But he didn't object. 'I've plenty of cash with me, Scott. We both had the same so we can split it straight down the middle.'

They stood talking for a while, standing between their cars, loath to leave. Scott took hold of her hand. 'Thanks for coming out with me, I've really enjoyed your company. We must do it again sometime.'

'Yes, OK. We will. I shall be glad you're here when Rose's baby arrives. I expect Dan will be taking a couple of weeks off, that's if he's back at work by then. Which he won't be, I suspect.'

'Delighted to be of assistance. Goodnight, Zoe.' He bent his head and kissed her cheek with the chasteness of a favourite uncle. 'See you in the morning.'

'Scott, I wish you could use your charm on Joy Bastable. She needs to be back and we need her back. If Duncan were here he'd sort her out. Miriam's doing a splendid job but it's not really her kind of work.'

'She's left because of me, so it's hardly likely I could persuade her. Perhaps sackcloth and ashes might do the trick?' He raised both eyebrows and gave her one of those smiles of his which made you smile in return. 'Where's Duncan gone?'

'Who knows. Gone in a flash he was and never a word

as to his whereabouts ever since. For all we know he could have been swept away in the Chess and floated out to sea.'

Scott leaned his back against the Land Rover. 'I suppose you can go on for so long loving someone and getting nothing in return.'

Zoe laughed. 'Listen to him! Marriage guidance, is it now? What a multi-skilled person you are.'

'Do you ever take me seriously?'

'No.' Zoe opened up her car. 'I'm just thankful Tiger was saved. Otherwise I think that would have been the last straw. By the way, will you come to Lord Askew's to-morrow? We'll go first thing. See you there?'

Scott saluted her. 'Yes, ma'am!'

Chapter 7

Zoe arrived at half past eight to find Scott already in deep discussion with Gavin the head stable lad and Lord Askew. They had one of his hunters out of its stable and Scott was examining one of its legs.

She felt etiquette demanded that she should not get involved, so she wandered off through the archway to find Chris and tell him she'd got Scott to come to examine Ruby.

Scott came through almost immediately after her and he and Chris shook hands like old friends.

'Hi, Chris, mate, am I pleased to see you again.'

'Couldn't stand the heat, then? Had to come back to where he belongs, eh, Zoe?'

Scott threw a mock punch at Chris's arm. 'Could do with some of the heat this morning. By God, it's cold.'

Grinning with pleasure, Chris said, 'Fresh, I think is the word for it.'

'Fresh! That's an understatement if ever there was one. Where's this Ruby?'

Chris went off ahead of them and into the cow byre. Ruby was standing by herself, disconsolate and obviously not well.

'How long since she calved?'

'Thirty-three days exactly.'

'Mmm.'

Scott examined her, running his hands over her, looking in her mouth, feeling her udder. She withstood his gentle examination without a murmur, only giving him the occasional sad look from her beautiful soft brown eyes. 'Did her blood tests indicate anaemia?'

'Not desperate but certainly present,' Zoe answered. You had to admit he had the touch where animals were concerned. She'd always admired the way Mungo's hands 'read' an animal's condition and here was Scott with exactly the same talent. But she'd bite her tongue off before she told him of her admiration.

'I bet if you took another blood test she'd be even worse. One month calved . . . it could be her fourth stomach has moved across. Displaced abomasum. Yes?'

Chris asked, 'What does that mean to Ruby?'

Zoe said, 'Ah!' feeling thoroughly incompetent for not having thought about that possibility. Damn him. Just damn him. 'It means we have to cast her on to her right side then roll her over on to her left. By then the stomach, with a bit of massaging and manoeuvring, will have gone into the right place and we make an incision and sew the stomach to the abdominal wall to keep it in place. That more or less sums up the whole operation. Right, Scott?'

'In a nutshell. I'd suggest, if I may, that we sedate her – make life easier for her and for us. Give Zoe a hand, Chris?'

'Of course. Could be interesting this could. Never seen it done before. You done it before, Zoe?'

'Of course.'

'Sounds like a magic trick, just rolling her over. It does work, does it?' He asked this question of Scott, as though he found it hard to believe that a slip of a woman like Zoe could know anything about this simple remedy.

Much to her relief she emerged unscathed from the procedure. With Scott's strength behind the ropes, Ruby was down before she knew it, then her legs were secured to prevent her kicking Zoe as she made the incision. Using the sedative and then a local anaesthetic where the incision was needed, the job was completed without a hitch. She always felt as though she was being tested when she had a procedure to perform in front of men, and if the praise for her success was too effusive it made her feel like a small child being praised by adults for her totally unexpected genius.

But she did appreciate the way Scott left all the instructions and decisions to her. Zoe emerged from the cow byre her ego back on track, after being deflated by Scott's almost immediate diagnosis. Scott, sensing she was not feeling her best, said, 'It could have happened to anyone, you know. I just happened to be the one who picked it up.'

'Thanks for being kind but I should not have missed it. It simply never occurred to me and that's not good news. Thanks for coming anyway.'

'The pleasure's all mine. Anytime you have a problem just send for Scott.'

Zoe kicked out at his ankle, but he nimbly stepped aside and she missed. 'I might do that very thing, with Francesca's pigs. It happens so spasmodically. I can't work it out. But she's beginning to lose faith in me so I've got to get serious.'

'You bow to my superior knowledge?' He was grinning at her and for one second she could have hit him, but just in time she remembered they had an audience. Gavin was leading the hunter back to his stable and Lord Askew was coming over to speak to them both.

'Good morning, Zoe. Called in the cavalry after all, then. Found anything?'

Zoe explained what had happened and Lord Askew nodded sagely. 'Good. Good. Glad you've solved it, Scott. You're an excellent all-rounder. Please me if you stayed. *Are* you staying?'

'Only till Dan is on his feet again.'

'How is he?'

'Doing well, thanks.'

'I'm glad, he's a great man for the horses, you know. Outspoken, but he knows his job. Coming to our dinner dance?'

'Haven't heard about it. Are you going, Zoe?'

She had to ask. 'Is it in support of the hunt?'

Lord Askew nodded.

'Not coming, then.'

'With your views on the subject that's par for the course. Will you come, Scott? Bring one of your lady friends? Eh? How about it?'

'I'd have to find someone.'

'Hundred pounds double ticket and cheap at the price. Wonderful food. Great band.'

'I'll think about it, my lord.'

Zoe stood there fuming.

'Good. Good. Need all the help we can get. Don't forget, it promises to be a good night.'

'Must press on.' Scott offered to shake hands, and found his hand engulfed by that of Lord Askew. 'I won't forget, though I may be on call.'

Zoe and he walked off towards their vehicles and he could feel, without even looking at her, how angry she was. Between gritted teeth she said, 'You're not really going, are you?'

'I might.'

' "I might". Huh!'

She got back in her car, shut the door, opened her window and said, 'You're a traitor to the profession. An absolute traitor. I despise you for that. You should have thrown his idea back in his face immediately.'

'Zoe! He's a client. We can't afford to lose him again.'

'And what about principles? Haven't you got any?'

'You know full well I don't object to fox-hunting. I've said so before.'

'But supporting it? That's going a step too far. I've *seen* a fox killed by hounds, *heard* the screams, *smelled* the blood. Have you?'

'No. But, look, I haven't said I'm going, have I? Just keeping him sweet.'

'It's all about money! Keeping his account, that's all you're thinking about.'

'So, if you feel so strongly about it, why do you attend his cows?'

Zoe stared straight ahead and thought about his challenge. 'Because they've nothing to do with hunting at all. Absolutely nothing.'

'That's not logical. What do you think pays for the hunters' food and their stable lads? Eh? What? The milk and cream and yoghurt those Guernseys produce, perhaps? I challenge you to tell Mungo you refuse to attend his cows.'

'I shall. Right now.' She fumbled about to find her mobile but Scott said, 'No. Zoe, don't be a fool.' He reached through the window and grabbed her arm.

'I will. I will.' They'd spoken very quietly up until then, but Zoe raised her voice when she added, 'Let go my arm.'

'We can't have this discussion on Lord Askew's property. It's not right. Please. Don't do this. Wait till you've calmed down. Please, Zoe.'

He spoke so softly and so reasonably that Zoe saw the sense behind his request for restraint. 'Let go my arm. I promise I won't do anything until I've calmed down.'

'That's my girl. I'm running late. Must be off. Don't do anything rash.'

He roared out of the stableyard like a man possessed. Zoe followed more calmly but was boiling over inside.

She popped into the Practice that afternoon and found Mungo, between operations, standing around talking to Phil Parsons and his wife Blossom.

'But you know, Phil, it takes money nowadays to keep a farm going. You need to take advantage of every trick in the trade just to keep your head above water. Every inch of land used to its full potential, a tight rein on outgoings and you've a chance. That field you never use, you could have stock on that for fattening.'

Blossom almost blenched. 'We couldn't do that! Just when you're getting to know them they're ready for slaughter.' She shuddered at the prospect.

From inside his balaclava Phil agreed with her. 'It's bad enough when they're too old or too ill and you've to have 'em put to sleep. Well, that's as maybe, but Blossom and me we do what we like and it seems to work.' He turned to speak to Zoe. 'Now, my girl, you're looking good enough to eat today. How's things?'

'Fine thanks, Phil. Busy, you know. Got to press on. Need to see Mungo. Can you spare me a moment?'

Mungo shook hands with Phil and Blossom and then headed for his office. 'Of course. I've got five minutes.'

'I'll get my bills paid and then Blossom and me's off to the George for a bite to eat. Be seeing yer.'

Mungo went to sit behind his desk and she stood in front of it. 'I've made a decision.'

'Yes?'

'I do not want to attend the Guernsey herd at Lord Askew's.'

'Why not?'

'I disapprove wholeheartedly of fox-hunting and as Scott pointed out this morning, the money the cows produce goes towards paying for the hunters and the eventers and all their paraphernalia and as I so disapprove of fox-hunting, I can't in all honesty attend the cows.'

'I see. What does Scott think?'

'It doesn't matter what he thinks, he's only temporary.'

Mungo persisted. 'I want to know.'

'He thinks I'm mad. He's even almost promised to go to the ball he's holding.'

'I'm going with Miriam. So's Valentine and Nadia, Rhodri and Megan, Graham and a guest and Colin and Letty. There's going to be quite a party of us.'

'So what do you say?'

'There is nothing to say. If you're needed at Askew Park then you're needed and if it's on your way, so be it.' Mungo stood up, implying the discussion was at an end.

'You're saying I have to go.'

'I'm saying it's all part of your job. I have clients I could cheerfully strangle, but it's not their animals' fault they belong to fools. The animals still need our attention if they're ill. We can't pick and choose who we will or will not cure. The animals come first.'

'I see.'

'OK, Zoe? How's young Oscar? I haven't seen him for ages. Bring him in sometime.'

Zoe muttered something unintelligible and left, with

panic rising in her like an erupting volcano. Bring him in? Definitely not! They'd all see. And then they'd know. Without a doubt. The prospect of everyone guessing took all thoughts of her stand about fox-hunting out of her mind. At first she'd been furious with Mungo, but he'd been so reasonable about the matter it had been hard to challenge him and insist on her own way. But she'd see Miriam and ask her to avoid putting Lord Askew on her list. That was it, a bit of subterfuge and she'd never have to go again. Colin could always go, of course, though he had a list of clients he preferred to attend and nothing short of being struck by lightning would persuade him to attend any of the others. Well, he'd damn well have to. She wouldn't kowtow to that rich, overfed, privileged, aristocratic, mountainous slab of a man ever again.

Miriam was in Joy's office as Zoe left so she went in, closed the door and said without even a word of greeting, 'Never again am I to be put down for visiting Askew Park. I've decided not to. Can you see to it, please?'

Hearing the pent-up anger in Zoe's voice, Miriam chose her words carefully. 'Is that what you've been in to see Mungo about?'

Zoe looked down at Miriam's sweet, smiling face. 'It is.'

'And he said . . . ?'

She couldn't lie, or could she? 'If it was convenient for someone else to go he didn't seem to mind. He didn't get angry about it. Didn't fly off the handle like he can sometimes.'

'I see. I'll make a note, but I don't promise anything.'

'Colin never goes. He could for a change.'

'Colin works his own way, and we put up with it. He has a big client list and there are some who will only have Colin visit, so that says something in his favour, doesn't it?

I'll do my best.' Miriam made a few notes on a piece of paper in a file marked Visiting Lists. 'Be good. Bye-bye.'

And that, thought Miriam, is the final straw. Joy had to come back, because she, Miriam, was not up to dealing with difficult people. She always felt so sorry for them that she usually ended up apologizing to them for their own bad temper. Today a dust-up between two clients, the cat that escaped and the hamster that died in Valentine's hands – it was all getting too much. Joy would have taken it in her stride, but she, Miriam Price, just wasn't up to it. The clients having an argument this afternoon in the waiting room had used up all her resources.

It had all begun with Miranda Costello bringing in her Goliath without a leash. 'He's well behaved, Mrs Price, he always does as he's told. Bunged him in the van and never gave it a thought.'

'Do keep tight hold, Miranda. They're all nervous when they come in here, anything could happen. Would you like me to bring a leash in from the back? We do have a few spare ones.'

'No, no, he'll be OK.' Miranda settled herself in the very last of the chairs. Her Goliath was the smallest adult Yorkshire Terrier anyone had ever seen. But in his mind he was the very largest dog anyone had ever seen, positively of donkey proportions. He sat quietly beside Miranda, looking as though butter wouldn't melt in his mouth. Eventually he laid down and apparently went to sleep.

Then, in came a client of Valentine's accompanied by her Llaza Apso named Chang, his long fur beautifully groomed and resplendent. His collar and lead were a bright scarlet and it set off his superior looks beautifully.

'I'm Mrs Bookbinder. I have an appointment at three

with Valentine Dedic. It's my first time. I'm a new client, moved to Barleybridge a few months ago.'

Miriam checked the name on the computer. 'That's right. Do take a seat. He won't be long.'

'I hope not. To me three o'clock is three o'clock and not half past.'

'Indeed. The thing is, we had a road accident in a short while ago and everything's got delayed.'

'Your problems are not mine, whoever you are. I'm under pressure like everyone else.'

'Of course, of course. Do sit down, please.'

'I won't, I shall stand. Tell him, please, I'm here.'

'I'm afraid I can't, he has a client in.'

'Then I shall go and interrupt. Three o'clock is three o'clock, and it is three o'clock.' Mrs Bookbinder drew herself up to her full height and began heading for Valentine's consulting room.

'Don't you think it would be better to wait your turn?' Miranda Costello said. Ever a champion of the Practice, she couldn't tolerate this client's haughty manner towards Miriam.

Mrs Bookbinder paused and turned to look at Miranda. As different as cheese and chalk they were. Miranda in one of her more eccentric get-ups and Mrs Bookbinder only too well aware she was dressed to kill. But then she always was. One shouldn't leave the house looking as though one had just finished scrubbing the kitchen floor, not that she ever did, but the principle was the same.

'And who might you be?' She gave Chang a tug on his leash and Miranda Costello the benefit of one of her 'put down' stares.

'A client with better manners than you apparently. Now sit down and shut up and wait like everybody else.'

Chang didn't notice that Goliath was keeping an eye on him, so being the brave dog he was, he began to growl at the angry tone of Miranda's retort.

Goliath sprang to life, jumped down from his chair and in an instant had Chang by the scruff. He hung on as though his life depended on it. Chang went to pieces; he positively crumpled to the floor. Goliath, not yet ready to accept his victory, kept growling and hanging on. Miranda shouted, 'Goliath! Come!' But he completed ignored her.

'Get him off! Get him off!' Mrs Bookbinder shouted. 'He'll kill him!'

Miranda got to her feet and tried to catch hold of Goliath's collar, but Goliath knew a trick or two. He hadn't subdued all Miranda's other dogs by giving in at the first move. He clung on and, exerting all his strength, he began swirling about so that Chang was slewing across the floor, unable to resist.

Stephie appeared at that moment and saw that a bucket of water would do the trick. She disappeared in the back and returned in a moment carrying the old firebucket filled to the brim. She threw it on the pair of them and it landed fair and square on its target – except Mrs Bookbinder had, at that moment, decided to bend over and try to pull Goliath away. The water soaked her all the way down the front of her smart imitation Astrakhan fur jacket.

But the water had achieved Stephie's objective and the two dogs separated, soaked to the skin.

Miranda could do nothing but laugh, which positively ignited Mrs Bookbinder's anger. 'You've thrown water all over my fur coat. You blithering idiot! You stupid girl! Look at it, ruined. Out of a filthy bucket too! Chang, my little darling. Come to Mummy.'

Stephie stood open-mouthed, too surprised to apologize.

Miriam rushed out from behind the reception desk and began a full-scale diplomatic onslaught on Mrs Bookbinder.

'I am so sorry. Please don't blame Stephie, it's our standard practice when dogs fight. It's the only way, believe me. Now look, I'll go get a towel and we'll dry your coat as best we can. Hold on to Chang's leash, and you, Miranda, hang on to Goliath. We don't want a repeat performance.'

Miriam had hurried away, glad for an excuse to remove herself from the scene. She found a dog towel freshly laundered but a bit holey and, bracing herself, returned to reception.

Goliath was confidently perched on Miranda's knee, surveying Chang from a great height with what looked like a smirk on his face. Miriam began rubbing the worst of the wet from Mrs Bookbinder's fur coat.

'I shall sue. I shall. First, this person for that nasty little dog being out of control and second, the practice for not taking sufficient precautions for the safety of the animals on these premises.'

Miranda couldn't take her seriously. 'For heaven's sakes. Just a bit of a dust-up, that's all. They were both to blame.'

'Chang did not start this fight.'

'He shouldn't have growled at Goliath. In any case, you're going to look a mite foolish bringing a case against a Yorkshire Terrier as small as he is. Couldn't hurt a flea. You'd get laughed out of court.'

'Don't you think I won't, because I will, he's totally out of control is that dog of yours, he should be put down, the sooner the—'

To Miriam's great relief, Valentine popped his head out of his consulting-room door at that moment and called out 'Chang Bookbinder'.

Valentine Dedic was lean and handsome in a very obviously Eastern European way and Miriam had never seen him looking more engaging than he did right now. With his thick, jet-black hair in one of its more turbulent moods, and those splendidly expressive deep, dark-brown eyes of his looking straight at Mrs Bookbinder, he smiled, showing all his beautifully even, snow-white teeth. She noticed Mrs Bookbinder's immediate reaction. Thank God it wasn't Graham or Rhodri, they couldn't hold a candle to Valentine where good looks were concerned, Miriam thought. Valentine bowed slightly, in the Continental manner, and stood aside to make room for her to pass through his door. Mrs Bookbinder, glad she'd made the effort to dress well, visibly melted and swanned towards him. If it had been a film there would have been violins playing as she disappeared into the consulting room.

But Miriam hadn't had quite such a successful ending to her experience, for it had left her shaking with nerves. That was when she decided she'd have a word with Mungo.

So Mungo heard all about it when they'd finished their evening meal. 'Because of all that, I want Joy back. In fact, she's got to come back, the place isn't the same without her. We all need her. So something has to be done. If Duncan doesn't reappear she'll need the money; savings don't last for ever. Shall I go see her again, do you think?'

'I've admired the way you've tackled Joy's job, my love. But at the same time I know it's not you. Looks as though I shall have to do something serious about it. No time tomorrow, busy all day, I'll go right now.' He got to his feet and kissed Miriam, saying, 'You've been a brick, and I love you for it.'

'Are you sure, on top of a busy day?'

'I'm sure. But don't expect success. At the very least I might find out if she intends coming back or not.'

Mungo drove to Joy's thinking she might not even let him in. He parked his car out of sight round the bend just as Miriam had done, got out and walked round to the front door and pressed the bell. He heard Joy's footsteps on the tiled floor of the hall and got his foot ready to jam in the door if she threatened to close it when she saw who was there.

He barely recognized her. She stared at him for a moment, opened the door wider and let him in. It was her hair, always so curly and pretty around her face, but now kind of stringy, and she'd lost weight, and it made her look . . . well . . . old. Was it only two weeks since she'd stormed out? No, it must be more. Even her sweater wasn't in Joy's usual kind of pristine cleanliness.

'Joy? It's me.'

'Obviously. I haven't forgotten.'

'Thought I'd call to see how Tiger was bearing up.'

'Liar.'

'Can we sit down?'

Joy led the way to the kitchen. Accustomed to Miriam's pretty welcoming kitchen Mungo had to close his eyes to the state of Joy's big farmhouse-sized one. What was the matter with the woman?

'I left home without having my coffee. Would you mind if I fixed myself one?'

'Be my guest.'

'Will you join me?'

Joy nodded.

Mungo found a space by moving some dishes into an already overflowing sink. All the time he fumbled to find things in her kitchen Joy never spoke. He didn't turn round to look at her, but he guessed she scarcely knew he was there. He had to empty the cafetière before he could use it and spotted an empty gin bottle in the bin. So that was how the cookie crumbled, was it?

He wiped a small tray, put two mugs, the only clean ones he could find, on it with the cafetière and some milk, which he'd surreptitiously sniffed before he'd poured it out, and sat down opposite her.

'You haven't heard from Duncan, then?'

Joy shook her head.

'Drink is never the answer, you know.'

'What do you know about it?'

'Nothing, I suppose.'

Joy wasn't looking at him. Her head was buried in her hands, her elbows resting on the table. 'That's right, you know nothing at all about it.'

Mungo pressed the bright red knob on the cafetière and watched the ground coffee get squeezed as the plunger went down, poured Joy's coffee out for her and served it to her black.

'You remember then?'

'Of course, we've been together too many years for me not to remember.'

'We have indeed.' Joy picked up her mug and sipped her coffee. 'You haven't lost your magic with the coffee.'

'Good. We had some good times, didn't we?'

'Some awful ones too. Working single-handed like you were, we worked long hours.'

'We did. You're right. Couldn't do it now.'

Joy half smiled. 'Certainly not. Too long in the tooth.'

The pair of them sat thinking about that.

Mungo broke their silence. 'I wonder where all that energy has gone?'

'No idea.' Joy continued drinking her coffee. She'd emptied her mug so she helped herself to a refill. When the comfort of the heat of it had finally warmed her she said, 'If he would only come back, if only I knew he was alive . . .'

'So he does matter to you, then?'

'I think he must.'

'Miriam's trying hard to fill your shoes. She reckons she doesn't come within an ace of your standards. Finds it difficult if there's a lot of dissension, you know.'

'Don't come that sentimental claptrap with me. I'm too old a bird to fall for it.'

Mungo poured himself a second mug. 'OK, then. You need to come back for your own sake. I know you disagreed about Scott, but I do believe he's changed, and the clients are delighted. He's doing a good job.'

'Is he, indeed?'

'There's one thing for certain – you can't go on like this.' He waved a hand round her kitchen. 'Something has to be done. How about if I give you a hand to clear up? At least, let's make a start?'

'You? The high and mighty Mungo Price?' Mimicking the high-pitched tones of a client of Mungo's, Joy added, ' "Oh! He's wonderful, Joy, truly wonderful, my Minnie-Lou isn't the same cat, he's given her back her life." How many times have I heard that?'

Indignantly Mungo replied, 'But I did give that Minnie-Lou her life back.'

Joy laughed at his indignation. 'You did, you're quite right, but even so, that kind of talent does not give you the right to believe what *you* think is always right.'

'But usually I am. And I am right about you getting back to work. You need to brace your shoulders, stand tall and give yourself a kick-start. How about it?'

Joy took a moment to reply and when she did Mungo was astounded. 'I've had a very good offer from the practice in the High Street. They're desperate for a nurse/ manager.'

Mungo shot to his feet, giving a very good impression of having been fired out of a cannon. 'You've what? You haven't accepted, have you?'

Joy had tears of laughter running down her cheeks. 'I've never seen anything so funny in years!' She was holding her sides and almost falling from her chair with laughter. 'You should have seen your face.' She pointed a finger at him and rolled about, laughing all over again.

'Well, I suppose I've served some kind of purpose if I've made you laugh. Do you mean it or are you pulling my leg?'

'I mean it. I have. Yesterday.'

'You applied?'

'No, they heard I'd left so thought, on the off-chance, they'd give me a ring.'

'What did you say?'

'I'd think about it.'

Mungo was about to say, 'You wouldn't leave me, never in a hundred years!' but remembered not to just in time. 'Well, of course,' he sat down again, 'of course, if that's what you want, you do what you feel is right.'

Joy dug the knife a little deeper. 'Much smaller practice, of course, no farm side or equine at all, much easier to manage. Only three vets.'

'Perhaps not quite so exciting, though. Our practice is very challenging. They referred a couple of clients to me last week. Very good of them.'

'Very *wise* of them.'

'Premises aren't a patch on ours.'

Joy studied over what he'd said. 'No, you're right there.' She glanced at the kitchen clock. 'Getting late. Should you be going home? Miriam will be wondering.'

'Miriam knows where I am.'

'You're a very lucky man. I hope you know it.'

'I do. Every day.'

Joy was silent for a moment, thinking how the fact she had loved him all these years had never been mentioned between the two of them through the long years of her devotion. 'I'd never have been right for you.'

Mungo looked up at her. So it had come out at last. He felt uncomfortable confronting it like this, as though she'd stripped herself bare in front of him.

'I know that now. I shouldn't have been such an ass all these years. Loving you and making the mistake of thinking there could be no one *but* you.'

'Pity Duncan can't hear you saying that.'

'I wish he could. Sometimes I almost hear him speaking to me and then find that, of course, he isn't here. I realize, and it's taken me all these months to realize it, that I could love Duncan and it would take hardly any effort at all.'

He reached out and clasped her hand. 'My dear. For your sake and Duncan's, I'm so glad.'

Snatching her hand away, Joy said forcefully, 'Off you go.'

'Oh! Right. But I did offer—'

'I know, but before I go to bed this kitchen will be pristine. I promise. Go on, off you go, back to where you belong.'

Joy stood up and Mungo also got to his feet. He went round the table and took her in his arms. They hugged and hugged each other and he kissed her cheek, and she thought how many times in the past she had longed for the deep, deep pleasure of having him hold her as close as this.

Then he stood back from her and looked at her face. 'Thanks for all the good times we've had. Coming back?'

'I'll think about it. Goodnight, Mungo.' She patted his cheek and smiled at him. 'And thank you.'

Before Joy went to bed she cleared up the kitchen, shook out the cats' bedding, gave them each a treat as an apology for neglecting them these last weeks, and before she switched out the light she looked round her kitchen and thought about Duncan's intense absorption when he was planning it. He really loved this kitchen so much. She wished she could see him in it, right now, saying good-night to his cats.

But Duncan lay huddled under his duvet with his coat piled on top to keep him warm, listening to the loud unwelcome sounds of the waves rolling timelessly on to the shore. He thought about Tiger and Copper, about his wood-burning stove, which warmed his heart as well as his toes. What he'd give right this minute to be snugly curled against Joy's back, his nose nuzzling her sweet-smelling hair. He crooked his arm as though it were wrapped around her waist, which made his imagination run riot. He'd had enough of this deprivation, and the cold, and the isolation. These waves, at first so welcome, were a total pain now and while at first they had lulled him to sleep, tonight they were keeping him awake. Yes! He'd go. Back home to Joy and accept with resignation and without recrimination, what scraps of love she had to offer him.

*

When Mungo got home he found Miriam waiting up for him. She was sitting reading in a chair with her feet tucked up in the skirt of her dressing gown.

'Darling! Well?'

'Don't know is the answer. She still hasn't decided.'

'Hell's bells.'

'She's had an offer from the High Street practice, as nurse/manager.'

'No! Really? It's years since she did anything on the nursing side.'

'I know, but she says it's a good offer.'

'You mean she might come back to us if we offer her a rise?'

'There is a limit. She's not forcing my hand by threatening to walk out on us. I might think about it if she comes back and looks like staying but not to entice her back. That's not even thinkable.'

'No, well, right, but—'

'No buts. She looked ghastly. Gone right down, drinking too.'

'Oh! That's bad news. No news of Duncan, then?'

Mungo shook his head. 'But she says she wants him back.'

Miriam brightened considerably. 'That's good news then. Very good, in fact.'

'But wanting him back and getting him back are two quite different things, I mean, where is he?'

'Poor Duncan.'

'Poor Duncan, my foot. He could at least have let her know he was still in the land of the living. It's totally thoughtless of him not to let her know. A postcard would suffice. He's selfish, you know.'

'He's desperately, desperately unhappy.'

'I suppose.'

'However, you've done your best. Joy must have got over you, then.'

'Mmm. What?'

'Joy. She must have got over loving you.' Miriam watched him closely while she waited for his reply.

'Oh! Yes. I'm sure. At last. I can't understand how I never recognized it all these years. But I genuinely didn't know.'

'Did she say anything about it?'

'Said she'd never have been right for me.'

'Oh! I see.'

There was a silence between them while they both absorbed the consequences of Joy's change of heart. It was Miriam who spoke first. 'Next problem is Zoe not wanting to attend Lord Askew's. It was all I needed today. She was very worked up about it.'

'I said she should. All in a day's work et cetera.'

'She said you didn't get angry about it and that if it was convenient she needn't.'

'That's a slight variation of the truth. I'll have a word tomorrow. She can be damned difficult. As a partner she should be above all this petty business. Time she grew up.'

'Mungo! Have you ever wondered who Oscar's father is?'

'No. It's her business. That poor child, if she's always as hard as she appears to be, I wonder if he gets enough loving.'

'He does have his grandmother there.'

Mungo snorted derisively. 'She's another one. Like mother like daughter. She's got a lump of iron where her heart should be. I've only met her once and that was once too many.'

'Poor Zoe. I feel sorry for her.'

'You'd feel sorry for a serial killer.' He got up and offered Miriam a hand. 'I'm going to bed. Will you come too?'

'Of course, I usually do. Perkins has already been out.' Miriam uncoiled herself from the big armchair and stood up. They smiled at each other and Mungo hugged her like he'd hugged Joy, but as well as hugging her he kissed her and said, 'I love you.'

'I love you. You're the apple of my eye.' Miriam kissed her finger and pressed it to Mungo's lips and they wandered off to bed.

Chapter 8

Exactly a week after Mrs Bookbinder had succumbed to Valentine's charms and become a permanent client of his, Miriam received a phone call from Joy.

She was making breakfast for herself and Mungo, but he hadn't arrived in the kitchen yet so it was Miriam who answered the call. 'Miriam Price speaking.'

'Glad it's you, it's Joy.'

'Good morning, Joy.' Miriam crossed her fingers.

'Just to say there's no need to come down today, I'm coming in.'

Miriam swallowed hard. 'That's lovely. I am glad.'

'Of course.' Miriam put down the phone and was dancing a jig round her kitchen table when Mungo came in. 'What's the cause of all this jollity?'

'Mungo! Joy's coming in this morning. She's just rung.'

'Good! She's seen the sense of it at last.'

Miriam flung her arms round him. 'Isn't it wonderful? Thank heavens!'

Mungo grinned. 'I've not lost my touch, then.'

'That is naughty. You went to see if she was OK, not to entice her back with a load of sweet talk.'

Mungo looked innocent. 'I didn't. I was very considerate.'

'I don't believe you.'

'It's true.' He delved into his bowl of muesli with enthusiasm, delighted that things were getting back to normal. 'Put the radio on. You'll be glad.'

'I am. Very glad. I couldn't have taken much more of it. If there's an argument or a complaint, I take full responsibility. It's ridiculous but I can't help it.' Mungo's toast shot into the African Violets again and she had to rescue it and dust it off.

'Are you ever going to buy a new toaster? I've had dusted-off toast for years now. Or better still, move the plant.'

'I know. I keep going out to buy one and then I remember buying this one when you and I were so unhappy, you know, when we lost the children and I can't . . . I know it's silly but . . . I'm deeply attached to it. And what's more, the violet doesn't thrive anywhere else but there, so there it stays.'

Mungo reached across the table and grabbed her hand, took it to his lips and kissed it. 'Never mind, darling, I suppose there are worse things in life than having one's toast dusted off. It's fine, I don't really mind.'

He got a trembling smile for his gentle consideration and she changed the subject and before they knew it they could hear the phone ringing downstairs and Joy calling out, 'Answer that phone, someone,' as she came in through the back door.

Miriam and Mungo smiled at each other. Miriam said, 'There's the difference, I would have raced in and answered it myself.'

Joy conducted herself throughout the day as though she'd never been away. The staff, although tempted to say something, anything to cover their embarrassment and delighted surprise, realized she didn't want anything said at all, so they carried on as though she'd never stormed out, glad to have the reins safe in her hands again. The embarrassing part came when Scott roared in late, seeking Miriam.

'Miriam! Sorry I'm late but the Land Rover wouldn't start. Too damn cold, I expect . . . Ah!' He came to a shuddering halt at the doorway of Joy's office. 'Joy! You're back.'

'I am. Maybe it's time it was dumped. A new reliable one would be good, wouldn't it?'

'Well, yes, it would. It was no end of trouble when I was here before, and it hasn't got any better. Could you wangle it with the boss?'

'I could have a try. Anyway, get your list and off you go.'

'Right, yes, I will. Be seeing you. Bloody cold this morning. Nice to have you back, though.'

'It is?' Joy smiled to herself. On the surface it seemed as though he'd never been gone, but he was not quite the carefree chap of yore. There was a kind of maturity about him, which was pleasing to her.

She sought out the rota file and spotted a list of reminders in Miriam's handwriting, one of which said she should avoid putting Zoe down for visiting Lord Askew's. So, who was Zoe to begin picking and choosing her visits? That would have to stop. As of now. If they began saying who they would and would not visit there would be mayhem.

Joy looked round her office and felt glad to be back. The brightly coloured files, with their neat labels, even her lovely blue filing cabinet which she'd chosen and was so dear to her heart . . . God! Things were getting out of hand if she'd fallen in love with a filing cabinet! Heavens above! She'd have to get a life. Briefly she rested her elbow on the desk and with fingers clenched under her chin she thought about coming back. She'd come back not because she wanted to see Mungo every day and couldn't exist without the heavenly vision of him and loving wallowing in his clients' appreciation of his skill, but simply because she needed to. If Duncan was away much longer and she had no salary coming in she'd have had to begin dipping into their savings in order to keep the house for when he came back.

It wasn't the only reason though. She loved the hustle of the Practice and all the people she met and the friends she made. She gave a great sigh. Mungo went past her door and gave her a thumbs up and a welcoming grin as he passed. So what had happened to her heart? It hadn't raced as it normally did. She must be over him? A great feeling of release swept over her. Free. Free as air she felt. But no Duncan to fill the gap. Ah! Well, back to the grindstone.

Unfortunately for Zoe, she called in with a message on her way to Porter's Fold and as soon as Joy heard her voice she went into reception.

'A word, if you please, in my office.'

Joy didn't wait to see if she followed her.

'Now, Zoe, what does this mean, you're not willing to attend at Lord Askew's? Mmm?'

'I spoke to Mungo. He didn't object.'

'Well, he's not the manager. I am and I want to know the reason.'

'Frankly, as a partner, I don't think I need to give an explanation. Colin gets away with murder, he picks and chooses where he goes, so I want to do the same. It's the only one I object to.' Zoe stood looking down at Joy with a belligerent look on her face.

'I'm well aware Colin is choosy, it's kind of happened over the years, but he does have a wide selection of clients. Colin's an excellent vet, and has been a partner for far longer than you and is years older. So he deserves a certain amount of leeway. Now, come on, enlighten me.'

Zoe explained her reasons and somehow, faced by Joy and not Miriam, they appeared rather lame.

'I see. Well, I'm sorry, it's not the cows' fault and that account is very valuable to us. I can't wait for Dan to be mobile again. I know Scott's been once to his horses, but Dan is the one his lordship really prefers, and it's up to us not to tread on his toes. So if it comes up and it's convenient for you to go, you will go. Right?'

'And if I dig my heels in?'

'Well, of course, that's up to you.' Joy glared at her and Zoe glared back.

But it was Zoe's eyes that dropped first. She spun on her heel and left the office, dashed down the corridor to the back door and left, slamming the door as she went.

Joy shrugged. You couldn't give them an inch. She'd turned her back for a minute and look what had happened. A rebellion. Choosing a black marker pen, she put a thick line through Miriam's reminder, and thought, She's far too kind is Miriam to be doing a job like this, good thing I came back. Joy could hear the clinic getting busier and in a moment of silence heard Miss Chillingsworth's voice.

'Why, Miss Chillingsworth, how are you?'

'Joy! How lovely to see you. Enjoyed your holiday? Mrs Price said you'd been away.'

'Ah! Yes. Glad to be back though. Cherub OK?'

'Of course, my dear, you won't have heard with being away. She's been in a dreadful fight and Mr Murgatroyd came very close to saying there was no hope. Well, he did say there was no hope, but he decided to have a go, as Wilfred Pickles used to say, and he and Mr Price operated on her and I've brought her in for a check-up.'

'Let me take a peep.' Joy looked into the door of Cherub's carrying basket and saw the long bald patch where she'd been shaved in order to be stitched and the blue plasters on her front legs. 'Oh my word! She's had a lucky escape.'

'She has. I've got Mr Murgatroyd and Mr Price to thank for that. I'll sit down now, it's seemed a long way on the bus. They've started the sewage pipe replacement on my side of town now and it's taken ages to get here.'

Joy went back into her office and suddenly realized that Miriam had been right. Tiger had had similar injuries but without the broken legs. My God! Whatever was it that had done this? It was no ordinary cat, she was sure. That long jagged tear! Some cat! If indeed it was a cat. No. It must have been a dog. Yes. That was it. She remembered that when Tiger had her operation she'd been so sad, so desperate that she hadn't cared whether Tiger lived or died. Had Duncan been here he would have been distraught by the thought of losing her. Joy remembered how Miriam had almost died laughing when Duncan admitted he loved Tiger, and her eyes filled with tears.

'I'm going for lunch. Having it at the snack bar. Look after the shop, Annette, while I'm out.'

The snack bar still glowed with the New York look it had given itself months ago and Joy went in there for her favourite BLT. There wasn't anywhere else that could get the bacon so crisp and the lettuce and tomatoes nearly so fresh tasting as they could.

The television high up on a shelf where it could easily be seen by the customers announced a newsflash was about to be broadcast. Apparently there'd been a terrible ferry disaster in the Irish Sea. Most of the passengers had been rescued but they believed that at least seven had drowned. The storm that caused it was beginning to blow itself out, but the rescue operation was hazardous. It drew Joy's attention and she watched while she ate her sandwich. The mountainous seas made Joy feel queasy and seeing the waves made her amazed that anyone could have survived, but apparently they had. Helicopters had winched up a lot of the passengers, others had been rescued by the lifeboats. The ferry was sinking in the huge waves . . . she couldn't wait any longer, watching the tragedy was giving her the heebie-jeebies . . . as if life wasn't difficult enough. Joy leaped to her feet, swallowed down the remains of her coffee and left.

At home, still having all the time in the world to watch the news, was Dan. Propped in an easy chair with a large upholstered footstool in front of it on which he could support his Meccano legs, as Rose called them, he was watching the pictures of the tragedy. The house was quiet, for Jonathan was having his midday sleep, Rose was taking the opportunity for a rest on the bed while she could and Lloyd had gone up to London for a few days on business.

Dan picked up the remote control, intending to change the programme but precisely at that moment, the BBC interviewer was speaking to some of the survivors. The first one he approached, tall and thin with a blanket around his shoulders, brushed him aside and waved his hands to indicate he didn't want to be interviewed. Dan peered closely. My God! It couldn't be. It was Duncan, surely it was. The tall, thin figure moved off into the background of the picture and Dan could see him being approached by an ambulance paramedic. But the man handed the blanket over and stalked away down the seafront, bag in hand. Just for a brief moment he turned to check the road before he crossed and Dan saw quite definitely that the man was Duncan, even thinner than before but definitely Duncan. No mistake. No, he must be wrong, you didn't see friends walking away from a drowning on TV. Did you?

He quickly switched to ITV and found they were reporting the story on there too. This time the picture was slightly different but it gave him another chance to look for Duncan and there he was, pictured as he stepped off a helicopter with the blanket round his shoulders. He brushed away a newspaper photographer as he did so, brusquely, no nonsense. He obviously didn't want to be photographed.

Dan felt hot and sweaty and bewildered.

Unable to believe what he'd seen.

But at the same time certain it was Duncan.

So, he'd been in Ireland.

And was coming home.

Well, perhaps that wasn't certain, but Joy deserved to know at least that he was alive.

Dan itched to tell someone and decided to ring Miriam and ask her if . . .

'Miriam Price speaking.'

'It's Dan.'

'How lovely, how are you?'

'Doing fine, thanks. And you? Oh, good. Joy's back? Wonderful. That's good news. Miriam, have you watched the TV, seen the Irish ferry disaster?'

'Oh, dear. No, I haven't.'

Slowly and deliberately, knowing he was tremendously excited for Joy, but needing to be absolutely clear about what he'd seen, Dan said, 'I hardly dare believe my eyes but I'm almost one hundred per cent sure that I've seen Duncan Bastable getting out of a rescue helicopter at Fishguard.'

When Miriam didn't answer him, Dan said, 'Did you hear what I said? Are you there?'

'Yes, I am. I can't believe what you say.'

'Neither can I. Shall we tell her?'

'Are you totally certain?'

'I saw him on BBC and ITV news. Once walking away with a blanket round his shoulders, and then giving it to a paramedic who was obviously wanting him to get in the ambulance but he wouldn't, and once climbing out of a helicopter. I saw him full face, there was no mistake.'

'But if we tell her and it isn't him?'

'I know, that's the worry. Have you got News Twenty-Four? We haven't here, you see. But you could watch on there if you have it.'

'We have. I'll put down the phone and take a look and ring you back.'

In minutes Miriam was back on the telephone. 'Oh, Dan, I'm sure it's him! I saw him checking before he crossed the road. Caught him full face, but he's so thin. He even walks like Duncan, you know, with his shoulders hunched. It *must* be him, mustn't it? What shall we do? What if he's come back to England, but doesn't want to come back to Barleybridge? It would be devastating for Joy. Wouldn't it?' Miriam was pacing about with indecision and excitement. 'What shall we do?'

'If we could get her to watch the news she could decide for herself if it was him.'

'Good thinking. I do hope it is. Oh, Dan! If he's coming

back, it would be wonderful. I'll ring you in a while. Keep your fingers crossed.'

As Miriam raced downstairs to find Joy, she came in from the car park.

'Ah! Joy. Had a good lunch?'

'Not particularly.'

'I want you to come upstairs with me for a moment.'

'Must press on.'

'I know, but please come upstairs for a moment, just to see something I have to show you.' Miriam took Joy's hand and pulled her as far as the bottom of the stairs to the flat.

'What are you being so mysterious about?'

'Just come, please.'

Miriam ran up in front of her, and Joy followed more slowly. 'I really shouldn't, you know.'

'They won't mind, the others. Sit down, I've got something to explain. I want you to watch News Twenty-Four with me, because Dan and I think there's someone on that you know. We could be wrong and we shall be devastated if we are, but you've got to see.'

'Look, Miriam—'

But she had switched on. The footage of the ferry disaster was being replayed.

Joy sat watching closely, puzzled by Miriam's excitement. She watched the lifeboatmen landing some survivors and then the camera switched to a helicopter and Joy saw a thin, weary figure with a blanket round his shoulders. Saw the paramedic go speak to him, the brusque refusal of help, the handing over of the blanket, saw him check before crossing the road. Got to her feet, hands over her mouth, a huge intake of breath, not believing what she saw.

Miriam caught her just as she collapsed, and pushed her into the chair. 'My dear! My dear!'

Joy sobbed, heartbroken. Not speaking, just giving vent to her feelings, bottled up for so long. Miriam poured her a brandy and urged her to sip it, giving with it a handful of tissues. With her arm around her shoulders Miriam waited for the storm to abate.

'Oh! My heavens! It was him. It was him. He's been in Ireland all this time. Oh! Duncan! Has he been ill, do you think? He looked so terribly thin.'

'I don't suppose anyone looks at their best when they've just been rescued from a sinking ferry. But at least he's still with us, so to speak. I'm going downstairs to tell everyone, they'll be so pleased. You stay here as long as you like. The girls will be all right, don't worry.'

Miriam raced down the stairs and went first into reception and told Stephie and Annette the good news. Before they'd had a chance to take it in she'd gone to tell Mungo, who was operating, and to tell Graham, who was doing a castration in room three. Then she got on the phone to Colin's mobile and Zoe's and Scott's and told them the news. 'Isn't it wonderful?' 'Isn't it marvellous news?' 'Isn't it just tremendous?'

Upstairs in the flat, Perkins had come into the sitting room and was resting a paw on Joy's knee, trying to lick her face. Sympathy oozed from him and Joy had to break off crying just to console him. 'Perkins! You are a love. A dear, dear dog. You know far more than we give you credit for.' Joy bent to kiss his head.

The ferry disaster news came on again and she watched every moment of it. Just think, if he hadn't survived I might never have known what had happened to him. Just a foot passenger, a nonentity possibly. Oh, Duncan Bastable, you owe me. You most certainly do.

Now she knew he was alive, did she love him? Like he wanted? Frankly, she hadn't time to answer her own question, she was too excited. He was alive. All the worry over with.

Perkins took his paw from her knee and she sprang out of the chair. Should she go to Fishguard to find him? When she suggested that to Miriam, Miriam thought no. 'You see, he might be on his way home as you're going there and you'd cross in the middle, so there'd be so much time wasted and confusion.'

'I never thought, he might ring home? And I'm not there.'

'He might ring here, he knows you're likely to be in work, doesn't he? After all, he doesn't know you haven't been in for a while, does he?'

'Oh, Miriam! I don't know what I'm doing. Of course you're right.' Joy paced about the room. 'Miriam! What if he isn't intending coming home? What shall I do then?'

There was no answer to that question and all Miriam could do was hug her.

Desperately and in the smallest possible voice Joy whispered, 'I shall die if he doesn't. That will be rejection, him being saved and not coming home. Oh God! I can't bear it.'

'You will. You will. You've no choice.'

'How wise. I have no choice, but to wait and see.' Joy went to the window with a view towards Beulah Bank Top. 'He loved it up there, all wild and lonely, the cold and the high winds. Spent hours huddled in sheep hollows thinking. Wishing. If he comes back he'll get all he wants and more. I've realized while I've been at home, how many years I've wasted waiting for . . . well, you know . . . when all the time I could have been loving

Duncan. I've been such a fool. It's his choice to come home or not, I shall just have to be patient. But I wish he'd hurry up.' Joy gave a great sigh, picked up her bag, twinkled her fingers at Miriam and wended her way downstairs to her office to spend all afternoon fretting, expecting that each phone call would be Duncan, but it never was.

Zoe and Scott talked of nothing else when they met for dinner that night. Scott said for the umpteenth time, 'I wonder what the hell he's been doing all this time?'

'Don't ask me. Apparently, Miriam says, he's even thinner than he was the last time we saw him.'

'I thought it could be lonely on our sheep station, so lonely you'd drive a hundred-mile round trip just to go to a party, but at least you've got the hands there and my pa's housekeeper, and things going on. But what is it, six months he's been missing? What the hell?'

'He's always been a loner, you know, ever since I've known him and of course, Joy loving Mungo hasn't helped.'

'I can't imagine what it must be like marrying someone and then finding out they loved someone else. What a kick up the backside that must have been for poor old Duncan.' Scott pushed his soup bowl away. 'Shouldn't have chosen oxtail. It's awful.'

Zoe with her soup spoon halfway to her mouth said, 'It wouldn't do for me. All or nothing, as far as I'm concerned. But as I'm unlikely to find someone who thinks I'm the bee's knees I can look forward to a single life.'

'What's wrong with you? Why shouldn't you find some-one?'

Zoe shrugged her shoulders.

'You're very attractive.'

'You think so, do you?'

'Of course. There's no one but you in the Practice at the moment I'd give any time to at all.'

'What should I do? Kneel down and kiss your feet?'

'Zoe! Why is it every time I say something pleasing about you, you turn it on its head?'

She paused for a moment before she replied. 'Habit, I suppose.'

'No, it's not, you're doing it to keep me at arm's length. Why?'

'How can you expect me to take you seriously with your record?'

Scott's face blanked for a moment.

'See! Mention the word "seriously" and you run a mile.'

'I do not.'

'You do. Commitment! Definitely not. That's not your stock in trade and you have to admit you have something of a record in that department. First me, then Bunty, then Kate and heaven knows who else besides. It's all in your genes. You can't help it. The thrill of the chase. That's what.' She finished her soup and pushed the dish away. 'You should have had chicken, it was lovely. Before you know it you'll be a randy old bachelor and a laughing stock among the girls, who'll all be twenty years younger than you.'

Scott looked hurt.

'Sorry, but it's true and by the looks of your face you know it's likely.'

Scott didn't answer her and they remained silent until after the waiter had served their main course. As Scott plunged his knife into the centre of his appetizing steak and kidney pie he said, 'Perhaps if I'd found the right person it would be different. I like the idea of fathering children and all that entails. I'd like a family. It must be utterly amazing seeing for the first time the child that you've created.'

Zoe was absorbed eating her steak and didn't reply.

Scott pursued his train of thought. 'Ever seen the Bridges boys all together?'

Zoe shook her head. 'Only in ones and twos.'

'All of 'em together is a magnificent sight and then you look at little Mrs Bridges and you wonder how on earth she managed it. Still less how she managed when they were all growing up. We had some laughs when I was here before. Going out shooting together and drinking. They could drink me to a standstill.'

'Could they?'

Scott laughed. 'I remember one night we—'

'For heaven's sake, Scott, not a drinking story. I can't bear men drunk and even less women drunk. They disgust me.'

'Only fun.'

'What's the fun when you're so drunk you don't know you're enjoying yourself? Eh? Tell me that?'

Hand on heart Scott said, 'Ah! You have a point. I promise faithfully not to tell you drinking stories.'

Zoe gave him a smile, she didn't want to hurt his feelings. 'Good. Are you going to Lord Askew's dinner and dance for the hunt?'

'Not thought about it. Are you?'

'No. I am not, as I told you.'

'Neither can I. I've no partner. I don't suppose you'd . . .' He raised an eyebrow at her, knowing full well she'd say no.

Zoe hesitated and for a moment Scott thought he must just have persuaded her.

'No, and don't mention it again.'

'That's all right with me. I'd have evening dress to hire and I don't go much for all that privilege bit. Cinema after? Shall we try the new ten-screen job? Give it a whirl?'

'Yes. I shan't want pudding. Shall you?'

Scott shook his head. 'No. I'll pay. No going Dutch.'

'I'll pay for the cinema then.'

'OK.'

They crossed the precinct hand in hand, window shopping as they went. She couldn't help but notice the admiring glances Scott got as they walked along. Well, he was good-looking, but he knew it, that was the problem, he damn well knew he was and lapped up the admiration. In fact, he thrived on it. Sad really. But somehow, cautious and wary as she was, she had to confess to enjoying holding his hand, and liked knowing him so well she could see his faults as plain as plain, but still enjoy his company. He had his arm around her shoulders while they watched the film, and she was intensely aware of him beside her.

Had Joy known Zoe was enjoying Scott's arm around her when she herself was sitting watching the pictures of Duncan and the ferry disaster on her TV time and again, she would have been incredibly envious.

Chapter 9

Everyone, except for Scott and his partner, going from the Practice to the dinner dance had agreed they'd hire a minibus between them so they wouldn't have problems over who drove and didn't drink. The starting time was seven for seven-thirty and the bus was to pick up Miriam and Mungo the last. Miriam came into the sitting room ready for leaving. 'Pour me a gin and tonic, Mungo, I might as well get in the mood.' She was wearing a slim, sleeveless pale-pink dress, perfectly plain but with an intricate design of mother-of-pearl coloured beads on the bodice. She glanced at Mungo and her heart flipped. He didn't look a day older than when she'd first met him. He was so handsome. 'I wonder who Scott's bringing tonight, he was very cagey about her name. You don't think it could be Zoe, do you?'

'Here you are. I've no idea. I doubt it with her being so opposed to fox-hunting. Just wish Duncan was here then Joy would be going. He can be quite good fun when he makes the effort.'

'It's strange, isn't it? Two weeks since he got off that ferry and still he's not home. I wonder where he is. She's even more upset now than when she didn't know if he was alive or dead.' Miriam looked up at him to admire how good he looked in his dinner jacket, and smiled at him.

'Let's forget about him, we're supposed to be enjoying ourselves tonight.'

'Got your bleeper?'

Mungo checked it was clipped to his waistband. 'Yes. Let's hope we don't get a call.'

'Let's hope so. That's the minibus tooting. I'm so looking forward to this. It's ages since we had a dressed-up night out.' Miriam gave Perkins a quick pat, whereupon, realizing he wasn't being included in the outing, he gave an excellent impression of a badly-done-by dog and went to sulk in his basket. Mungo followed her downstairs, thinking how beautiful she looked and wishing it hadn't been him with the defective gene, which had caused their children to die.

He and Miriam squeezed into the two front seats of the minibus and with a loud rallying call on a hunting horn Colin had dug up from somewhere, they left for the George Hotel.

By the time they arrived at the hotel, everyone in the party was looking forward immensely to the evening. Valentine and Nadia must have had a good few drinks before they'd got on the bus because, unusually for them, they were full of jokes and laughter, and even teased Letty about how being a mother had changed her. 'Probably lack of sleep,' she answered, unperturbed by their joking.

They all spilled out onto the pavement outside the George with eager anticipation only to be faced with an anti-fox-hunting protest. And there, right at the front of it, was Zoe Savage holding up a huge banner, skilfully constructed and its message plain:

BAN FOX-HUNTING FOR EVER! STOP THE MURDER!

Mungo stalked past and went up the steps, seething with anger but not prepared to tackle a member of his own staff in full public view when he knew there was nothing he could do about it; after all, he had no jurisdiction over what Zoe did in her free time. The rest of them, except for Miriam, who gave her a nod, ignored her and followed Mungo inside.

Scott was already in the bar when they went to order their pre-dinner drinks. He was full to the brim with good spirits and when Miriam asked if he was on his own he answered, 'No. Ah! Here she is.'

It was Joy in a lavender dress with a deep décolleté neckline, and a wide, multi-stranded pearl choker clasped round her neck.

Scott's eyes almost popped out of his head. 'Wow! My word! What an honour to be partnering you, Joy. You look wonderful, doesn't she?'

They all had to agree she did. For someone whose husband was on the missing list, so to speak, she looked fabulous.

At the first chance she got, Miriam asked Scott how he'd persuaded her to come.

'Thought she'd feel out of it so I said I wanted to go but I'd no partner and would she come just to please me.'

'Well, full marks for persuading her, it's just what she needs. I had hoped you'd bring Zoe, but I saw she came on a very different mission.'

'I asked her to come with me, but she said no. She has good reason for not wanting to support hunting. She's damned stubborn. I never thought she'd be protesting in front of everyone. There must be loads of people who recognize her. But she is free to protest if she wishes.'

'She is.' Miriam pressed her lips together and Scott saw

she was annoyed. He glanced at Mungo and saw the inscrutable look on his face and guessed he wouldn't enjoy himself tonight. Blast Zoe! But he had to admire her determination.

The gong sounded and dinner was announced.

The food exceeded expectations. It was a pity, thought Scott, that it would have to be spoiled by speeches. He just hoped everyone who spoke recognized the need for brevity. With the tables swiftly and expertly cleared, Lord Askew stood up to speak. 'My lords, ladies and gentlemen, may I take this . . .' As he did so, there was a commotion at the door, resolved by someone thrusting herself into the hall carrying her placard. Zoe! Scott groaned. What was she thinking of? He didn't dare look at Mungo. Zoe, in comparison to the people attending the dinner, looked scruffy and dishevelled. She hastened across to the nearest table and began tossing leaflets on it, spreading them out so no one could miss reading their message. The restaurant manager, foreseeing there might be trouble, had employed two 'heavies' who rapidly lunged in after her, but she was far too fleet of foot for them to catch her straight away, and she was halfway down the hall, approaching his lordship, by the time they caught hold of her arms. Scott thought she couldn't have timed her entrance better. He leaped to his feet. He wasn't going to stand by and see her man-handled by those two thugs. His chair crashed back on to the floor, leaving him no space to rush forward, but he disentangled his feet and ran between the tables, which in itself caused a fluster.

'Leave her alone! Take your hands off her. Zoe! You've made your point.'

The restaurant manager dashed through from the kit-chens on winged feet to aid the heavies, but Zoe was fighting like a wildcat, kicking, struggling, trying to throw her leaflets out over their heads. Some of the guests were finding it amusing and were calling out encouraging hunting cries like 'Tally-ho', but others, along with everyone from the Practice, were acutely embarrassed.

In the midst of the struggle Lord Askew called out, 'That will do. You men, release her!'

The restaurant manager, after years of bowing to his lordship's every whim and fancy, let go immediately, but his two henchmen were under no such obligation. Scott, still trying to force their hands off Zoe, was becoming wilder by the moment.

His lordship's powerful voice boomed out again. 'Firth! Did you hear me? Leave her be!'

Finally the manager made the men understand that the fighting was at an end. Scott, much relieved as he didn't enjoy being on the losing side, stood to one side and whispered, 'Zoe, just go out.'

She looked at him defiantly, but seeing him shake his head ever so slightly, the fight went out of her. She was breathing heavily, nevertheless she managed to shout out, 'Murderers! The lot of you! Murderers!'

Scott put a hand under her elbow and walked out with her. As her final act of defiance she was still scattering her leaflets as they went out of the door with shouts of 'Gone to ground' following them out. As the door shut behind them a heavy silence fell in the restaurant.

Someone at the first table began collecting the leaflets, not bothering to read them. The restaurant manager bent to gather the ones littering the floor, helped by a waiter or two, and Lord Askew began his speech again as though there had been no interruption. But all the guests could sense the anger in his tone and if anything his speech was more passionate than anything he'd ever said in defence of his cause. He spoke with real depth of feeling about the abuse of an Englishman's right to hunt, of the despicable state of affairs whereby those who knew nothing of a countryman's life had the gross arrogance to interfere in such a devastating way. 'By what right?' he shouted. 'By what right?' He was applauded long and loudly, so in a curious way Zoe's protest had stiffened everyone's resolve.

Outside the hotel Scott was trying to persuade Zoe to ignore the clamour of her supporters, all wanting to know what had happened to her in the restaurant, and allow him to drive her home.

'Leave me alone.'

'I *am* taking you home.'

'You're not. I have my car and I shall drive myself home.'

'Well, at least let me sit in the car with you for a while until you calm down. You can't drive in this mood.'

'I'm not a child, Scott, I can drive perfectly well.'

But he didn't like the way she appeared to be on the point of hyperventilating. Patiently he answered, 'I know you're not, but I'm doing it just the same. Where is your car parked?'

'On the market car park.'

'Come on, then.'

Scott sat in the front passenger seat and didn't speak. Gradually Zoe's breathing became steadier, but he remained quiet. Their silence was broken by Zoe saying, 'I showed 'em.'

A mite sarcastically he asked, 'You did, did you?'

She looked at him.

'As Sheilas go you're a toughie and I admire you for that. But I thought it was verging on the ridiculous.'

'Ridiculous! What was ridiculous about it?'

'You've probably made them all even more determined to beat you rabble-rousers.'

'Rabble-rousers? I'm serious.'

'I know you are, but . . .'

'What?'

'But in those circumstances you did your cause no good.' Scott looked out of the side window. 'And you put me in the position of looking a fool, because I couldn't stop those two louts from manhandling you, which I don't like.'

'That's not my fault. I didn't ask you to help.'

'I know you didn't, but I couldn't stand by and watch you being humiliated.'

'Whoops! He's got a heart. I'm sorry I upset everyone, you know Mungo and the rest. It didn't occur to me about them being there, and it should have done. I've spoilt it for them, haven't I? And I'm sorry I did.'

'Yes, you have. You're hot-headed, you know.'

'I *feel* so strongly about it.'

He turned to look at her. 'Look, I'm going back to the George now, because I mustn't leave my partner on her own any longer. She's only come because I promised to stick by her. Remember to eat humble pie for breakfast, you're going to need it.' He opened the car door, but before he got out he said thoughtfully, 'You look splendid when you're roused.' She turned her head to see just how much he meant what he said, so he took his chance to kiss her and she didn't object.

'Thanks for supporting me.'

'I don't support your cause, but I do support your freedom to protest, but only if you behave yourself. Nothing ever again like tonight. Too damaging to yourself. Goodnight.'

Through her rear-view mirror Zoe watched Scott walk away. She had to admit that in a dinner jacket too he looked splendid. It niggled at the back of her mind that he thought her courageous plan to bring the protest right into the heartland of the fox-hunting clan had misfired. He couldn't be right, could he? She never thought she'd ever feel grateful for Lord Askew's existence, but she did; he'd saved her from an ignominious and exceedingly public exit.

Who had partnered Scott? She'd given him a half-hearted refusal and it wouldn't have taken much to have gone as his partner. Was she going soft in the head? Of course she couldn't have gone, not with her beliefs. Mungo no doubt would have plenty to say for himself tomorrow. But what the hell – if he wanted her to leave, well, then, no problem. The problem was all his, because he'd have to buy her out, and she wouldn't go quietly.

So who *had* partnered Scott? Not that it was of any interest to her. Definitely not. She didn't care.

Mungo was intending to be breakfasted by 7.55 a.m. and waiting in reception to see Zoe when she came in. His head was roaring with the drink he'd had last night but nothing was going to stop him from being there to see Zoe arrive. Even Miriam's gentle chatter felt like a steam hammer working on overdrive right inside his head and he had to ask her not to talk. So she said not a word of apology when his toast leaped into the African Violets again, nor did she chastise him when the jar of marmalade slipped from his hand and smashed on the tiled floor; she quietly replaced it with a new jar without a word.

But when he went to kiss her before he left for his confrontation with Zoe he could sense her holding back her laughter.

'Oh, Mungo. Your bad head serves you right.'

'Mmm.'

'It does. You drank far too much last night but no wonder.'

'Wish me good luck.'

'Good luck. Remember she has a right to her own opinions.'

'Not when it embarrasses me, well . . . both of us, and she makes a fool of one of our clients.'

Mungo went down the stairs in a bad mood, made worse by the fact that he could hear Zoe was already there, so it took the edge off his dominance in any battle royal.

She was in Joy's office asking who had been her partner last night.

'Scott.'

'Oh, I see. Well, I think that was great. It was good, was it?'

'Well, it was until you turned up. Whatever made you do it, for heaven's sakes? Knowing who'd be there and not only him but other clients too.'

'I feel very passionately about the whole thing, hare-coursing, whatever, it should all be stopped. At least I took the fight right into the arena, didn't I?'

'Oh! You did that all right. I still think you—'

Mungo stood in the doorway. 'Zoe. My office, if you please.'

She followed him in and was sitting in a chair before he had sat down in his own. Deciding not to be browbeaten, she got in first. 'I do hope you're not expecting an apology from me because there won't be one. I behave according to the dictates of my own conscience and as I was in no way representing the Practice I consider you have nothing to say to me. The hunt is cruel beyond belief and I shall never give in until it is totally stopped.'

Mungo, ignoring every word she uttered, said firmly, 'One, I insist on you apologizing to Lord Askew. And I mean apologize. I mean grovel, crawl, submit, do homage and if necessary genuflect to his lordship, because I know of nothing else that might appease him. Your behaviour towards him was a disgrace. More worthy of a sulky teenager than a mature professional woman. I am ashamed of you. Second, you can thank him for stopping those men hauling you out like a strumpet off the streets. Third, *I* want an apology from you too. The damage you have done to the Practice will only be revealed as the days go by. I dread to think how much business you have lost us by your antics. Well?'

'Antics! Is that what you call it? Antics! I'm serious. I'll do anything to stop it.'

'Miriam was very distressed about what you did, but she's more thoughtful than I am and she understands your reasons. However, I don't and won't even try.' Mungo stood up. 'You'd better think very seriously about your position at this Practice. For now, I have nothing more to say.'

He left, calling out cheerfully to Scott about last night and the raffle prize Scott had won. 'A weekend in a five-star hotel. Are you up to it?'

'Of course.'

'They'll all be begging you to take them.'

Scott grinned. 'I've already got someone in mind.'

Scott met Zoe in the corridor. In a low voice he asked how she had got on. 'He seems chirpy enough.'

'Empty threats. But I do have to apologize to his lordship. Damn and blast.'

'Get it over with, Zoe, today, while you're still hyped up. It will be harder the longer you leave it.'

She changed the subject. She wouldn't be dictated to, least of all by Scott. 'Did I hear Mungo say you'd won a raffle prize, a weekend away?'

'I did. For two. Will you help me out of a difficult spot?'

'What do you mean?'

'Come with me. No commitment.' He held up his hands, palms towards her.

'When?'

'Whenever we choose. Have to be a weekend when Colin's on call.'

'OK.' Should she have agreed? Only time would tell. 'No commitment, like you said.'

Scott nodded. 'That's right, mate, no commitment.' As he turned away he smiled, and was whistling by the time he got to his Land Rover. He enjoyed getting his own way.

Zoe, however, was not nearly so cheerful. She looked at her list of calls and decided to fit in visiting Lord Askew at the start of her day because he should be back from his morning ride shortly. Better to catch him out in the yard; she felt more comfortable with that.

Gavin was about when she got there so she zoomed down her window and called out, 'Is his lordship back yet?'

'Any minute now.'

'Thanks.' Zoe waited in her car for his return. She turned on the local radio just at the moment when they were reporting on the dinner at the George. The way the protest was reported annoyed her. Even worse was the fact that they interviewed Lord Askew and he gave a very good account of himself. All in all it would appear her protest had fallen flat on its face. They all kowtowed to him, that was the trouble. Every word that fell from those fleshy lips of his was treated like some precious pearl of wisdom. How unfair!

Above the noise of the radio came the heavy clop-clopping of his hunter. She leaped out of the car and waited, hands in pockets, for him to appear through the arch.

When he saw her he touched his riding hat, pulled up, dismounted and, still holding the reins, came across to speak to her. 'Zoe! No worse for last night, then? You're a feisty young woman, I admire that in a girl.'

Zoe swallowed hard. 'I've come to apologize. I should never have—'

'Every Englishman, and woman come to that, has a right to express their opinion. Can't fault you on that.'

'Thank you for saving me from an ignominious removal. On your part it was most kind.'

'Couldn't have someone I admired being hoisted out like a common criminal. No, you did right to protest. I'm sorry we don't have more like you on my side. Think no more about it, my dear.' Gavin came across at this point to take his hunter away, and Lord Askew turned towards the house and breakfast. He looked back to say, 'You did us a good turn anyway, made us more resolved than ever to get our own way.' She got a wave of his riding crop and was left standing on the cobbles feeling humiliated, with all the heart taken out of her. What was the point? She was prepared for him to rant and rave and being able to respond in kind with plenty of ripe phrases stored away in her head ready to bring out, but there he was being so charming to her and then right at the last taking the wind out of her sails. Damn him. Damn him. But she gave a wry smile when she thought about it being her, 'the rabble-rouser', who was getting the weekend in the five-star hotel. It made an interesting twist to the whole affair. She'd apologize to Mungo wholeheartedly at lunchtime.

But he wasn't there because he'd been called away by an important client unable to bring their dog into his clinic. So instead Zoe went up to see Miriam. She was seated in her kitchen eating a solitary lunch. 'Sorry, I'll come back later.'

'No, share this salad with me, I need the company anyway. Please?'

'First though I'm going to apologize.' So while Miriam found a plate for her and a glass and cutlery and put a thick slice of cold roast beef on Zoe's plate, Zoe explained why she'd come, finishing with, 'I have a nasty feeling I've made a complete fool of myself. Just possibly my demonstration did my cause no good whatsoever.'

'You didn't get hurt by those thugs, did you? Help yourself, please do. I thought they were far too heavy-handed.'

'No, not at all. Scott, I think, saved me from the worst of it. But you haven't said anything about my apology. I know Mungo's not here but I have to get it off my chest.'

Miriam spoke after she'd put more mayonnaise on her hard-boiled egg. 'Have you done as Mungo asked?'

'Oh, yes! His lordship was very gracious about it, then walked away saying I'd done him a good turn as my protest had made everyone even more determined.' She laughed ruefully at herself and looked up at Miriam for her answer.

'Well, then, that's all right.'

'Your voice doesn't ring true, Miriam.'

'No, it doesn't. I had thought that having Oscar had made you grow up, but judging by last night it hasn't. I was very disappointed in you, but on the other hand the Practice doesn't own you body and soul. Do you know, I haven't seen Oscar since before he could walk. You should bring him to see us sometime. During the day when everyone's here. They'd like that.'

Zoe quickly scotched that as an idea. 'He's at nursery every day till six, you see. Unavoidable really.'

'Of course. Will you apologize to Joy? Just a casual one, I think she'd appreciate that. She feels responsible for you all, you see.'

'Joy? All right then. But that's it. I've finished with apologizing for something I firmly believe in.'

Miriam patted her arm. 'Quite. Quite. Another bread roll?'

You couldn't be cross with Miriam for long and before she knew it Zoe was telling her stories about when she was at college, and how much she hoped Kate would be having as exciting a time as she had had. 'It was damned hard work, never seemed to have any time to spare, but so worth while. Such fun. I just hope Kate's enjoying herself.'

'I'm sure she is. How's Scott coping?'

Miriam noticed Zoe's slight hesitation before she replied, 'Fine. The clients are delighted. Some swear by him, you know.'

'He's a great chap. I find him delightful, and he's matured since he was here last. Always full of life, as though he has to watch all the hours he has to get the most from them he can. Don't you think so?' Miriam offered Zoe cheese and biscuits. 'Or would you prefer fruit?'

'Cheese, please.'

Zoe didn't say any more about Scott, and carried on eating her lunch and finishing her apple juice, so Miriam drew her own conclusions; sometimes silence told her as much and more than talk.

The clock on Miriam's kitchen wall said it was time for Zoe to go. 'I'll see Joy before I leave, best get it over with. Thanks for lunch, it was lovely.'

Having determined, as Miriam had advised, to say how sorry she was to Joy, Zoe went straight away to find her. She was on reception while the girls had their lunch and accepted Zoe's apology generously. 'Mind you, I was blazing at the time. But I have to admit to having a great deal of sympathy for your views. It must have been hard going with Lord Askew.'

'Not too bad actually. He was most gracious.'

'Good. Always fair-minded, I would have thought. We'll put it all behind us now and start with a clean sheet. OK?'

'Agreed.' Zoe left at the gallop, having spent more than enough time lunching with Miriam.

Joy watched her leave, glad she had been able to be magnanimous about the whole matter when inside herself she was feeling anything but. She'd recorded the arrival of Duncan on the mainland and watched it time and again. It definitely was Duncan, or he had an identical twin, and it hurt so badly. Sometimes there was a real live pain gnawing at her innards and it made her mean and judgemental.

Right now, Joy wished she were at home where she could brood in peace and watch the pictures of him all over again, but there'd be another four hours before she could leave. A busy afternoon gave her no time to dwell. All in all, she knew that Dan's idea of a long afternoon clinic had definitely paid off. They were busier than ever. That Mrs Bookbinder had recommended her friends so when Valentine was doing consultations they had all on to fit everyone in.

Finally Joy could escape. She popped in the supermarket

for a few things for the cats and herself and then drove home through the darkened streets and the pitch-black lanes closer to home. Usually Tiger and Copper came to greet her, slipping out through the cat flap at the sound of her car, but tonight they didn't. A nasty scrunched feeling started inside her. Surely they hadn't come across whatever it was that had attacked Tiger? She still wasn't over the fear that had caused her. Tentatively she put her key in the door and as she pushed it open Tiger came running, closely followed by Copper. What relief! Joy bent down to stroke them. 'My beauties! My little darlings! How are you both? Spent the day curled up in front of the stove, have you, while I'm out in the world earning a crust? And I can't blame you. It's been a bitch of a day.'

She took off her coat and hung it in the hall cupboard. Deciding she'd get something to eat before she collapsed in Duncan's chair in front of the stove for the evening, she went down the hall and round the corner to the kitchen. The cats beat her to it.

Joy stood in the doorway thinking it must be a trick of the light.

It must be.

Like hallucinating in the desert and imagining one could see an oasis.

But the kitchen was brightly lit.

She wasn't mistaken. He was cooking the dinner as though he'd never been away.

Chapter 10

All the desperate anxiety she'd suffered these last few months welled up like a great volcano inside her chest and she flew across the kitchen and beat him with her fists. 'How could you do this to me? How could you? Where have you been?'

Duncan turned round to grab her to stop her pounding him. But he couldn't. Her fists were driving at him with such fury, his arms, his chest, his face, his head all came in for a hammering until finally she ran out of strength and stood in front of him, weeping and crushed.

'Joy!'

She croaked a reply between her tears. 'Joy? Joy! You say? How dare you come back after all these months without a word? Have you gone mad?'

'I'm sorry.'

'Sorry? Is that all you can say? I didn't know if you were alive or dead.' Joy plunged down onto a chair with such force it almost overbalanced. Duncan reached out to save her and she cringed at his touch. 'Don't. I can't bear you to touch me.'

'Well, I am sorry. I don't know what else to say except that I was devastated and couldn't cope any more. All I wanted was for you to love me, but it was always Mungo, Mungo, Mungo!' Duncan put a pathetic pleading tone to his voice when he said the word Mungo, which trivialized her feelings and infuriated her. 'If that's how you feel that you can't even bear my touch then—'

'That's right. Give up at the first hurdle. Go on, then, off you go, back to wherever you've been. Don't think for one moment about how I've felt all these months, oh no! Selfish to the last. Always have been and always will be. I saw you on TV coming off the helicopter and *still* you didn't come home. What was I to think?'

Joy dragged a tissue from her pocket and vigorously scrubbed at her face.

'So, how have you felt all these months?'

Joy sniffed unattractively and wiped her nose. 'Do you really want to know?'

'Of course.'

'In a word, devastated.' She wasn't looking at Duncan because she knew she looked her age. More than her age, if the truth be told.

So she didn't see his tentative, hopeful smile. 'I do believe you missed me.'

She glanced up to see if he was mocking her and saw his face soften. 'Just why did you go? What's more *where* did you go? Something's burning.'

'Oh, hell! It's the beans!' Duncan picked the pan up from the stove and tipped the runner beans into a colander. The ones burned and sticking to the bottom he doused in water and left it to soak.

'Oh well! Damn it. Small sacrifice to make. Steak, onions, potato wedges and grilled tomatoes and a very small portion of beans. Will it do?'

Joy nodded bleakly. She knew she wouldn't eat a single mouthful of it.

He took the steaks and onions from the pan and placed

161

them on their plates, drained the chips on kitchen paper, placed the grilled tomatoes decoratively on their plates, shook the remaining beans out of the bowl and pronounced it ready to eat.

Surprisingly she found her appetite, wolfed her food, swilling it down with the wine Duncan had opened. A rich, dark, fruity wine, which warmed her through and through. She felt as though she'd never been so warm since he'd left.

'Fill my glass again, please.'

The glasses were big and she never had more than one, but tonight she could have drunk the whole bottle.

Duncan had called in at the patisserie in the town before he came home and bought two of their cream cakes, the really glorious gooey ones, which Joy found so very hard to resist.

They didn't speak again until they'd finished their meal, each avoiding the other's eyes for fear of what they might see there.

Joy, once she had consumed the food, began to feel better disposed towards him. After all, he was back and that had been what she'd looked forward to almost all the months he was away. In a soft, shaky voice she suggested they clear up the kitchen, but Duncan stood up, took hold of her hand and led her into the sitting room where he'd had the doors of the wood stove open. The logs were burning furiously, and the colossal heat of it was so comforting. He sat in his favourite chair and squeezed up and invited her to sit in beside him. Joy hesitated for a moment. Things were moving all too quickly and nothing had been sorted out between them. With bad grace she accepted his invitation.

With his arms locked around her he said, 'This is what

I've been looking forward to, sitting here, the fire burning fiercely and the heat pouring out on you and me, at peace.'

The heat from the fire lit their faces and gave each a rosy glow. Lost in their own thoughts for several minutes they both began to speak together.

'No, you first.' Duncan said.

'Where have you been all these months? Exactly where?'

Duncan shuffled himself around to achieve greater comfort. 'On the west coast of Ireland, living in an abandoned hovel right on the edge of a beach. With the sea pounding all day and all night. It had a roof but that was about all.'

'But why? Why so . . . *basic*?'

'Escape. From the misery I was in, to escape from the pain, which was making me rot inside. A kind of very welcome hairshirt.'

Joy took hold of his hand and pressed it to her cheek. The idea of him rotting inside for lack of her love crucified Joy. 'I've done you wrong, terrible wrong. I should never have married you knowing what I knew. I can never recompense you for it. I'm sorrier than you'll ever know.'

Duncan kissed her on the side of her head. 'I'd five miles to walk to the nearest village. It was hard going but it cleansed me. Some days I sat in the pub all day, then walked home with my shopping. The baker in the village did some very good meat pies. I tried every variety he baked.'

Joy felt his ribs. 'You've lost weight and no wonder, living like that. In winter too. What did you do all day every day?'

'Walked along the coast. I had the isolation I'd yearned for but it makes socializing impossible. However, eventually, I was so desperate for company I could have held an intellectual conversation with a sheep.'

Joy had to giggle at that. 'I know what you mean. I talked to the cats. It's quite easy once you get the hang of it. Duncan, why such deprivation? I can't understand the need for it.'

'No demands. No obligations. No rules. No time scale. No bills. No structure. Only myself, needing healing.'

Joy forced herself to ask. 'Are you healed? Now, this minute?' Her guilt about her neglect of him and her ghastly lie of marrying him when she still loved Mungo made her desperate to have an answer.

'I do believe I might be.' They fell silent again, deep in their own thoughts until Duncan asked, 'Why has Tiger had her fur shaved?'

'Ah! Well, she got in a fight and had to be stitched up. She was quite ill.'

'In a fight. What with? A donkey?'

Joy smiled up at him. 'We don't really know, but Miss Chillingsworth's Cherub came in with similar injuries. It's a mystery. Tiger was really quite badly mauled.'

'Weren't you worried?'

'Of course. Well, no. I'd given in my notice and left the same day. I'd enough problems of my own. Life was very bitter just then.'

Duncan raised an eyebrow at this. 'Gave your notice in and left the same day?' He dragged the whole story from her. When she said it out loud to Duncan it felt to have been the stupidest thing to have done.

'I stormed out. I must have been crazy. Well, I think perhaps I was. We do such daft things when we're deeply upset, don't we?'

Duncan squeezed her tight. 'We do. I'll put some more

logs on.' He struggled carefully out of the chair, not wanting to disturb Joy any more than he needed, knelt on the floor and took logs from the basket beside the fire. The new logs going on chilled the atmosphere immediately; gone was the red-hot glow and the sparks. Joy shivered. 'I've longed for you to come home. I couldn't believe that having realized how much I cared for you, I'd never have the chance to tell you. Why didn't you let me know where you were, at the very least, that you were alive.'

'I honestly believed you didn't care.'

'Well, I did.'

'I'm glad for that.' There was a pause. 'And Mungo?'

Joy didn't answer.

Again she was faced with the question, 'And Mungo?' more forcefully this time.

'We had that terrible row when I resigned, and I was at such a low ebb with you missing, suddenly he didn't seem to matter any more. *Really not matter.* He's still a colleague and a friend, but that's where it ends. I think I've been chasing shadows all these years. I shall understand if you can't forgive me for it.'

'I came home determined to make the best of whatever crumbs you could offer me.'

'Well, it's not crumbs I have to offer, it's a whole cake and then some.'

The fire was burning briskly now, and the logs were springing to life.

Duncan, still kneeling on the floor, looked up at her. 'Is that so?'

Joy nodded.

'Do you want to know where I've been these last weeks?'

'Of course. I waited hourly for you to ring.'

'I was getting myself de-fleaed for one thing. Scrubbing myself clean, buying clothes, eating copiously and . . . getting a job.'

'Getting a job!' Joy couldn't believe her ears. 'What kind of a job?'

'Working full-time for the company I've done all the freelance business with. I decided working alone was making me strange.' He was sitting on the floor now, leaning his back against the chair that was usually hers, so she could see him full face. He was smiling the dearest smile she'd seen in years.

Today was a day for being truthful. 'It did. You were strange. A complete odd bod.'

Duncan's face registered rueful agreement accompanied by a smile. 'Thanks. So I thought, during all those long hours alone in my little hovel, that working in an office with like minds might be a better option. So that's what I'm going to do, go to work every day, like a real person. I start Monday. So you see, it's a whole new beginning.' He smiled triumphantly at her, and Joy smiled back. Those deep-set eyes of his held more life in them than she'd ever seen since she'd known him. They shone with promise. She slid down off her chair and joined him on the carpet. Joy kissed his mouth tenderly and relished him.

Next morning Scott found Joy in her office, hanging up her coat, singing. He couldn't let this pass unnoticed.

'So, why the singing?' She turned to look at him. 'You look like someone who's been thoroughly,' he hesitated, 'kissed?'

'Cheeky boy!' Joy winked at him and gave him the thumbs-up, a broad grin on her face.

'If I didn't know different I'd think . . .' Scott closed the door behind him and said softly, hardly daring to say it in case he was wrong, 'Is he home, then?'

Joy nodded.

'He is?'

Joy nodded again.

'That's brilliant news. When?'

'He was home when I got in last night.'

'I'm so pleased.' He took a piece of paper from his pocket and using a pen from Joy's desk, made a mark on it.

'What are you doing?'

'It's my list of eligible girls in Barleybridge, and I've just crossed you off.'

'Scott!' Joy came round her desk, flung her arms about him and kissed him. 'I'm so glad you're back. I should never have been angry that you were coming back to help us out.'

The office door opened and Mungo stood there, watching them embracing. 'Is this a private party or can anyone join in?'

Joy threw her arms round him and kissed him too. 'Anyone can join in. Duncan's back!'

Mungo released himself. 'Never! And where has he been, then? On some South Sea island enjoying the sun?'

'No, in Ireland living in an abandoned fisherman's cottage or something, in total poverty. But he's back and he's a changed man and he's got a job and he starts Monday!'

'That's wonderful news. I'll tell Miriam.' Mungo left the office to stand at the bottom of the stairs leading to their flat and shout up, 'Miriam! Duncan's back.'

Miriam's answer floated down the stairs. 'Tell Joy I'm so glad. I'll be down soon.'

Accompanied by Perkins, who, sensing something exciting had happened, proceeded to make a tremendous fuss of Joy as though he hadn't seen her for months, Miriam burst into Joy's office, her arms held wide ready to embrace her.

Having kissed her, Miriam whispered in her ear, 'Well?'

Joy said, 'Everything's fine. Absolutely fine!'

They both sat down and Joy told her the whole story of Duncan's lost months. 'So now he starts Monday for the company he's been freelancing for all these years. Said he thought being at home programming was sending him crazy.'

'Well, it was, wasn't it?'

Joy nodded. 'I agreed with him.'

'And you and him? Things have got sorted I assume?'

'Oh, yes! Definitely.'

Miriam smiled. 'I'm so glad, so very glad. No more heartache, then?'

Joy was about to answer but at that moment they both became aware of sounds of panic in reception.

Joy rushed through to find Mrs Bookbinder clutching a cat basket and crying. Stephie and Annette were attempting to reassure her but were having no effect.

'Mrs Bookbinder, whatever is the matter?'

'It's Jai, she's . . . I think she's . . .' The floods of tears began again and she became incoherent.

'We'll let Rhodri examine her. We'll pop you in first.'

Dabbing her eyes vigorously, not having bothered with mascara this morning Mrs Bookbinder gasped, 'I would prefer Valentine.'

'Day off today, sorry. Rhodri's just as good. Honestly. Here he is. Rhodri, can you see Mrs Bookbinder first, please?'

'Of course. Come in, Mrs Bookbinder, then. Who have

we here?' Rhodri's strong musical Welsh accent appeared to soothe Mrs Bookbinder's fears. She staggered into his consulting room, placed the basket on his examination table and said, 'It's Jai, she's been in a fight. I'm sure she's dead. Will you look? I can't bear to.'

Jai made no move at all, so Rhodri gently lifted her out. She was a perfectly splendid specimen of an Asian leopard cat, but it was all too obvious she was dead. He glanced up at Mrs Bookbinder and found she'd turned away, not daring to watch.

'She's not a house cat then?'

'Oh, no. That's cruel. I prefer her to have her freedom. She's never been in a fight before, though. Never. But that's what it is, isn't it? She's been fighting?'

Joy crept in, carefully closing the door behind her. Rhodri looked at her and she recognized the signal he gave her; she didn't need him to say it out loud.

To Mrs Bookbinder Rhodri said sorrowfully, 'I'm sorry, but you're right, she is dead.'

She broke down again when she heard Rhodri's confirmation of her worst fears.

'Yes, yes, I'm afraid so. What killed her, it's hard to say. Do you want to hear the details?'

Mrs Bookbinder nodded.

'It's clawed her badly down both of her sides, bitten her throat, and she's lost a lot of blood by the looks of it from this bite on her stomach. She's the third cat we've seen in the last few weeks with similar injuries.'

'Were the others . . . dead?'

'No, but very close. I'm so sorry.'

'Well, then, we've to find out what's doing it, haven't we? It isn't one of these big wild cats people keep saying they've seen? Puma or jaguar or something?'

Rhodri shook his head. 'No. If it had been, well, let me see, how can I put it, er . . . they wouldn't have been brought in, if you get my meaning.'

Mrs Bookbinder shuddered. 'Ugh! I see. Well, it comes to something when one can't even let one's pedigree cat out for fear it won't come back. She cost five hundred pounds two years ago.'

'She was very beautiful. She must have given you a lot of pleasure.'

'She did. You're right. It's just me getting all upset.'

Joy asked if she would prefer to take Jai home for burial.

'Yes, thank you. Yes. She can join the others at the bottom of the garden. I'll have a headstone made for her. But I do think something should be done about these attacks.'

'So do I. I'll get in touch with the police and the RSPCA. See if they've any experience of this. I'm sorry. So sorry.'

Rhodri patted her arm and Mrs Bookbinder gave him a weak smile. 'I've no doubt I shall have another cat in a few weeks. But not a rare breed this time. I do like cats, you see.' As she was turning to go, Mrs Bookbinder said to Joy, 'I must apologize for making an exhibition of myself. I don't usually, I'm not that kind of person, so sorry.'

'Not at all, it's perfectly understandable in the circumstances.'

Mrs Bookbinder smiled. 'You're all such lovely people here, so much nicer than that grumpy lot in the High Street.'

Rhodri placed the deceased Jai in the basket, and handed it to her.

'Thank you. Thank you for being so compassionate.'

After she left the consulting room, Rhodri carefully

closed the door and said, 'Joy, I have a nasty feeling I know exactly what it was that killed poor Jai.'

'Who or what exactly?'

'I could be completely wrong, but . . . you know my Megan has feral cats she feeds, well, for months she's been feeding a new cat, a massive male, and I mean massive, never seen one as big. He was affectionate and even allowed her to stroke him. Then he didn't turn up for a few weeks but last Monday he returned and she spotted him attacking one of her other feral cats while they were waiting for her to feed them, and before she could get him he'd dispatched it in a very efficient manner. She said he was completely ruthless, and had obviously done it before, she thought. Megan was terribly upset, and so was I. But they're always spitting at each other and having fisticuffs so in a way it was no surprise. Never occurred to us he might have been the one that attacked Cherub and now Jai.'

'And our poor Tiger.'

'Yes, of course. It does make you think.' Rhodri leaned against the examination table, reflecting.

'Well, you've no alternative have you? None at all.'

'None. Trouble is my Megan is so . . . well . . . it's her hormones, you see, she hasn't settled down properly since the baby. The slightest little thing upsets her. It's like walking on hot coals with her. It's not her fault, you understand. However, I'll have to tell her and get it over with. Damn and blast it.' He went to his computer to enter in Jai Bookbinder's case.

'How will you catch it?'

Pointing at the screen, Rhodri said, 'Look, you see, Mrs Bookbinder lives the same side of Barleybridge as your Tiger and Beulah Bank Farm. North side. It could be him.'

Joy reminded him his next client was waiting.

'Sorry, then. How we'll catch him I've no idea. He's like greased lightning and very twitchy about humans. I wonder if Scott would lend a hand this weekend?'

Scott agreed he would and from what he said next he appeared to be enjoying the idea of a hunt. 'Shall I bring my gun? I'm a crack shot.'

'No, thanks all the same. Old Man Jones won't have guns on the farm at all. None whatsoever.'

'In the right hands—'

'I know, but he won't. Has a brother he never talks about and I wonder sometimes if he got shot or something accidentally, he's so adamant about it. Anyway we'll give you lunch on Sunday if you'll help me, and we'll lie in wait for them when they come to be fed about three.'

'Thanks. I will. Be glad to have a good nosh. Will it be all right with Megan, me coming to kill one of her cats?'

'It will be when I've talked to her about it.'

'It's a date. Always fancied your Megan, lovely girl. Real woman through and through.'

Rhodri looked a bit askance at his observation. 'Is that supposed to be a compliment?'

'Of course, what else?' Scott winked at him.

Rhodri had to smile. 'See you then, we eat at one. The old man will be there, but don't let him bother you.'

But Scott did have his gun with him when he went on the Sunday, locked in its case, hidden under his veterinary belongings in the back of the Land Rover. As back-up, he thought.

When he saw Megan and the quiet contentment Rhodri and the baby had brought to her he couldn't help but find her attractive. Off limits but still very attractive.

'Megan!' He kissed her in the fashionable social way, one kiss to each cheek.

'Scott! How lovely to see you. When Rhodri said you were back, the blood pressure of every farmer's wife in the district shot up at least ten points.'

'Get away! You're flattering me. Where's the ultra clever baby called Owen? And your father?'

'Da will be in shortly and Owen is sleeping, hopefully until after we've had lunch.'

'I'm looking forward to seeing him, the baby, I mean. Is he like that ugly devil of a husband of yours or does he look like you? I hope for his sake he looks like you.'

Megan pretended to pout. 'My Rhodri is distinguished looking.'

Scott grinned. 'Is that what you call it?'

'You'll have heard the news about Rose? A baby girl? They're calling her Serena. Rose was almost three weeks late and refusing to be induced, but eventually they insisted on an immediate Caesarean or wouldn't be responsible for the outcome.'

'Yes, fantastic.'

'Isn't she lucky? Dan says she's beautiful. But then, what else can one expect with Rose for a mother?'

'Exactly, if Rose doesn't have beautiful children, I don't know who will. Present company excepted, of course.'

'Flatterer! I understand her stepfather, Lloyd, was distraught about her and has said no more babies because he can't face it again!'

'We'll drink a toast when we have lunch, shall we?'

'Yes, of course. Here comes Da.'

Old Man Jones came in, shaky but defiant. 'Hello, Scott. Nice to see you again. Couldn't keep away from the old country, eh? Care for a whisky with me?'

'Good afternoon, Mr Jones. I'd prefer a dry sherry, if you wouldn't mind.'

'Oh! Didn't think you Australians would be so civilized.'

Scott raised an eyebrow at that and couldn't stop himself from saying, 'We wear ties too, sometimes.'

Mr Jones struggled to pour the sherry. Scott almost offered to help but decided not to. The chap needed to be treated like a man, he could sense that. 'Thanks. Your good health, Mr Jones, everyone. Where's Rhod?'

'Coming.' Megan went to open the oven door and check the lunch.

'Scott, come with me while Megan potters with lunch.' When he'd got himself safely seated in his chair and had waved a vague hand at the sofa to tell Scott to sit down, Old Man Jones said, 'Now about this cat, that Megan calls Samson. I want rid of it. Megan hasn't said anything today, but he killed one of her own cats yesterday right in front of her. So it's now two he's killed. My poor girl was very upset and it mustn't happen again for her sake. She's still delicate after the baby; she missed post-natal depression by a whisker, you know. The cat that died was her favourite, she was lovely and a great ratter, but not big enough nor strong enough to stand up to that great brute. I say great brute but one has to admire him. He's majestic, though something has obviously gone very wrong with him. You'll have a surprise when you see him. Not fond of cats, I'm not, but he is a magnificent beast. However, he has to go. How do you propose to go about it?'

'Has Rhodri no ideas?'

'He's brought something he uses for putting cats down, but how the blazes he'll get close enough to stick the needle in I've no idea.'

'Ah! Right. Perhaps that's where I come in.'

After lunch Megan went off to feed the baby and Rhodri decided now was their moment.

As soon as she'd shut the door behind her, Rhodri said, 'We'll have to get the blasted thing in the stable with a bowl of food, and keep the others out till we've got the door shut. You be waiting in the shadows, completely still, and as we slam the door, throw this over him and hold on tight, on the floor. Shout when you've got him and I'll come in with the syringe and Bob's your uncle.'

'Well, I don't know who my uncle Bob is but it seems to me I've got the major job, catching the damn thing. What if I don't and it starts on me? I could be in shreds.'

Rhodri leaned back in his chair and roared with laughter. When he finally got himself under control he said, 'Well, you'll have to be quick. I'm the small animal vet so I'm the best one to do the injection, am I not? He's usually the first to arrive so it should be easy to keep the others out of the way. They're very wary of him, as you can imagine.'

'I don't like the sound of this.'

Rhodri found Scott's attitude amusing. 'Nothing to it, man, nothing at all.'

'If there's nothing at all, why don't you catch him?'

'Ah! Well, I'm not as sharp on my feet as you are. You've had more experience dodging irate fathers and husbands than I have.'

'Hey! Steady on. It's half past two already. He could be here any minute.'

Scott went to look out of the kitchen window and saw the cat in question sauntering along and then placing himself outside one of the stables. He was a huge, all-black cat with an extra long, very furry tail, which he kept twitching, and long, snow-white whiskers. He turned his head and looked towards the kitchen window as though checking if the food might be coming any moment.

'He's just come,' he said. 'Walking kind of sideways. Has he always done that? He has the most frightening eyes I have ever seen in a cat. Are you sure his father wasn't a puma? He's massive.'

Mr Jones laughed out loud. 'Strong pair of gardening gloves required, I think, Rhodri, eh?'

'Tell you what, Rhod, I'd like to do a post-mortem on him. I'm serious. Don't you think it would be interesting?'

'It would, you're right. I'll get a bowl of food for it before the others arrive.'

He came back with a large pair of heavy gloves and handed them to Scott, who put them on. 'All right, I'll do it, if you'll let me take him back to the Practice and PM him. Deal?'

Rhodri nodded. 'Come on then, before Megan finishes feeding Owen and sees us.'

'Mind you don't stick that lethal weapon in me in the struggle.'

Rhodri raised his eyebrows and smiled. 'As if I would.'

Scott marched towards the stable with the gardening gloves on and a large old bath sheet folded and stitched to double thickness that Megan used for drying her dogs. Rhodri followed him with the bowl of food and a fully primed syringe. The cat watched warily. While Rhodri distracted him by pretending to be putting down the bowl of food outside, Scott opened the stable door and slid quietly in.

The stable was lit by a single small window, which was covered with dust so the light inside was really quite dim. Scott stood by an old manger with his face half turned to the wall. He decided to dump the gardening gloves in the manger because they were too awkward and bulky for the job and made his fingers as useless as a bunch of carrots.

Rhodri came in with the bowl of food, put it down, then left, leaving the stable door wide open as he'd seen Megan do, so as not to alert Samson. Scott daren't breathe because the light coming in through the open stable door was making him very obvious. He turned ever so slightly so that out of the corner of his eye he could just see Samson making up his mind to come in. Twice he almost entered the doorway, twice he backed off, and then slowly but surely the smell of the food tempted him in and he headed straight for it.

Suddenly the stable door slammed shut and Scott flung himself, towel in hand, full length on to Samson. All hell was let loose. The squalling of the cat mixed with Scott's serious swearing and shouting as he was clawed, and the desperate struggle to hold him down and not let him escape was terrible to hear. Outside Rhodri was shouting, 'Ready? Are you ready?' Inside Scott was still struggling. The cat had no intention of being imprisoned by anyone and was putting up a good fight. Scott tenaciously held his grip and shouted, 'For God's sake, man, hurry up.'

Rhodri shot into the stable, leaving the door open. Scott screeched, 'Shut it! Shut it! You fool!'

The stable went dark again with Scott still holding on for dear life. Poor Samson was fighting his last desperate battle. He wasn't going to give in easily and for that Scott admired him. Rhodri clamped a hand on Samson's neck, flicked the towel back and managed to press the needle into his scruff. In the time it took to empty the syringe Samson bit Scott's hand.

The struggling slowed almost immediately and in a moment Samson was completely still.

Scott keeled over backwards on to the floor, sweat pouring off him. 'My God! That was a near thing.' He scrambled to his feet just as Rhodri turned on the light and the two of them looked down at Samson. Scott bent to move the towel away but it was caught on Samson's big claws, so he had to extricate him from the towel. Samson lay harmless in death, a pathetic shadow of himself, his threatening eyes closed for ever. 'You can't help but feel sorry, can you? Such a spirited creature. Like Old Man Jones said, "a magnificent beast".'

'Thanks for that, Scott, bach. Needed to be done. If you still want to do a PM let's pop him in your car before Megan sees him. She's seen enough of dead cats lately.'

Scott picked up Samson and went to open up the Land Rover to place him carefully underneath his calving suit. It was only then he looked at his hands. They were almost as he had suggested he might be – shredded. There were long tears on the back of his hands where Samson's claws had dug in, blood was running, and in the soft flesh down the side of his hand where he'd been bitten, blood dripped. 'Look at this! Stone the crows! You owe me.'

Rhodri had to smile. 'And there was I thinking what a tough Aussie you were. Come inside, Megan has an excellent first aid box. She'll see to them.'

When they got in they found Mr Jones in the sitting room nursing a well satisfied Owen Hughes with Megan sitting close admiring him. She sprang to her feet when she saw Scott's hands. 'Scott! What a mess. Come in the kitchen and I'll sort them out.'

'I'm dripping, I'm afraid. Bit of soap and water will do. Good scrub, you know.'

'Come!' Megan held open the sitting-room door and pointed sternly to the kitchen.

Scott said, 'I love masterful women!' winked at Mr Jones and meekly followed her.

Megan brought out a large important looking green box with 'First Aid' printed on the top. By way of an apology for her apparently over-the-top equipment she said, 'Health and Safety. Sorry. I'm not about to operate, don't worry.'

Her red hair and his blond mingled as they studied the severity of his wounds. 'This here on the side of your hand is very deep, where he bit you. Are they painful?'

'No, well not much.'

As she disinfected his hands, which made Scott wince, Megan asked if they'd finished Samson off.

'Well, yes. He wasn't ready to go, but he had to. Superb creature.'

'I know. I'm truly sorry about him. For a feral cat he was so friendly. You should have heard him purring; I needed ear plugs.' She smiled sadly at Scott and then said with a tremor in her voice, 'But he'd become a maverick and no mistake. My poor Buttons . . .'

Scott patted her arm with the hand she'd already attended to. 'It's hard to witness that. I'm sorry you did. Still, that's it now. I'm doing a PM on him, in the interests of science.'

Megan dried his hands and decided to put antiseptic cream on both of them. 'You can't be too careful with cat scratches.'

'Don't put dressings on. I want them to dry out. Thanks.'

'Thank you, Scott, for today. I do appreciate you coming. It was a two-man job.'

He smiled. 'Not at all, and thanks for the lunch.'

They returned to the sitting room and Scott went

across to look at the baby. 'He's a grand little chap, isn't he?'

Mr Jones nodded. 'He is. Such a good little boy.' He offered for Scott to take the baby and much to everyone's surprise he welcomed the idea. Scott walked across to the window and spent a few minutes talking to Owen about what he could see in the farmyard.

Megan became quite emotional and tears came into her eyes. She looked across at Rhodri and they raised their eyebrows to each other and smiled. When Owen got that glazed look in his eyes, which, in a baby, signifies a readiness to sleep, Scott handed him to Megan. 'He's tired.'

'How do you know that?'

'My sister has twins. Must be going. Thanks again for the lunch and for this.' He held up his hands now streaked with dried blood. 'I won't shake hands, if you don't mind, Mr Jones, hands a bit tender. Bye!'

Megan and Rhodri came to the door with him, to wave him off and Scott left, eager to start the post-mortem on Samson. When he got to the Practice, although there were no clients with it being Sunday, he found both Joy and Duncan there and also Zoe.

'What's this? Can't keep away? Nice to see you, Duncan. Won't shake hands, glad you're back though. Very glad. You've been greatly missed.'

It was Joy who answered him. 'We could say the same to you. Just look at your hands! Who did that?'

Scott explained.

'Well, we're here to do the rotas for next month, and Zoe's looking up some research on the computer as hers has crashed.'

'I'm here to PM the cat Rhodri and I have just put

down. We're fairly certain it's the one that's been knocking off half the cats in the area, including your Tiger. Just thought I'd spend my Sunday afternoon taking a look.'

Duncan claimed he could find more sizzling occupations for a Sunday afternoon than opening up a cat.

Sceptically Scott looked at them both and replied, 'Doing rotas, for instance?'

Duncan laughed. 'Mmm. Well. All depends, I suppose, who you're doing it *with*. If you don't mind I'll stay well out of the way.'

'That's fine.' Scott, surprised by Duncan's unfamiliar jocular conversation, went to look for Zoe, who was tapping away on the computer in the staffroom. 'Fancy helping me with a PM on a feral cat?'

Zoe didn't even look up. 'No.'

'OK.'

Scott got himself organized and went out to bring in Samson. He laid him on the table in an ops room, found some plastic gloves and began.

He became totally absorbed and didn't realize he was talking to himself. When he came across a large tumour invading Samson's brain he said loudly, 'Eureka!'

Zoe, unable to resist the excitement in his voice, went to see what he had found.

'Just look at this, Zoe. No wonder the poor chap had gone crackers. The pain and confusion in his head with this thing growing in it. Look, it's wrapped right round this side. I'm so glad we got him today, otherwise he'd have died a slow, agonizing death holed up somewhere, quietly starving to death. It doesn't bear thinking about.'

'He'd get as he couldn't coordinate his thoughts, wouldn't he?'

'Exactly. He'd be hungry but wouldn't know what to

do about it. Perhaps that's why he latched on to getting fed with Megan's cats, because he couldn't hunt any more. The poor old chap. I'm glad I've done this because Megan knew he had to go but couldn't face up to it. I can ring her now and tell her we did him a good turn.'

'I wonder he could coordinate enough to walk straight. Look! It's reached here . . . and here. Did you see him walking?'

'Yes, he was weaving about a bit as he walked, which you would expect with pressure like this.'

The two of them studied Samson's brain for a while longer, following the path of the tumour as it had developed inside poor Samson's skull, long enough anyway for Joy and Duncan to finish the rotas.

'You'll lock up?' called Joy over her shoulder before leaving.

As they drove out into the country, hoping to get the Sunday lunch they'd not yet managed to eat, Joy said to Duncan, 'Those two seem cosy, don't they?'

Duncan glanced at her and smiled. 'You're not matchmaking?'

'No, just hoping. They both need someone.'

'Anyone who catches Scott will need to run fast.'

'You're right there. But Zoe needs someone, bringing up a child on her own.'

'I see you're full of your new-found contentment and want everyone to feel the same as you.'

Joy patted his leg. 'I don't know about contentment. My highly charged emotional state might be more appropriate.'

'Happy?'

'Yes, of course I am. All these years that I've wasted, I

can't believe it of myself. Duncan! We're not going to find anywhere pleasing, are we, this time in the afternoon. Let's turn round and go home, have a quick sandwich and I'll cook us Sunday lunch tonight. How about it? Mmm?'

Chapter 11

Once Duncan and Joy were out of earshot, Scott commented, 'They seem very happy, don't they?' He realized his hands felt very uncomfortable and looking down saw that his blood had made the plastic gloves stick to his hands.

Zoe said, 'They do, you're right, and not before time. That looks nasty. One quick pull and it'll all be over.'

Scott winced and said, 'I know.' He took a deep breath and ripped off the gloves. The scratches began bleeding even more, so Zoe went to get the Practice first aid box.

Scott protested vigorously. 'I don't need anything doing to them. They'll be all right.'

'They won't. You know and I know you need to take care.'

Scott began clearing up the remains of Samson and received a broadside from Zoe as she returned carrying the box. 'Are you mad? Touching all that when you've got open wounds. For heaven's sakes, Scott, I thought you would have had more sense.'

'I love you when you're mad.'

'Don't be mushy.'

'I do. There's a fire in your eyes, which is normally kept under very tight wraps, in fact, you're under tight wraps all the time. Zoe? What is it you're hiding from me?'

Absorbed in cleansing the scratches and putting dressings on Scott's hands, Zoe took a moment to answer. 'I don't know what you mean. Hold still while I get sticking plaster on. There, now let's do the other one.'

He took in a deep breath as he winced at the treatment he was receiving and breathed in her perfume. There was a pleasing, clean, clear smell about it overlaid by a deeply sensuous perfume, with oriental undertones. She caught his eye and he saw she was very conscious of his scrutiny. He was delighted when a blush came to her cheeks. Her head was close to his face, he only needed to bend slightly and he'd be able to kiss her hair. He remembered Megan's smell of motherhood and fresh flowery perfume, but that hadn't had quite the same effect on him as Zoe's smell was having.

She finished the dressing on his other hand and when she looked at him, their faces were only six inches apart. He couldn't help himself – he'd have to kiss her. She looked as though she wanted him to. His bandaged hands went round her so she couldn't escape, his blue eyes looked long and hard into hers and then they were kissing frantically. They drew apart when Zoe began to laugh.

'What's funny?' Scott asked.

'Us. Where's the soft lights, where's the violins? All we've got is a powerful light, a dismembered cat, a strong smell of disinfectant and a few scalpels. Honestly, we'll never get it right.'

'We can soon make it more romantic if that's what you want. Go somewhere special, I know a nice place—'

Zoe backed off. 'Oh, no! You're not going to catch me a second time.'

'What does that mean?'

Zoe shook her head. 'I didn't mean anything. Well, I

did. I meant not like when you were here the last time. As far as I'm concerned, you're off limits for evermore.'

'But that was fun, we both knew that. Why can't two adults have fun together without hurt?'

Zoe took a deep breath, 'Must get back to the computer . . . it's printing out and can get a bit temperamental. That weekend is off. I'm not going. Sorry.'

Scott cleared up after Samson, kicking himself for having misinterpreted her feelings towards him. He only meant it as fun, so why hadn't she seen it that way. But *did* he only mean it as fun? He honestly didn't know what he'd meant, except she'd excited him like no woman had for a long time. He bagged Samson up ready for the incinerator, and using the phone in Joy's office, rang Megan.

'Hello, Megan. It's Scott. I've done the post-mortem on Samson and to put your mind at rest, I thought I should tell you I found a huge tumour on his brain. That was the reason he'd gone peculiar and begun attacking cats. We've done him a good turn, really, before things got too bad for him. So, he's out of his misery now.'

'Thank you, Scott. Thank you for letting me know. I feel a bit better about him now.'

Scott felt as well as heard the break in her voice. 'Good girl. Must go. Tell Rhodri, won't you?'

Scott went to check if Zoe was ready to leave. Just as he entered the staff room door, Zoe's mobile rang. She went flapping round trying to find her bag, when she did the phone wasn't in it and she eventually found it with Scott's help, right beside the computer under the papers she'd printed out.

'Hi! Zoe here.'

He watched her listening to her caller, full concentration, nodding as she listened. 'Right! Right! I'm

coming. Take me fifteen, twenty minutes, Mrs Goodwood. See you!'

She stood up, picked up the papers she needed,
switched off the computer, gathered her coat and gloves,
and remembered Scott was standing watching her.

'Oh! I'm off to Quarry Mount. Pigs dying, *again*.'

'I'm coming. I'll drive?'

Zoe pondered the idea and decided yes, he couldn't get
up to much looking at pigs, now could he? And it would
be nice to have some company, to say nothing of a second
opinion. 'OK.'

'I'll lock up.'

As they took the right turn off the Magnum Percy Hill
to get to Quarry Mount Farm, Zoe said, 'I do dislike
Magnum Percy. There's something about that village
which alarms me. It's a bit sinister and the people are
strange and not half.'

Scott glanced at her. 'Never thought of you as a nervy
type.'

'I'm not. It's just that it feels threatening, gloomy sort of.
Architecturally the houses are completely different from
the other houses round here, haven't you noticed?'

'Never gone there. Don't need to.'

He pulled up and waited for Zoe to open the farm gate
for him, then slid through, giving her just enough room to
shut it before she climbed back in. 'When we leave we'll
go take a look at Magnum Percy. I'm curious.'

Together they went to knock on Mrs Goodwood's
house door. Cecil answered it. 'She's up the field waiting
for you. There's two died already.'

'Thanks, Cecil,' said Zoe. Then she turned briskly
away, anxious to get on with the job. 'Damn and blast. If
you can sort it, Scott, I shall be dead pleased. The whole

episode is making me look a complete incompetent. It appears to be pneumonia although when I've taken lung samples, it isn't. But their breathing is bad.'

'Have you thought about poisoning?'

'No. Who the blazes would take pleasure in poisoning pigs?'

'Someone who lives close by and hates the smell of 'em.'

'You've got a point, but I don't really think anyone would. I mean why?'

They climbed the gate into the field where the pigs roamed and spotted Mrs Goodwood waving to them. She was leaning on one of the corrugated-iron pig shelters, at the bottom of the field close to the boundary fence.

'Sorry,' she shouted, 'don't like calling you out on a Sunday but you said don't wait till they've died.'

Zoe called back. 'No problem. I'm on duty anyway.'

They were breeding sows that had died. She'd left them where they'd fallen for Zoe to see. Trundling about obviously in some confusion and pain were five pigs in varying degrees of being half alive and almost dead. They staggered about looking ill and disinterested, their breathing laboured, and there were some already laid down and apparently giving up on life. Scott spoke up. 'Have you any enemies, Mrs Goodwood?' She treated his question as though it was a joke, but beneath the carefree manner of her reply Scott felt he might have hit the nail on the head. 'I'm serious. Just one look at their behaviour and I've a suspicion they've been poisoned. Could be entirely wrong but I'm making the suggestion because Zoe has investigated all the other avenues and drawn a blank.'

Zoe said, 'I'd thought of that possibility, but it seemed ridiculous. What do you think, Mrs Goodwood?'

None of them realized that Cecil had arrived and,

contrary to a lifetime of leaving Mrs Goodwood to deal with the livestock, which left him free to idle at will and attend every race meeting within reasonable driving distance, he'd come to see what they had to say. Before she could answer, he'd said vehemently, 'Only them damn beggars at Crossways.'

'Cecil! Just shut up. You don't know what you're talking about.'

'I won't shut up. If I've said it once I've said it a thousand times, it's them to blame. But would you listen? Oh no! If I was another foot taller I'd be round there telling 'em what we think.'

Scott was grateful Cecil was only five feet high. 'I didn't say they *had* been poisoned, I said it was a *possibility*.'

Zoe asked, 'But why would they want to, Cecil?'

'They's namby-pamby townees come to live the country life so long as it's all clinical and sweet-smelling. Well, farming i'n't like that, is it, as you well know. You 'ave animals and there's smells, which they thinks is disgusting. I've lived with the smell of pigs all my life and what harm has it done me?'

Zoe felt like suggesting 'Stunted your growth' or 'Made you completely drone like', but didn't. A nice chap like him wasn't someone she wished to insult. 'Have they been round here complaining?'

Mrs Goodwood laughed. 'No, they invite us round to their place and then they give us it straight from the shoulder. Twice now we've been invited round, but we shan't accept the next time, not to be berated like they do. Thing is, they knew we were here when they bought the place, so they've not a leg to stand on.' She folded her arms as though to say that settled the matter.

'Paid half a million pounds for the place. Bit sickening

for 'em, isn't it?' Cecil laughed like a drain and set off back to the house, scratching the odd pig behind the ear as he went.

While they'd been talking, Scott had been walking about, looking in general at the pigs that were staggering about and the ones that were apparently as yet unaffected.

'Look, Francesca, I'll be in touch tomorrow when I've had time to think around the matter. Thing is, I can't think of anything it might be other than deliberate poisoning. We'll get one of these that's died to the veterinary service, get them to do a post-mortem, eh?' He smiled at her and Zoe watched the effect; Mrs Goodwood melted. She'd have agreed to almost anything he said.

'All well and good, but them pigs is our breeding stock, they're all in pig and that's money to us. Big money. Not that there's that much money in pigs nowadays, leastways not till they get wrapped in cling film and polystyrene in the supermarkets, then they don't know what to charge.'

Seeing as Mrs Goodwood was her own client Zoe said, 'You've got a point there. *I'll* be in touch tomorrow when the two of us have had time to discuss what they find. But I have an idea he's right.' Zoe was tempted to add, 'He usually is', but didn't as it would inflate his ego more than ever. 'We'll put down these staggering about before we leave, OK? Can't leave them suffering like this.'

When they departed, Scott could have taken the left-hand turn down into Long Lane, but he kept going and turned for Magnum Percy. Uncomfortable at the prospect of what he intended to do, Zoe said, 'Must we?'

'Just out of curiosity, that's all. I'm not going to get out.' When they reached the junction at the top of Magnum Percy Hill he turned right and they were in the claustro-phobic High Street immediately. The houses were tall, some three storeys high and terraced, flat-faced and identical, crowding the pavement without front gardens to lighten their threat. Zoe cringed. The houses seemed to loom over her, guarding their terrible secrets.

'Hey! They're only houses, you know.'

She shivered. 'They're ominous. Something nasty has happened here at some time, like black magic or murder or some dreadful tragedy to do with children. I can feel it in the air, the houses are keeping the secret for fear we find out. Let's go . . .' Her voice trailed off.

'Zoe! For heaven's sakes, we'll turn round and leave if it's as bad as that.' He spun the steering wheel and backed into a car parking space in front of a shop, paused for a moment to look at her face and saw her horror plainly obvious. 'Zoe! There's nothing terrible here, honestly, believe me.'

She shouted, 'Get out of here. Now!'

Patiently Scott responded to her fear. 'Fine, fine, that's just what I'm doing.'

Some of her panic infected him and he drove as fast as he dare down the narrow street. When finally they were clear of Magnum Percy he slowed down and pulled into the side of the road.

'No, don't do that, please. Just go, take me back to the Practice. Right now.'

'Very well, I will, but it's all nonsense.'

Zoe's excess of panic had been caused by having spotted her mother coming out of a house only three or four doors away from the shop where Scott had reversed the Land Rover. She only began calming down when she knew there was no possibility her mother's car would be close behind them, as she'd have to turn off down Gorge Way to get home and not drive into Barleybridge town. She had been carrying Oscar, as though he'd fallen asleep while she was visiting whoever it was. What on earth had she been doing taking Oscar to Magnum Percy? Thank heavens Scott had offered to drive them in his Land Rover, or she'd never have got away with it; her mother would have recognized her own car immediately.

By the time they got to the Practice car park she was back in charge of herself.

Scott squeezed the handbrake on, turned to look at her and said, 'Better, now?'

'Yes, thank you. Sorry for being such an idiot. Don't you find it even a little bit sinister?'

'No, I don't. Sorry.' He patted her knee.

'I've never liked it.'

'About the weekend I've won. I've booked two single rooms. Will you come?'

Zoe stared out of the windscreen not answering him.

'Well?'

'Don't expect a passionate weekend, because it won't be.'

'Of course not. We're friends, that's all.'

'And . . . that's how it's going to stay.'

'Just exactly what is it you're afraid of? I'm not going to slit your throat at the first opportunity, am I?'

Zoe gave a little smile. 'No.'

'So what is it?'

'Nothing for you to bother your head with.'

'Is there someone else I don't know about? Are you harbouring a secret passion for Gab Bridges? Is that it?'

She turned to look at him and snapped, 'No, I am not, for heaven's sake.' In a completely different voice she added, 'I'll come on the weekend and we'll see how we go. Right? More than that I cannot promise.'

'Well, that's something anyway.' He leaned towards her and just before he kissed her he said, 'We won't rush things, eh?'

'I don't know that there is anything to rush.' Zoe got out, gave him a nod, picked up her bag and the papers she'd printed out earlier from the well of the front passenger seat and walked towards her own car. Scott watched her go and found himself thinking about her and her reaction to his trip to Magnum Percy. He was sure she'd seen something when he'd reversed that she didn't want him to know about. But all he'd seen was an older woman coming out of a house carrying a sleeping toddler. What could be frightening about that?

By the time Zoe got home, her mother and Oscar were back. He ran to greet her, flinging his arms about her shouting, 'Mummy! Mummy!'

Joan called from the kitchen, 'I'm just putting the kettle on for a cup of tea. Want one?'

'Yes, please.' Zoe went to stand in the kitchen doorway, Oscar hoisted onto her hip. 'Sorry I've been a long time, got a call out just as I was ready to leave.'

'We've only just got in. I was glad to go out. The Whitworths had been arguing all morning. I'm absolutely sick of the pair of them. I've no sympathy for her, she must be mad to stay with such a brute. I'd have dumped him quick years ago.'

She went to get the cups out of the cupboard. 'We've been out to lunch with a woman in Magnum Percy. I met her in Barleybridge in the coffee shop at the church and we got talking and she said how much she'd like to meet Oscar, because she'd always longed for grandchildren and it looked as though she wasn't going to get any, so she rang me this morning and invited us for lunch. She's one of those people I hit it off with straight away. So we've been enjoying ourselves in very pleasant company, but Oscar fell asleep because we took him up the hill behind the village and he ran himself to a standstill. She's a thoroughly nice person. Biscuits?'

'Yes, please.' So that was why they were there. Narrow escape. She didn't want the added complication of Scott seeing Oscar, because the moment he did he'd recognize that Oscar was the spitting image of himself . . .

Or for that matter her mother seeing Scott. She might be what her mother classed as an 'older woman', but she was quick-witted even so. She'd know and then the inquisition would begin. She sent up a prayer asking Dan to get on his feet quickly, the quicker the better, then Scott would go and things could get back to normal. If they could ever be normal again.

Oscar tickled her face with a feather he'd found while he was up the hill in Magnum Percy. She had to laugh. 'Oscar, where has that feather been? Not on my face. I shall tickle *you* if you do.' She pulled it off him and tickled the bare skin revealed by the gap between his socks and the bottom of his trousers. He shrieked with laughter. 'Mummy! 'gain 'gain!' Zoe put him down and chased him round the room, pretending to be a big bird coming to catch him.

'Who's put the smile on your face?' Her mother put down the tray of tea things. 'Well?'

'No one. Just glad he's had some fun.'

'Wish you got some fun. How about this Scott who's come back? I've never met him but he sounds nice. Mind you, it might not be a good idea, he'd want to take you back to Australia and that won't do.'

'Why not?'

'Think how I'd feel? You're selfish, you really are, you've no thought for anyone but yourself. I'd never see you for years and I can't manage to fly out to Australia.'

'You could always live there.' That was a damn stupid thing to have said. 'Anyway, you're safe, the matter won't arise. He has dozens of women who'd give their eye teeth to go out with him, believe me. By the way, would you mind me having next weekend away?'

There was a small silence while her mother poured the tea out. 'Here you are.'

'Thanks. Well?'

'No, dear, that's fine. Where are you going?'

'The Cotswolds, with some fellow vets I knew at College. We're all meeting up at a hotel, all been decided in a rush. Said I'd go if you didn't mind. Reunion, kind of.' Zoe thought, 'reunion' was a misnomer if ever there was one. Why did she have to tell lies? It wasn't in her make-up to lie, not until Oscar.

'That's fine. You deserve some time off. Oscar and I can entertain ourselves, can't we, darling?' She held out Oscar's beaker and helped him to drink from it. 'Biscuit?'

It was all far too easy. Once before she'd asked her mother to do this for her while she went to a conference, and there'd been a holy war over it and she'd finished up not being able to go. What had her mother got up her sleeve? Some scheme or other. Zoe thought about her mother's drinking and seriously wondered if she was wise planning to go away with Scott. She'd be on tenterhooks all the time. Though, just lately, she'd not been nearly as bad for it as she once was.

Oscar smiled at her in triumph, as his granny gave him a forbidden second biscuit. When she returned his smile she had to acknowledge for the umpteenth time there appeared to be no part of him that was hers. He was all Scott Spencer, every smiling, blond, fair-skinned inch of him; his thick golden hair, the brilliant blue of his eyes, the smile, his height, at the top of the scale for his age, the way he saw fun in everything, good and bad. What a heritage Scott had given him; and she loved him for it. Oscar that was, not Scott.

Mentally Zoe shook herself. Dwelling on Scott simply would not do, it would only cloud her judgement.

'There's a curious smell in here, whatever is it?'

Zoe answered. 'Oh! It could be me, I've been to a pig farm.'

'Well, go get a shower if you don't mind. Bringing your disgusting farmyard smells here, it's a disgrace. It'll be permeating all the furniture and the curtains and I've only just had them cleaned.'

'Me! Me!' Oscar shouted.

'All right then, it's instead of a bath when you go to bed. Right.'

'Right!'

'Thanks Mum for having him for the weekend. Much appreciated.'

As Zoe picked up Oscar she noticed the smile on her mother's face when she thought Zoe wasn't looking and Zoe knew for certain she had something planned for the weekend, which she didn't want her to know about. Well, that made two of them.

They got away from the Practice about half past four on Friday. Zoe had spent the week fretting about leaving Oscar with her mother, but finally decided she was being ridiculous. Either she trusted her to look after him properly or she had to make up her mind to find someone else, and that she could not face. He had a birthday party to go to on Saturday, and she'd left his clothes and the present neatly wrapped so it would be a question of dressing him and getting him there on time. She couldn't do any more.

Scott broke into her thoughts. 'Stop worrying! We're going as two old friends to a lovely hotel and there's no point at all in us taking a break if you're not going to enjoy it.'

'Worrying? Who said I was worrying?'

'You are.' As they paused at the traffic lights, Scott looked at her and smiled encouragement. She smiled back and thought of Oscar. If he knew! Zoe looked out of the window and decided he'd be on the first bus that passed his door; a highly appropriate phrase she'd borrowed from Mungo. Commitment? The marrying kind? What were those words Scott had used? *I'm not husband material.* And he wasn't, though he was more so than when he'd been here last.

They were on the by-pass now and sailing on at a great rate of knots. Once the Land Rover had got up speed it went quite fast. He'd polished it, scrubbed its wheels and despite its age it was putting up a good performance. The fact that he'd had the thought to get it cleaned must mean something, although there was still that all-pervading smell that a vet's vehicle has. It was hard to describe. To her it wasn't offensive, but other people to whom she'd given a lift from time to time always mentioned it.

Zoe glanced at Scott. God, he was handsome. That beautifully straight nose, neither too long nor too short, the curve of his mouth and that splendidly moulded chin and his strong, proud forehead. Even in old age, when everything had sagged, she guessed she'd still find him attractive. What was she doing thinking of Scott in old age? She must be mad.

Aware of her scrutiny Scott grinned. 'Looked your fill?'

Zoe, to her annoyance, blushed. She'd half a mind to ask him to take her home again. Worried about Oscar would be her excuse. Oh, no, she couldn't. Blast. All this deception was getting on her nerves. But the decision she'd made when she was pregnant that he was never to know was still the best one. She wouldn't give him the chance to walk away from both of them. Complete humiliation of that kind she did not need. If he didn't know, he couldn't do it. Nor would she give him the chance to marry her for Oscar's sake.

As they turned through the gates of the hotel she just knew she was going to have a good time. The whole of the front was floodlit and the mellow Cotswold stone façade stood the test of the exposure the lights gave. As an example of an early nineteenth-century stately home it couldn't be bettered. The wonderful symmetry of the house, the glow of lights from inside promised a weekend of sheer pleasure.

Standing in the hall they were not disappointed. Elegance and good taste went hand in hand. It was almost like being guests in someone's very beautiful home. At the discreetly placed reception desk they signed in, received their keys and made their way up the long flight of marble stairs to the first floor. As they walked up, Zoe took her chance to admire the oil paintings hanging all the way up the staircase as though they might be portraits of the ancestors of the current owners. Zoe hadn't stayed in a hotel since long before Oscar had been born and she revelled in it. She inspected her room, went into Scott's and compared his with hers, admired the luscious toiletries laid out in their bathrooms and drank in the absolute luxury of the place.

Scott said, 'Not bad. What do you think?'

'It's wonderful. I can't wait to eat. Didn't get my lunch today.'

'We can always find somewhere else if you're not satisfied.'

'Not satisfied? How can I be anything else but satisfied? It's beautiful.' She went to stand at his window and look out onto the grounds. She admired the pieces of statuary, softly lit to accentuate their classic shapes and the parkland with its floodlit trees. Close to the house itself small lights like stars illuminated the pathways and the magnificent fountain tossed water up into the night sky from a curved stone pond, lit with underwater blue spotlights. 'So romantic. It's kind of *Pride and Prejudice*, isn't it? Remember the ball they had? You can imagine the carriages arriving can't you, sweeping round the fountain to the front door. Whoever designed it was a genius. I just hope for their sakes they knew it while they were alive.'

Scott went to stand beside her. He put a hand on her shoulder. 'Some prize.'

The two of them stood looking out of the window, not speaking. Mrs Goodwood and her pigs, Samson and his agonizing pain, Lord Askew and his fox-hunting protest all seemed a million, million miles away.

The wonderful peace of the place affected them both. At the same moment they turned to each other and held out their arms. Scott rocked her gently as he hugged her, not speaking, not kissing. He stroked her lovely, gleaming black hair. He drew in a big breath to smell that sensuous perfume of hers.

'I like the perfume.'

'So do I. Birthday present.'

'I said I'd find somewhere romantic, didn't I?'

'But you didn't, it was the prize.'

'Oh yes!' He grinned at his self-conceit.

She could feel his ribs under her hands and she played them like piano keys.

'What tune are you playing?'

'Anything you choose, I can't play the piano.'

' "Moonlight Becomes You" ? "Dancing in the Rain" ? "Till We Meet Again" ?'

'They're awfully old-fashioned.'

'Meaningful, just the same.'

Zoe's stomach rumbled so loudly Scott heard it. 'Wow! I'd better get this lady fed or she might expire on me.'

They broke apart.

Zoe said. 'Half an hour.'

'Half an hour? What are you going to do? Have a nap?'

'Quarter of an hour then.' But it was twenty-five minutes before he saw her again.

He felt proud to be escorting her. He loved the elegant, wide-legged black silk trousers she wore with the short-sleeved top in a warm raspberry pink that flattered her dark looks.

She was delighted to be escorted by a man who dressed so smartly. Gone were his usual half-country half-outback clothes, replaced by a fashionable suit with a pale, pale lavender shirt and a matching tie with a grey stripe that toned with his suit exactly. He caught her looking at him and he explained the transformation by saying sotto voce, 'London tailor persuaded me. Cost me a bomb. It's not me at all.'

'Oh but it is. It's worth every penny. See the admiring looks?'

She annoyed him by her assumption that he enjoyed everyone admiring him. 'Shut up, Zoe. Table for two in the name of Spencer.' The head waiter led them to a table in the window where they could look out on to the beautiful gardens. 'I ordered Champagne.'

'That's correct, sir. It will be with you in a moment.'

Zoe waited until the waiter had left and said quietly, 'Champagne! Scott, have you gone mad?'

'I can't bear Sheilas who tell me I'm being extravagant, as though they consider themselves to be not worth a cent.'

'Ah! All I can say by way of an apology is I love being treated like this. It makes me feel special.'

'That's why I want to go out with you.'

'Thank you for that.' Zoe felt the conversation was getting too intimate so she changed the subject. 'Do you have any plans for tomorrow?'

'Oh, yes. If it's fine I thought . . .' Scott was interrupted by the arrival of the Champagne and they never did get back to discussing their plans for Saturday until Scott was saying goodnight to her in the corridor outside their rooms.

'I've had the loveliest evening of my life. Truly, I have. Thank you so much, Scott.'

'So have I. Absolutely perfect. The food, the surroundings, the ambience and especially the company. See you in the morning. Goodnight, Zoe.'

'Breakfast? Nine o'clock?'

'Fine. I'll tell you my plans for the day then. Thank you for being such a delightful friend.' He bent his head and kissed her on her lips, a firm but gentle kiss, which she felt was as good as all the passion in the world. Then Scott turned, unlocked his door and went into his room, closing the door firmly behind him.

Zoe felt almost peeved. She'd expected to have a fight on her hands. In some ways it was a disappointment. A serious disappointment. Not that she had any intention of succumbing to his charm, but it would have been a pleasure to have had the opportunity to tell him what he could do with his advances.

But then, by the time she was in bed, she decided she liked the idea of him standing off and giving her space. It was positively gentlemanly of him. She laughed at herself, switched off her bedside light and in moments was asleep.

They enjoyed each other's company all day Saturday. Not a moment was spent when Zoe wished they weren't together. They walked along a stretch of the Cotswold Way, had lunch in a wayside pub, where the local football team gathered before going off to a fixture and they could enjoy listening to their banter, they rowed on a lake, chilled to the marrow, but it was fun, had afternoon tea in an old world teashop in the High Street, and finally went back to the hotel to sit in the bar to talk.

All day there'd been intense looks between them and both of them had become embarrassed. Zoe avoided looking at him by picking up an abandoned newspaper and pretending to read it. Because she was so acutely aware of him she had difficulty concentrating on the print, so had to try very hard to make any sense of what she read. When she did sneak a look she found he was staring at her with a strange appraising look she had never seen him use before. This time it was Scott who blushed, very faintly.

'Are you wanting the paper?'

Scott shook his head.

Zoe returned to her reading and Scott to his whisky.

Eventually when she couldn't stand the tension between them any longer, common sense took over and she said, 'Is there something you're wanting to say? If so, say it.'

'I was just wishing we'd stayed together the last time . . .'

'Stayed together! That was just a blip.' She could have died. The word blip reminded her of Oscar, that was how she'd described him before he was born. A blip. 'You went straight off after Bunty and then Kate. Why ever should we have stayed together, as you call it?'

'I know now we should. I usually prefer blondes and here I am with you.' His wicked eyes sparkled and his face creased into a grin.

'Please, Scott, I'm not going to sit here and listen to this . . . I'm well aware I'm only one of a string of your conquests, but do you have to remind me so blatantly? I'm worth more than that and so are you. I'm going to my room. See you at dinner. Half past seven here in the bar?' Zoe got to her feet, flinging the newspaper on his lap. 'We're only here to take advantage of your stroke of luck with the prize draw, remember?'

She stormed off across the bar, mistook the exit to the hall, turned on her heel, came back in looking flustered then disappeared through the correct archway.

Scott watched her. So all his chickens had come home to roost and Scott Spencer found himself at a loss. Years of playing one girl off against another, flirting, bedding, teasing, enjoying the adoration, and being fully aware girls found him irresistible and playing it for all he was worth, had finally become ashes in his mouth.

He couldn't understand this new feeling he had. He'd treated her like a harlot that time, no wonder she was angry. He was ashamed of himself. Deeply ashamed. His mother dying had somehow made him different, struck a chord somewhere, made him realize he wasn't immortal, far from it. Did he really want to spend the rest of his life like some kind of ageing Romeo, as Zoe had so bluntly remarked to him that night when they went out to dinner in Barleybridge? There must surely be more to life than that.

Dinner that Saturday night was a chilly occasion. Neither of them could forget what he'd said nor her acid reply and neither of them wished to resurrect the matter. They didn't have Champagne, nor the lively chatter of the previous night. Zoe wondered how ever she was going to get through the rest of the weekend. Then Scott remembered an incident with Phil Parson's bull and before they knew it they were off down a trail of reminiscences, which took them right through to coffee and went a long way to restoring their good feelings for each other.

'We'll have a liqueur, shall we? In the bar?' Scott leaped up to pull Zoe's chair back for her and took her elbow as they left the restaurant. He caught a glimpse of the two of them in a floor-length mirror in the hall and was thrilled by how perfectly splendid they looked. He in his dark suit with a pale apricot shirt this time and coordinating tie, and she in a knee-length soft green floating thing, which swirled at her knees, with sleeves that gently flared out at the wrist. He knew she must have seen the two of them also.

'Cointreau, please, Scott.'

'Right.'

Zoe watched him standing at the bar waiting to be served, and wondered if he'd noticed the two of them in the mirror. Damn and blast the man. Damn and blast. She was succumbing just when she'd decided not to allow his charm to affect her. He walked carefully towards her balancing the two liqueurs, handed the Cointreau to her and looked as though he was about to speak, but changed his mind. Their conversation was desultory – practice matters, mothers, politics, Barleybridge, Australia. But when they went upstairs, he took her in his arms and waltzed her all the way down the corridor to their rooms.

'Scott, someone will see us!'

'And won't they be jealous?' He kissed her with more fervour than the previous night, and she knew it wouldn't have taken much encouragement on her part to find herself with an invitation to sleep in his bed.

But he quashed that idea by saying, 'We'll play it cool, huh?'

Zoe nodded. 'Let's do a tango, shall we?'

So they did, all the way along the corridor to the top of the stairs and back. They swirled and stamped their feet, Scott clicked his fingers as though he had castanets and they snapped their heads first one way and then the other.

'Oh, hell! I shall have to stop, I've run out of breath!' Zoe couldn't stop laughing.

Scott said, 'One more turn?'

'Absolutely not.'

So instead he leaned her backwards over his arm and kissed her, one hand in the small of her back, the other supporting her head. Before he released her he said, 'We do have fun together, don't we?'

'Yes. Goodnight, Scott. Thanks for a lovely day.'

Zoe went to bed, thinking it was a long time since she'd felt so carefree. She hadn't felt like this since before Scott had blithely walked away from her and gone straight into Bunty's eager arms.

Somewhat mysteriously on Sunday morning Scott insisted

they went to morning service in the cathedral. 'Be a wonderful experience for us, you'll see.' The immense building dwarfed them and proved enormously inspiring and it amused and surprised her that he could find his way around the prayer book and actually knew some of the hymns. The magnificence of the cathedral and the beauty of the Service were uplifting. It improved their spirits and released some of the tension between them. Then on to a farmer's market where Zoe picked up cheese and wines and butter for home, and they had lunch in a pub on the way back.

'I must say I've enjoyed myself this weekend and have to thank you for asking me.'

'The pleasure's all mine. The hotel was lovely, wasn't it?'

'Marvellous. Just the place to go when you want a pick-me-up.'

'Exactly.'

She'd left her car in the Practice car park. Scott said as he pulled up, 'I'll wait to make sure it'll start, then you won't be stranded.'

But it was stone cold dead. Zoe gripped the steering wheel and swore. Scott got the bonnet up, tried a few things but the engine was not having any of it. 'Must be the cold weather, or a very tired battery, and I've no jump leads.'

Zoe, suddenly reminded of her anxiety about her mother left to care for Oscar, said, 'Neither have I. I've got to get home.'

'No fret. I'll take you, it's not far.'

'No. I'll get a taxi. No need to bother.'

'You're being ridiculous. Of course I'll take you.'

Zoe accepted the inevitable. 'I could borrow my

mother's tomorrow and get the garage out in the morning.'

'Don't you have membership of anything you could call out?'

'No, never have done.'

'Well, then, your carriage awaits.'

As they drove home, Zoe said to herself, 'There's no way he's coming inside.' Even if her mother and Oscar were out, there were his toys all about the house. If he asked her whose they were she'd lie all over again and her deceptions would get more complicated by the hour. No, she'd get a lift to the bottom of the lane and walk up, it was only four houses up to her cottage, and if he offered to carry her bag she'd refuse.

The moment Scott switched off the engine she heard her mother's screams.

Chapter 12

'What's that?'

Zoe was out of the car and racing for home almost before the words were out of Scott's mouth. She reached the Whitworths' cottage and saw her mother hammering on their door screaming, 'Give him to me! Give him to me! Please let me have him.'

As Zoe reached her mother she heard a voice inside the house bellowing savagely, 'Go away, you stupid bitch!'

'Where's Oscar?'

Joan collapsed against the door at the sound of Zoe's voice. 'He's got him. He's got him.'

'Oh, my God!' Fear like she'd never known shook her like a terrier.

Scott was beside her, puzzled. 'Can't your mother get in? Haven't you a key?'

Zoe didn't know she was screaming. She stopped long enough to say, 'He's got him.'

'Who?'

'Oscar.'

'Oscar? Who's Oscar?'

But Zoe was too distressed to answer sensibly. 'He's mad. He'll kill him. Oh, God!'

Joan was now crouched by the door, feebly banging on

it and still calling hopelessly, 'Give him to me. Give him to me.'

Zoe put her hands on Joan's shoulders and shook her, demanding, 'How long has he been in there, Mum? How long?'

'An hour at least. Give him to me. Give him to me. *Please.*'

Scott, totally unable to understand what was going on, took hold of Zoe's arm. 'Tell me. Tell me.'

Zoe was gasping for breath.

'He's kidnapped him. Get the police.'

'Who's been kidnapped? I'll have to tell them who it is.'

'Oscar Savage. He's only a baby still.'

Overriding the sound of Joan begging for his return was Zoe's howling.

Scott ran down to the car for his mobile with the words 'Oscar Savage' running repeatedly through his head – he must be hers, Zoe's, she'd never said – then came racing back up the hill. 'They're coming.'

Zoe was at a front window shielding her eyes, trying to see inside. 'They're not in there.' She tried the window the other side of the front door, but the curtains were almost drawn so she couldn't see anything at all.

Scott raced round to the back and peered in the kitchen window. He was horrified to see the blond head of a child just showing above the back of the kitchen chair to which he was tied. Lounging on the other chair was a big brute of a man and there was something laid on the table, he could just see the handle. A knife perhaps?

The blood drained from his face. The man with his back to the window hadn't seen him peering in. Nor had the child because it was crying. Scott crouched down below the window to think. Calm. Positive. Crafty. That was what he had to be. Sweat was flooding his eyes as it ran down his forehead. It felt like a river was pouring down his back, wetting his shirt. Keeping low, he crept along to the back door, tried the handle but it was locked. Then on past the back door and round to a side window.

To his relief it was slightly ajar.

Small with frosted glass, the john or a pantry.

There was someone banging on a front window.

That's it, Zoe's mother, keep him thinking you're trying to get in at the front.

He squeezed in at the pantry window with no room to spare.

He knocked a loaf of bread with his foot as he slotted in but caught it halfway to the floor.

Musty smell.

Softly, softly.

Ouch! Trod on a nail.

Hold your breath.

Door's open.

Gaping hole in floor right outside door.

Floorboards up.

Get one.

Grip tight, both hands.

Gingerly across passage.

Blink sweat from eyes.

Must see.

Kitchen.

Child crying.

Blood on knife!

Floorboard. Hit man. Turned surprised. Got second heavier blow. Reeled. Groaned. Collapsed.

Child crying.

Someone banging on back door.

Key in. Open it.

Zoe! Eyes ablaze with fear. Scott pointed to the kitchen. She flew past him into kitchen, showered kisses on child. Went to pick up knife, to cut rope to release him, saw blood on blade.

Scott went to open front door to stop Zoe's mother screaming. 'I've knocked him out. It's safe to come in. The baby's all right. Get up. Come on, get up. Please.'

But she couldn't stop, she screamed and screamed and screamed. Scott patted her lightly on her cheek. 'Come on. He's OK. Zoe's got him.'

Joan gave a long, shuddering groan as she fought for control. Silent at last, but shaking in every limb, she whispered hoarsely, 'Where is she?'

'Zoe's with the baby.'

'No. Where's *she*? *Mrs Whitworth*? She was in the house, shouting.'

Scott said, 'You go in the kitchen. I'll look for her.'

He opened the door to the room with the curtain almost closed.

He was accustomed to blood for heaven's sakes, seen gallons of it in his time, but this.

This was above and beyond all.

She'd been slashed time and again. The sofa was soaked with the stuff. The carpet, her clothes. Sprays of blood decorated the wall behind like the handiwork of a demented painter. There was a ghastly, sickening smell of warm, newly shed blood.

He slammed the door shut, paused while the shock abated a little, then dashed for the kitchen.

'Go home. Go on. Do as I say. *Now*.'

Zoe had found some scissors and cut the rope fastening Oscar. She clutched the baby to her, pushed her mother in front of her, down the passage and outside. 'Lock your doors, *remember*.' Scott stood by the front door to make sure they didn't come back in. Checked his watch. Fifteen, twenty minutes yet. But then he heard stirrings in the kitchen. The knife!

Fingerprints! He squeezed past the man just coming round. Craftily Scott snatched a dry tea towel folded on the edge of the sink and grabbed the knife with it from where Zoe had dropped it. He carried it into the hall, took the mortise key from the locked front door, returned to the back of the house, took out the key in the back door, locked it behind him, raced round to the front of the cottage, placed the knife still in the tea towel by the front gate and headed for what he assumed must be Zoe's cottage.

He shouted, 'It's me, Scott.' Her mother cautiously opened the front door for him and locked it behind him when he'd entered. She'd aged a hundred years, Zoe's mother had. The baby, sobbing, was still clutched in Zoe's arms, just as he'd been when they'd run to freedom. Zoe was beside herself, rocking back and forth like an automaton.

'Wash my hands?'

All he got was a nod in the direction of the kitchen. Tea, he thought. Brandy perhaps. Both, he decided.

The brandy wasn't in the kitchen. He made tea and took the sugar in too.

'Brandy. Where's the brandy?'

Zoe, still incapable of speech, ignored him, but her mother found it in a corner cupboard in the sitting room. He poured out three glasses, and also having found a baby beaker, he poured tea and milk into it and sweetened it for the baby.

'Here, Zoe, drink this brandy. *Now.*'

She shook her head.

'*Now.*'

Her mother needed no such prompting. The brandy relaxed her and some of the colour came back into her cheeks. 'He'd been playing in the sandpit in the garden, that's all, and I'd been keeping an eye on him from the French windows and then . . . and then . . . suddenly he wasn't there.' Another sip of her brandy and she added, 'I ran out straight away but couldn't see him. Then I guessed what had happened because their front door is always open, summer and winter, but now it was closed. Zoe! I wouldn't have had it happen for the world. I truly wouldn't. Not for the world.' Tears flooded her eyes and her bottom lip trembled. 'I knew, I knew where he was and I banged and I begged till I was exhausted. I can't ever forgive myself.'

Silence fell because there was nothing to say that would ease her guilt. The baby began to slurp down his warm, sweet tea, his head pressed against Zoe's shoulder as though he couldn't bear to be parted from her.

Scott sank into a chair to drink his brandy, but he'd only taken one sip when he heard the police car arriving. 'Stay here. Don't come. I'll speak to them. Keep the door locked. In case.'

When he got outside he could hear the man hammering on the front door, and shouting obscenities through the letterbox.

A second police car arrived.

Scott explained what had happened.

'You're the child's father?'

Appalled Scott answered, 'No. No. I'm just a friend. His mother and I have been away for the weekend and his grandmother was looking after him and we've just got back and that's how we found them. But there's worse. Inside, in the room on the left at the front, there's a woman, murdered. This is the knife he used, here look.'

Zoe took Oscar with her when she went to bed; he was still so petrified he couldn't be separated from her. She'd been exhausted before in her life but never so deeply as she was this night. The emotional tension between her and Scott had been draining enough without finding Oscar tied to a chair facing a bloodied knife. When she looked back on events during the past year she should have guessed something dreadful might happen at the Whitworths, but murder!

She was so grateful for Scott. If she'd been in her right mind she'd have kissed him and clung to him before he left. He volunteered to stay the night if need be, but she really couldn't face his presence in her cottage any longer, so she'd refused. The comfort of his arms around her would have been so welcome . . . but there was Oscar to consider. He'd spent most of the time Scott was there with his face buried in her shoulder, clutching her, refusing to be parted and not eating. Perhaps as well, because whenever he was distressed whatever he ate he sicked up again.

He'd fallen asleep now, still holding on to her, but Zoe, exhausted though she was, couldn't sleep. Thoughts raced through her head without ceasing. Why on earth had her mother let him out of her sight? She knew the problem with the Whitworths. Funny Scott hadn't recognized Oscar for what he was. But then they were all traumatized and not thinking straight. Her mother had fallen asleep in her own bed, exhausted by all the emotions of the day, and knocked out by drinking on an empty stomach.

Exactly how much could she rely on her mother in the future?

But Scott! Now he must have majored in reliability. Whatever would she have done if her car had started and she'd come home alone? It didn't bear thinking about. And Mrs Whitworth. When Scott had told her Mrs Whitworth was murdered she'd seen in her mind's eye the knife laid on the table covered in blood and thought – What if he'd used it on Oscar? Thinking about blood reminded her of that time when two horse boxes had been involved in a road accident, and she'd been called out to put the badly injured horses out of their agony. She cringed inside at the thought of that night. Such beautiful animals! In such pain.

But tonight it was her in pain. She'd never acknowledged that she loved Oscar more than anyone in the world, but her reaction to what she'd gone through today had frightened her and forced her to face facts. Fear for him had shaken her rigid. Terrified her, in fact. Zoe turned over again only to find Oscar following her across the bed. So she turned back towards him and put her arms around him. She cuddled his little feet with her hands, and cherished every one of his ten little toes. She felt for his fingers and counted them to make sure he was still perfect, stroked his cheek, felt his soft breath against her palm. A tremendous peace came over Zoe and she slept.

But in the early hours she became a victim of nightmares in which Oscar and Scott featured. She was running frantically in search of the pair of them, but never quite catching them up.

Scott was at the door by quarter to eight the next morning. 'Come to take you into the Practice. Do you feel up to going into work?'

'Yes. Oscar's going to nursery. A friend from up the lane is taking him. Best keep him occupied.'

'Feeling better?'

Zoe nodded. 'He's just finishing his breakfast. I shan't be ten minutes.'

'Your mother?'

'Dead to the world.'

Scott smiled and so did she. He went to check how he looked in a long mirror in the sitting room. He'd had a bad night being so upset by the day's events. He straightened his tie, took out his comb and tidied his hair and decided he'd scrubbed up quite well considering. Bit gaunt looking around the eyes but not bad at all. Then through the mirror he saw Oscar standing behind him, watching.

Scott's body jerked with the shock. His pulse raced. His heart thumped. His eyes misted over and then cleared. He couldn't take his eyes from him. He'd had a bad night, so this was surely some strange, mystical illusion, brought about by lack of sleep. Because, Scott swallowed hard, because there was himself, a little boy all over again. A little boy with thick fair hair, bright blue eyes, *his* forehead, *his* chin, lean and bright. Surely it was seeing him through the mirror that was making him think that he . . . perhaps when he turned round the illusion would prove to be a mistake. Very, very slowly, hardly daring to face the truth, Scott turned around from the mirror and there was a little chap gravely studying . . . his father?

Scott's first word at this auspicious moment was hardly awe-inspiring. 'Hello.'

'New shoes.' Oscar pointed to his feet.

Scott admired them. 'Very nice. Do you like new shoes?'

Oscar nodded.

'I like new shoes too.'

This was a stupid conversation to be having with one's own . . . son. Surely something of importance, something memorable, should be said at such a moment. But what? She couldn't deny he was his. No way. What's more, why hadn't Zoe told him? This then was what she'd been keeping from him all these weeks.

Oscar heard his mother calling about cleaning his teeth and he disappeared upstairs. Scott paced the floor, thoughts racing through his head faster than he could comprehend them. Had he ever had a clue about Oscar and not seen it for what it was? No, he hadn't. Not even a hint of a clue. Though what was it she'd said once about being caught a 'second time'? Hell!

They came back into the sitting room together hand in hand and Scott looked at her and she knew. She knew he knew.

After a long moment he very softly asked, 'Why didn't you say?'

'Not right now. Please.'

'Zoe, are you sure he's all right to go to nursery? He had a terrible shock yesterday.'

'He isn't but it's better than having time to brood.'

'You know best.'

'Better than you, anyway.' She walked up the lane with Oscar to her friend's house and in a few minutes was back and joined him in the Land Rover. Scott could hear him screaming as she left him. Zoe was torn to shreds by his screams. She should never have expected him to go to nursery but what choice was there for her? If she stayed at home every time he was a bit down she'd never have held down a job.

'Are you sure about this? He doesn't sound any too happy?'

'What alternative have I got?'

'None, I suppose. But don't you hurt when you hear him?'

'Of course, but as I say, I can't help it. Sometimes we working mothers have to close our ears, however upset we are. I hurt inside too and shouldn't be going, but I must. It's already eight o'clock, we're late.' Zoe stared straight ahead, completely ignoring this most shattering event of his entire life.

'Not only that, you're late, *two years* late, telling me about Oscar.'

'So I am.'

'Well?' He stabbed the engine into first and with a lurch and a grind they set off down the lane. He braked hard at the junction and almost catapulted her into the wind-screen. 'Sorry!'

'Well? What would you have done about it, Scott? Walked away? Left me to it? Shaken the dust from your feet and gone without so much as a backward glance? Perhaps caught that bus Mungo talks about when he thinks of you. Oh, yes, I think so. Rather, *I know* so.'

Once clear of the junction he began to protest, but shut his mouth before the words got out. Of course he would have done . . . then. But now?

Zoe, after all her heartbreak of yesterday, couldn't face this discovery. Two years of keeping her secret, gone in one perceptive moment. But she'd always known he'd only to get a good look at Oscar to realize.

'You weren't going to tell me, were you? If I'd never come back you'd never have told me, would you?'

'No.'

'Right.' A mind-screeching thought hit him. 'Just to clear the lines, do they know back at the Practice?'

'No. When I realized how like you he was becoming I never took him back for them to see.'

A second thought hit his mind and caused him to lose his concentration. When he righted the car he asked, 'Does your mother know?'

'No, she doesn't. She'd never seen you until yesterday and she was too upset to realize anything at all. I've never known her be so genuinely upset.'

'There's absolutely no question that he *is* mine, is there?'

'Oh, no! You can't deny it.'

'I don't want to deny it.'

'Oh, right!'

But they were pulling into the Practice car park now and the conversation had to stop.

There was a van there from a garage and a mechanic looking at Zoe's engine. 'I didn't ring anyone.'

'I did. This morning before I called for you. You'd left the keys in.'

Zoe was almost blinded by her fury. 'Don't think for one moment after this morning that you are taking over my life. Because you're not. I am not in need of a prop. I've managed all this time without your help and will continue to do so. If I need a garage, I shall ring them, not you. OK?'

'Just trying to help.'

Zoe marched across to the back door and let herself in.

'Zoe!' It was Joy. 'Zoe, my dear, it was on the local radio this morning. A murder, of all things. Right next door to you. My dear, what a shock! Did you know them well? Were they friends of yours?'

'Not really, just to speak to, you know.' Zoe almost mentioned about Oscar being in there but decided against it. Telling would bring Scott's discovery even closer and she didn't want that. More deception.

The strain showing in Zoe's face worried Joy considerably. There were dark, dark circles under her eyes and frown lines on her forehead. 'Are you sure you're all right to work? Such a dreadful shock, especially after having such a lovely relaxing weekend. Was the hotel good?'

Zoe nodded. 'Yes, thanks. Best keep busy. Sorry we're late, my car wouldn't start when we got back yesterday, so Scott rang a garage first thing. Got my list?'

'Yes, here it is. Look, if you find you can't carry on, please ring in, perhaps we could put off some of your appointments until tomorrow.'

'Thanks, Joy, but I shall be all right. Best not to have time to think.'

'Perhaps you're right. But remember what I've said.'

Scott ambled in. 'He's fixed your car.' He put the keys on the desk. Zoe snatched them up and whisked herself away before anything more could be said to her.

Hardly the actions of two people in love, thought Joy. Surely they must have something going on between them though, because from what Zoe said, he appeared to have stayed the night at her cottage.

Before Scott had a chance to leave for his day's work, the two police officers from yesterday arrived.

'Ah! Mr Spencer?'

'Yes.'

'Good morning. We'd like a word about yesterday.'

Joy said, 'Use my office.'

'Thanks.' Scott led the way and closed the door behind the three of them. It was a squeeze because the two police officers must have been the tallest and widest that could be

220

found at Barleybridge police station. Briefly Scott mused that maybe they were specially kept for intimidating witnesses in murder cases and only let out as and when.

'Yesterday at Mr Whitworth's house, when you broke in, were you aware of there being someone else in the house?'

'Besides little Oscar?'

'Yes.'

'There was no one as far as I was aware. But then I never went upstairs.'

'Where did you go?'

'Like I said, I got in through the pantry window, went in the kitchen and then because Mrs Savage kept saying, "Where's Mrs Whitworth?" – I heard her shouting – I opened the door to one of the rooms at the front and saw . . . the murder.'

'Right. No other woman?'

'Absolutely not. I would have said when you questioned me if I had. But, as I say, I never went up the stairs. There could have been an army up there for all I know.'

'Had you met Mrs Whitworth before?'

'No. It was the first time I'd been to the Savages' house.'

'So that was why you thought it must be Mrs Whitworth. You assumed it was from what Mrs Savage said?'

'I did, because Mrs Savage said she'd heard her shouting after little Oscar had disappeared into their house.'

'I see.'

'Why? Is there someone else involved?'

'The murdered woman was not Mrs Whitworth, but a friend of Mr Whitworth's.'

'Oh! So where is Mrs Whitworth? He hasn't murdered her as well, has he?'

'We don't know where she is.'

Scott raised his eyebrows.

'However, thanks for your time, Mr Spencer. We'll be in touch.'

'I've had nothing to do with this at all, you know. Damn it. Like I said Zoe Savage and I had been away for the weekend. I have an account for the hotel over the weekend and a petrol bill I got on our way back. If that doesn't prove it I don't know what does.'

They ignored his protestations. 'You say the little boy they kidnapped wasn't your son?'

Scott, feeling extremely pressurized, decided to put his cards on the table. 'When I spoke to you yesterday I said he wasn't mine, and that was the truth *then* as far as I knew it. But, just this very morning I have been told he *is* mine. Sounds like a pack of lies, but it's absolutely true.'

The pair of them looked sceptically at him. The larger of the two policemen looked at his watch, implying there didn't seem to have been much time for such a moment-ous disclosure. Scott suddenly felt threatened. Had he now turned from a reliable witness into an unreliable one with secrets to hide?

'That's all for now.' They made to leave.

He hurried to his own defence before they took their leave. 'Just a moment. No one knows what I've just disclosed. It's entirely private between his mother and me.'

'Good morning, Mr Spencer. If we need you later in the day where will you be?'

'Doing the rounds of the farming community.' It crossed his mind to give them his mobile number but he decided against it. 'Ring the Practice, they'll find me.'

After they'd left he stood looking out of Joy's window. He'd had run-ins with the police back home when he was in his teens, but none of those had felt to be as threatening as this one this morning. Still, he was totally innocent, that must count for something. Pigs, he thought, which brought to mind that he should have spoken to Zoe to tell her the results of the post-mortem of the Goodwoods' pigs.

'Joy! Is Zoe down for going to the Goodwoods today?'

'Er . . . no, she isn't. She won't go because she's got a very full list. I'm not sure she should be working today, not after what happened.'

'Neither am I, but she won't be told. I'll go. I've come up with the solution about their pigs dying.'

He went there first thing. Cecil answered the door. 'Good morning, Cecil. Got the results. Is Francesca about?'

'Feeding the pigs.'

'Right! I'll go find her.'

Cecil rapidly closed the door, trapping his dressing gown as he did so. He released himself and went back to the roaring fire, his comfortable chair and the racing papers.

Scott found her in the feed shed, strategically placed in the middle of the field to facilitate the feeding of the pigs.

'Hi, Francesca.'

'Wasn't expecting you this morning. How come?' She was emptying a feed bag into a kind of state-of-the-art wheelbarrow ready for putting in the troughs.

'Results of the post-mortem say poisoning with weed killer. I'm here to find out how it's being administered. Need to inspect your feed bags.'

'There's nothing wrong with the feed. It's organic feed for organically raised pigs.'

'I'm well aware of that. Just checking something. Do you keep the shed locked?'

Francesca scoffed at the very idea. 'No! Who'd want to pinch pig feed round here? There's only me keeps pigs.'

'Well, I wasn't thinking of stealing, more interfering.' He bent down and dragged a feed bag out into the light. He examined it closely all the way round and from top to bottom. Put it back and proceeded one by one to drag them all out into the light and examine them thoroughly. 'Gotcha! Look! This one right at the back, not so easy to spot. Look!'

Francesca followed the path his finger was taking about halfway up the bag. 'Can't see anything.'

'You can. Look closer, a sort of big circle of pinpricks. Size of a dinner plate.'

Francesca dug into the back pocket of her dungarees, and brought out a filthy spectacle case from which she extracted a pair of gleaming, gold-rimmed glasses. She put them on her nose and examined the bag again. 'By hell! You're right. Who the hell's done that? What is it?'

'Pneumonia they appeared to be dying of, eh? Zoe said. But the antibiotics weren't effective and they died?'

Francesca nodded.

'Well, I think they're being poisoned, like Cecil thought.'

'Then he could be right?'

'Oh, yes. There's more to Cecil than meets the eye.'

Francesca said scathingly, 'Not much, but he could be right for once.'

'They've been injecting it into the bags, that's what the pinpricks are. I'm going to open up this bag and see what's inside. Mind if I spread it about to take a good look?'

'Here, spill it out onto this.' She dragged out an old feed bag, which she'd slit open one wet day to absorb some of the muck on her boots. 'Here, I'll spread it out.'

Scott used her knife to open the bag at the top and began shaking the feed out.

'What are you looking for?'

'Wet, brown crumbly bits. Where the feed has stuck together with whatever they've used. The crafty devils have injected the poison into the feed and then left you to give it to the pigs. That's why it's been so random.'

'No! There! Look! Look, and another. That's damp and crumbly like you said.'

'Don't touch it.'

'The nasty evil beggars.'

'Oh, yes!'

'The devils. What to do now?'

'I'll take some of these blobs and have them analysed to back up the results. We should know within the week. I'll get some plastic pots from the car. Won't be a minute.'

Francesca watched him marching up the field. If she was twenty years younger she could quite fancy him; such vigour, and so prepossessing. She saw Zoe coming through the gate. Oops! She didn't look too pleased. She could hear their raised voices but not what they said. Scott looked placatory, while Zoe looked wild with temper, gesticulating furiously.

And she was. With a finger stabbing him on his chest at every word.

'How dare you take over my case? How dare you?' Scott tried retreating but she followed his every step and he was caught backed up against the fence. 'What did you suppose I was checking on the other day when I was on the computer? It wasn't for a recipe for fairy cakes.'

'I'm so sorry. I beg your pardon. Joy said you had a full list so I thought I'd—'

'No, you didn't. You thought, she needs help, I'll show her how to solve it. Well, I have solved it. It's just that I've been too busy to get here until today. I was coming to examine the feed bags. Look.' Zoe dug in her pockets and brought out a collection of lidded, plastic pots. 'What you were going to get, are they?'

Scott agreed he was going to get what she'd had the forethought to put in her pockets.

'Well, you can go now. Go on. And never, ever try to take over a case of mine again. Bring back Dan, I say, and it won't be long before he can work. I understand he's walking about and doing quite well at it. So it'll be goodbye, Scott.' Zoe stormed off across the field to the feed shed, wanting to burst into tears but holding herself in check; her whole life was spinning out of her control.

Mrs Goodwood said, 'Good morning, Zoe. Saw the sparks flying. There's electricity between you two and no mistake, I could sense it from here.'

'Is there indeed. Now I suppose Scott has told you the story.'

'Yes. But is yours the same as his?'

'Poison. That's why the antibiotics didn't work. All the appearance of pneumonia but not that at all. Someone's getting it into the feed.'

Francesca showed her the feed Scott had tipped out. After that Zoe worked in silence, while Francesca wheeled out her barrow load of food for the troughs. She'd come back to reload before Zoe had finished.

Zoe stored the last of her samples in her pockets. 'There we are. I think it's going to be a police job, actually, you know, by the looks of it. Cecil was right after all.'

'And that's a first. If idleness was a profession he'd be at the top of the list.'

Zoe had to laugh. 'You've been too kind to him, too capable and too efficient all these years.'

'No, I married the wrong man. Make sure you don't make the same mistake. That Scott, I know he's a beggar for the girls but my God! What a wonderful life you'd have. Never two days the same. Added to which he looks gorgeous.' She caught the look of annoyance on Zoe's face and decided to say no more.

Zoe left cheerfully enough and promised results in a few days. 'Here, look, give me a hand and we'll get this lot back in the bag, and then it wants dumping at a tip somewhere. No, no, second thoughts, of course not, it must be incinerated. For heaven's sake, don't leave it lying around in case you feed it to the pigs by mistake. Check every bag before you use it, please. They do it inter-mittently to cause maximum upset, the nasty devils. And please, keep it locked up in future. As of now. This minute.'

Mrs Goodwood waved her off and Zoe strode up the field in turmoil.

She'd boil his liver if he did anything else to annoy her. Yesterday couldn't have been worse and today wasn't much better. How dare he. How dare he take over her case without so much as a consultation. She'd kill him. She would. Then she thought of Oscar and how she'd finally had to face up to how much he meant to her, and a smile spread over her face. But that brought Scott to mind again and the murderous feelings were back in strength. Still, not long to go, Dan would be fully operational shortly and it would be goodbye, Scott.

Her mobile rang. It was the nursery. 'He's been terribly sick, all his breakfast and then some. He's terribly upset this morning. I'm afraid you'll have to collect him and take him home. It's the other children, you see. We have to be so careful.'

'Of course, I'm coming straight away.' She could pick him up, take him home and hope her mother had finally surfaced from her drunken stupor.

When Oscar saw her the sun came out in his face. 'Mummy! Mummy!' He leaped upon her and clung like a limpet.

'Darling! I'd no idea he was ill. He seemed perfectly all right when he got up.'

'That's OK, Zoe. Hope he soon feels better.'

She strapped him in his seat and hurtled down the road for the cottage. Outside was a car she didn't recognize.

Zoe unstrapped Oscar and carried him to the front door. 'Mum! It's me. Oscar's not well. I've had to bring him home.'

She tried the kitchen first, and then the sitting room. Settled in an easy chair was an older man she didn't know. 'Hello. I don't think I've had the pleasure of meeting you before?'

He got to his feet. 'I'm Ivan Holt. From Magnum Percy. It's a pleasure to meet you.'

As they shook hands, Zoe said, 'I'm Zoe Savage, Joan's daughter, and this is her grandson Oscar.'

'Hello, Oscar. We've met before, haven't we? She's always talking about you. She's so proud.' The man held out his hand to shake Oscar's but he stuck his thumb in his mouth and hid his face.

'Oh! Right. And my mother? Where is she?'

'Upstairs getting ready to go out.'

Zoe tucked Oscar onto her hip and raced up the stairs. 'Mum!'

Joan was just putting her jacket on. She was made-up,

smart and apparently totally revived from her drunken stupor of the previous night.

'Mum! What's this?'

'I meant to tell you. It's Ivan downstairs.'

'So he said.'

'I'm going for my interview with the police. What's he doing home?' She pointed at Oscar as though he was something unpleasant the cat had brought in.

'He's been ill at nursery and they rang to ask me to collect him. You can't go. I've a visiting list as long as your arm and I've not even started it yet and I'm supposed to be going in for my interview too, sometime today. Can you take him with you and ask this Ivan to look after him while you do the interview? Who the hell is he anyway? I didn't know you knew anyone.'

'He's the brother of that woman I met in the church coffee shop. He's a widower, and he's very nice.'

'Well, I'm sorry, but I can't have Oscar all day. You'll *have* to take him with you. I know he's upset, but what can I do? You've recovered quickly, I must say.'

'Slept it off. I'm dreading this interview. They might trip me up. My memory of what happened is very muddled. I was so frightened. There's nothing for it, he'll have to come with us. Though he's so scared I doubt he'll come.'

'He'll have to even if he screams. I'll go down and square it with *Ivan*.' She rather over-emphasized his name and it sounded like a criticism of him, which she hadn't intended, but somehow that's how it turned out and she could have kicked herself.

'There's no need to be rude. He's nice.'

'Sorry. Sorry. I'll transfer Oscar's seat to your car.'

'No. Put it in Ivan's.'

'Oh! Right. Of course.'

'We're going for lunch afterwards, if they don't arrest me, to that new garden that's opened. They have a restaurant and we were going to stroll round the grounds and perhaps buy some plants in their shop.'

'OK. That'll please Oscar, being able to run about. Perhaps it'll help him to forget. Sorry, I can't help it. It's annoying when you've got a date.'

Joan bridled. 'I don't think it's a date . . . not yet . . . though it might be, given time.' She called downstairs, 'I'm just coming, Ivan.'

Zoe and Oscar followed her down the stairs and Zoe was just in time to see her mother give Ivan the sweetest smile that had been on her lips in years. Being so disturbed about the murder and Oscar's extreme distress about it, Zoe didn't initially realize the significance of that pleasing smile. She was just glad that her mother was drinking less and in such a good mood lately. Then, in one great illuminating flash, Zoe saw her whole life in turmoil. If things went her mother's way and Ivan got serious there'd soon be no one to look after Oscar while she worked. As for being on call in the night . . . Damn and blast the man. And from Magnum Percy too.

She waved them off with as much eagerness as she could muster, torn to shreds by the fact that Oscar was sobbing, trying to drag off his safety straps and reach her. They drove away, leaving her with the sounds of Oscar shouting, 'Mummy, Mummy!' Zoe felt guilt and despair in every fibre of her body. But what else could she do? She thought taking him to nursery would take his mind off what had happened, but in fact she had only made it worse. Life grew more bleak as the day progressed. The police were still at the Whitworths' so, having screwed down the lid on her feelings to get on with a day's work, she rolled down the window to have a word. 'Did he do it, then?'

An officer strolled across to speak. 'Don't know yet. You haven't seen Mrs Whitworth, have you?'

Puzzled, Zoe said, 'How could I have? She's dead, isn't she?'

'Well, no, she may not be. The woman we found dead in the house wasn't Mrs Whitworth. We can't find her.'

Feeling she couldn't cope with any more horror, she stammered, 'My God! Has he murdered both of them?'

'We don't know, but she isn't around.'

'If I see her I'll give you a buzz. I'm going in later today to give my statement.'

'We'll need to see the little boy too. See what he can tell us.'

'My mother's going to give her statement right now, and she has him with her. But he's only a baby and very frightened, I don't really want him to—'

'We still need to see him. He'll feel better with his mum. Anything else that strikes you as odd, let us know.'

'So what's happening to Mr Whitworth?'

'We're still holding him for questioning.'

'That's a relief.'

'Take care.'

Zoe drove away, aghast at the day she was having. A wonderful weekend and then to come home to this. It simply wasn't fair.

Chapter 13

The following morning Joy was the first one to arrive for work. She opened the back door, switching on the lights as she went, for the morning was dark and gloomy. She sniffed the air to check that the cleaning had been attended to properly and enjoyed that gorgeous addictive antiseptic smell she so loved.

She hung up her coat, and went to collect the post. There was a pile on the doormat. Heavens above, where did it all come from? Joy carried it into her office and laid it on her desk. Then she went round, switching on the lights in reception and included those new ones over the knick-knack shelves so beloved of Dan. It had been Miriam's idea to highlight them a little, in the hope of increasing trade. Though Joy had been so against the idea at the beginning and refused to have anything to do with stock control or pricing, she had to admit Dan's idea had been a good one. There was a tidy profit to be made and they needed every penny. She thought of Dan. He was coming in today, bless him.

She'd no sooner thought it than in he walked. Cautiously and stiffly and without his usual gusto, yes, but he looked more like the old Dan she knew. 'Dan! How lovely to see you.' Joy rushed across reception and kissed him on both cheeks and gave him a hug. 'My dear Dan! I'm so thrilled to see you. Well, go on then, let me see you walking.'

Dan walked right down towards the clients' chairs and back again, relying heavily on his stick. There was a little something of his old vigour and he obviously needed more physio but the improvement was unbelievable.

'Wonderful! You must have been working hard at your exercises.'

'The incentive was me longing to get back to work. You've no idea how much I've missed it. Can't bear not to be working. Added to which I miss the fresh air and meeting everybody.'

'All in good time. And how's the family? Rose and little Serena?'

Dan brought out a photograph from his top pocket. 'Here, look. I took this the first day she was home from hospital.'

Joy looked at the photograph and saw a picture of complete happiness. There was Rose, glowing with pride, sitting in a chair holding baby Serena with young Jonathan perched on the arm of the chair, leaning against his mother's shoulder and stroking the baby's head. 'Why, Dan, that's lovely. Perfectly lovely. Rose looks thinner. Is she?'

'Been quite poorly what with the Caesarean and the serious haemorrhage she had. Frankly it was hectic for a while and with me not being able to help very much . . . still, at least I had the time to give Jonathan special attention.'

'Is he fine about Serena?'

'Well, we watch him very carefully because he isn't old enough to understand about not hurting her, but he's doing fine.'

'I can't see who she's like.'

'Mercifully she takes after Rose.'

They both laughed at that. 'Well, that's a blessing then.' Joy handed him the photo back and he stored it away in his jacket pocket.

'No, don't do that, put it on the reception desk and we'll show everybody, they'll all be delighted, believe me.'

The clients started arriving and the whole building began to hum with activity. Another gloriously busy day, thought Joy. 'Take the weight off your feet, Dan. Why not sit down in here? They'll all be delighted to see you.'

'Mungo about?'

'I thought I heard him. Go have a word.'

Mungo was studying his appointments for the morning and broke off when he saw it was Dan knocking at his door.

'Dan! Come in, come in. Welcome back!' He pumped Dan's hand with enthusiasm. 'This is great. We've all missed your ugly mug about the place.'

'Mungo! Glad to see you. I'm not fully restored but I'm almost there.'

'Here, look, sit down. Sit down. How's the sleepless nights?'

'To be honest, excellent. Of course, the baby needs feeding during the night but apart from that you can almost set your watch by her. Every three hours and then out like a light. She's brilliant.'

'Good. Good. I'm glad. We'll be delighted when you're passed fit for work. Missed you.'

'About that. I've been thinking. Me coming back will mean Scott leaving. Do we really have to finish with him? Straight away that is. I might not be up to full time, and nights too at first, and I rather hoped the insurance would cover a couple more weeks. On the other hand, assuming we've kept all of our equine clients while I've been laid up, or maybe I'm flattering myself, perhaps they've thankfully crept off in the night to another practice, could we keep Scott on? We might be financially stretched for a while but I'm sure the equine side could be expanded. Scott's good with horses so perhaps we could both do farm and share the equine.'

Dan waited a full minute for Mungo to answer and when he didn't he got to his feet. 'Think about it? Mmm?'

'We could try it for a few weeks, see what happens. Trouble is, I'm never quite sure of Scott. Always have the feeling he could disappear into the sunset unexpectedly. He's done it once, might easily do it again. I'll have a think. It would mean we'd have eight full-time vets. That's a huge wage bill. Glad you're improving, Dan. Nice to see you. Don't come back before you're ready. Rose OK?' He picked up his morning appointments list and put on his reading glasses.

'Fine, absolutely fine.'

'Go see Miriam. She'll be delighted to have a chat.'

'Thanks. I will.'

Somehow or other Dan's brief visit turned into a whole morning and as he was getting into his car, Scott raced into the car park, intending to eat his lunch in the staff room. He leaped out to have a word.

'Hi, Dan! How's things?'

'Fine thanks. I've been standing quite a lot this morning, I'd be grateful to talk if you'd sit in the car with me a moment.'

'Of course.'

They chatted of this and that, about the Practice and Rose and the baby, and then Dan asked him how long he intended staying in England.

'For ever. If that's possible.'

Dan smiled. 'No sneaking home on the first bus that passes the door then?'

Scott grumbled. 'You've been talking to Mungo. That's

what he says. No. I've decided I'm staying here in good old England. In fact, I might even buy a house. Between you and me, do you think Mungo might agree to employing me full-time?'

'He might, I don't know.'

'Oh! That's what I want.'

'But anywhere would do wouldn't it, so long as it was England? It doesn't have to be Barleybridge.'

Scott looked out of the windscreen and then nodded firmly. 'Honest to God, I'd like to stay in Barleybridge.'

Dan was surprised. He turned to face Scott to assess if he was teasing. 'You mean it, don't you?'

'Oh yes! I do. Definitely. Ma left me money so I'm free as far as that is concerned. Gave Pa a bit of a jolt when he found out my sister and I had got half her money each, when he'd expected to inherit all of it. Strewth! Was he astounded! Though he didn't say a word, just looked more bewildered than usual. But there we are.'

'Right. I'm tired and Rose will be wondering where on earth I've got to. Must go.'

'How's the baby?'

'Serena's doing fine. We're thrilled.'

'Makes a difference does it when you have children?'

'Difference to what? Free time? A full night's sleep? Happiness?'

'I mean all of it. You know the inheritance thing, like looking like you or like Rose. Or knowing your genes will be carrying on. Or you've proved yourself to be a real man or something like it. Or just plain and simple pride.'

'All of that and then some. Suddenly life takes on a different meaning altogether.'

Scott by now was eating his club sandwich from the delicatessen and looking as though he'd taken root.

'You feel tremendous responsibility, I expect. Like you wouldn't do something stupid like microlite flying, or caving? Feel you can't take the risk.'

'Something like that. Yes. What's brought this on?'

Scott ignored the question. 'Fancy sharing my lunch?'

'Thanks for the offer, but Rose will have it ready for me.'

'It isn't boring, keeping to the same Sheila?'

Dan had a wry smile on his face when he said, 'No, but then I'm married to Rose not Sheila.'

'If it's the right woman, you mean.'

'Exactly. If your spirits lift and your heart does a flip when you see your beloved then . . . you've got something there and no mistake.'

'Right. I'd better let you go. I might even ask Mungo if I can buy a partnership.' Scott brushed the crumbs from his sandwich on to the floor of the car, gathered up his packaging, flung the door open and swung his long legs out of the car in preparation for leaving. Before he hoisted himself out he said, 'A few hints in Mungo's direction wouldn't go amiss, if you get the chance. Bye. Come back soon.'

Dan had to wait a moment before he could leave, as Zoe had just entered the car park and was looking for a space. Dan watched as Scott went straight across to her, she put her window down and they held a conversation both so enrapt they didn't think about Dan waiting to leave. If he could have heard what they were saying he'd have heard Scott's whole-hearted apology about upstaging her at the Goodwoods'. An apology that was gracefully accepted. Dan watched the two of them amble towards the back door still deep in conversation. Like a flash it occurred to Dan that Scott was thinking of Zoe when he talked of buying a house and staying in Barleybridge.

He asked Rose what she thought when he got home. But she was more concerned that he might have overdone things and insisted he sat down and ate lunch immediately and she'd make him a drink once she'd changed Serena.

'Where's Jonathan?'

'Asleep in his cot. I'm trying to plan it so he isn't seeing me feeding Serena as often. Jealousy, you know, that's what I'm worried about.'

'I don't think he has a jealous bone in his body.'

'I guess that's something you find out only when it's too late. So I'm doing my best.'

Rose put down a mug of coffee for him and said as she flopped in a chair, 'I wondered about Scott and Zoe too. Been away for the weekend together, and I understand from a reliable source, Scott was at pains for everyone to know they were having separate rooms. Incredibly strait-laced for him, considering his record, though that might mean he's serious for once.' Suddenly Rose sat bolt up-right and said, eyes wide and sparkling, 'Dan! You don't suppose that little Oscar is his?' She began counting on her fingers and working something out. 'It is possible, you know. And added to which, she's never brought him to the Practice, has she, for everyone to see, except when he was new. I wonder! What a turn-up for the books if I'm right.'

'Honestly, Rose. You've lived too long in Barleybridge. You're getting as bad as everyone else. As if!'

Rose wagged a finger at him. 'You might laugh, but just you wait and see.'

'Actually, come to think of it, I did wonder if they might have something between them when I watched them this morning. Just something about their body lan-guage. And . . .' He paused deliberately to tease her.

'And? Yes, go on.'

'He did ask about staying on and perhaps buying a house.'

Rose was triumphant. 'I'm right. See. I guess I am. He'll have had the most terrible shock will fancy-free Mr Scott Spencer and no mistake. On the other hand, he might not know. She might never have told him.'

'She told me she hadn't when I first came here. Said she was never going to tell the father.'

'But she must. That's not fair.'

'It's her affair, Rose, not ours.'

'I know, but gee, what a thing to do to a man. He has rights.'

Jonathan could be heard shouting from his cot, 'Mama, Mama.'

'Coming, Jonathan.' As she went up the stairs she called out, 'How can we get a look at Oscar without it being too obvious?'

'You'll do no such thing.'

'I will.'

'Rose! You mustn't!'

But she'd already reached the top of the stairs and she pretended not to hear his warning.

Rose dwelt on the matter for a few days and then the fully hatched plan came into her head at dead of night when she was sitting up in bed feeding Serena. Of course! They never had a 'do' for Jonathan's christening because she was so ill at the time, so they could have an extra special party for Serena's christening. Of course! Invite everybody! Or was she being cruel? No. Facts are facts. If she wanted a party then a party she should have and not have to ask anyone's permission. Well, she'd need Dan's cooperation but that wouldn't be difficult to get. Dan was so proud of the two of them. They'd make it a celebration of his recovery too. After all, Zoe didn't have to bring Oscar if she really didn't want to.

They invited everyone from the Practice to the christening and of course Lloyd, Rose's stepfather, would be there, as proud as any grandfather could be. Duncan, Joy, Miriam and Mungo were to be the godparents to baby Serena. Somehow Rose had tracked down a very old fine cotton christening gown in an antiques shop, which specialized in old linens. It had minute, hand-sewn pleats on the bodice and down the front, and was trimmed with exquisite broderie anglaise all down the skirt of the gown. It flowed well over thirty centimetres beyond Serena's feet and made her look positively royal. They were holding the party afterwards at the George because their own cottage was far too small for such a large number.

The invitations included Zoe, and Oscar, of course. As Zoe read hers she sighed with exasperation. Now what? Just what should she do? Take him and the news would be round like wildfire. Not take him? How unkind. With her mother spending every hour she could spare with Ivan Holt the chances of her wanting to have Oscar all Sunday afternoon were highly unlikely.

That romance had blossomed in a matter of weeks. For her mother's sake, Zoe was glad. Joan had been a widow twenty years and there must be something to Ivan that Zoe couldn't see because the bitter edge to her mother's tongue had definitely been sweetened since she'd met him. Joan still insisted there was nothing in it, but Zoe guessed differently. She turned the invitation card over and saw Rose had written on the back, 'Do come! Rose.'

Zoe gave herself twenty-four hours to think it over. She

could just go and leave Oscar with her mother. She'd have to persuade her. Although Oscar behaved very well in company, it seemed as though he already knew, even at his young age, that he had an audience to impress and with very little effort he drew people to him like bees round a honeypot, and the attention made him shine. Who does he get that from? thought Zoe. Not me. No need to ask. His father.

She stretched out on her bed and thought about Scott. He'd saved her sanity the day of the murder, for which she would be for ever in his debt. But did that mean she should take him seriously, which was apparently what he wanted? Since that day he'd tried so hard to get into her good books it was almost laughable. But she'd had two years of guarding her secret and it was desperately difficult to put that behind her and allow Oscar to be what he was: her son and his. What the hell. Scott would be like a dog with two tails if she took him. She'd better warn him. No doubt about that. Couldn't just arrive. But did she, who had been the sole support and guardian of Oscar since his conception, need to ask Scott's opinion as to whether or not Oscar should attend the christening? Of course not. If she wanted him to go then go he would without Scott's agreement or otherwise.

But was *she* ready for the big disclosure? She never would be absolutely ready for everyone to acknowledge she was yet another notch on Scott's bedpost. But Oscar couldn't be hidden for ever. So she might as well bite the bullet here and now before Oscar himself would be aware of people's shock at seeing him. She got up and leaned over his cot to look at him. She ought really to convert it into a bed now, he was far too big for a dropside cot, but that would mean he was growing up and she wanted to keep him a baby. But as sure as the sun rose in the sky every morning, he would grow up and she would have to accept that. He was so adorable right now. He was still lying as she'd left him, on his side, his covers still neatly tucked in, one hand up close to his face holding his piece of cuddly blanket to his cheek.

Zoe tentatively stroked his hair and thought about how close it had come to him being killed that day at the Whitworths'. She went cold as ice and had to choke back her cry of anguish for fear of waking him. At least that terrible time had forced her to acknowledge how precious he was to her. That had been something she'd deliberately kept buried deep down right from the day he was born, the love she bore him.

She moved the shade on her bedside lamp to a more acute angle so it wouldn't get in his eyes when he turned over. He was just like her for not liking the dark. But what else was there of her in him? Nothing that sprang immediately to mind. She left him to sleep, took the invitation card downstairs to compose an acceptance. Her pen hovered briefly, and then wrote '*Oscar and I* . . .'

She sealed and addressed the envelope, stuck a stamp on it and called to her mother, 'I'm just walking up to the post.'

'Take this letter for me, dear.' Joan, now much more caring since Ivan Holt, suggested she needed a coat. 'It's not spring yet, you know. You don't want to catch a cold. It's very late. Take care. You don't know who's about.'

'I'll be all right. Heavens above, who'd be out in our lane this time of night? Only an odd neighbour or two coming home from the pub.' Zoe turned left out of her gate and walked steadily up the hill towards the post box. She suddenly felt as though she was being watched. A brief glance over her shoulder told her she was being a fool.

There was no one there, though the shadows were deep as there was no moon and no street lights in the lane. She pressed on, telling herself she'd gone very fanciful since that final altercation of the Whitworths.

Her hand poised with the acceptance half in and half out of the letterbox, Zoe debated again and then decided yes, and stuff Scott's finer feelings, he'd have to put up with the surprise.

She set off back for the cottage, still uneasy that there might be someone about in the lane, but there was no one to be seen. So she went home, to a cup of tea and bed, still debating whether or not she'd done the right thing. Too late now. The die was cast.

She arrived at the church ten minutes before the ceremony began, dressed in her light grey suit, her hair gleaming, her make-up immaculate but discreet, her heart thumping a little. Oscar, glowing, was wearing yet another pair of new shoes because he was growing so fast, and a smart little overcoat his grandmother had bought him for the event. Unused to grown-up social occasions he was subdued and sat perched on the pew cushions, clutching cuddly blanket and watching everyone arriving.

There, sitting three pews ahead of her, was Scott. He half turned and greeted someone he knew across the aisle and Oscar spotted him. In a loud voice he said, 'Look. Scott, more new shoes! Look!' He pointed down to his shoes, thinking Scott could see through the pews.

Scott froze, half turned.

Oscar stuck a foot out into the aisle so Scott could see better.

Zoe took hold of his foot and pulled it back in saying, 'Shhh!'

Scott turned further round and saw. He whispered, 'Excuse me' to the people he was sitting with and stood up, walked back to Zoe's pew and dutifully admired Oscar's shoes.

'I didn't think—'

'You've a habit of that. Go back and sit down where you were. Please.'

The organ was at its most majestic and reaching a magnificent climax, wonderful chords pouring out and drowning any hope of a normal conversation.

'Oh, dear, how sad, someone's sat in my place. You've plenty of room in your pew. Shove up.'

Through gritted teeth Zoe said, 'No, I shan't.'

'Then I shall climb over and make an exhibition of myself.'

'Don't you dare.'

'Then shove up.'

'I have to be at the end in case Oscar needs taking out.'

'Then, let me pass.' As he squeezed by the edifice of her self-confidence, so carefully constructed before she left the house, collapsed. With pleasure? With anger? Delight? Despair? She didn't know which. But she trembled from head to foot. This was the public acceptance of what was between her and Scott and she didn't know if she could withstand the trauma. Why on earth hadn't she followed her first instincts and left Oscar at home? She'd wilfully ignored that instinct and now . . . Oscar fell off the pew with a clatter, picked himself up, squeezed past her and went to sit between them. He climbed up onto the pew without help, shuffled round and stuck out both his feet. 'Like my shoes?'

The organ went silent. Scott's loud whisper fell into the anticipatory silence. 'I do indeed. Another pair, you are a lucky boy.'

The vicar announced the first hymn but for Zoe the whole event passed by in a glorious haze.

Serena behaved beautifully, smiling benignly when the vicar carried her down the aisle for everyone to see. She was followed by lots of 'oohs' and 'aahs' so Oscar, curious, stood up on the pew seat to get a better view. As he did so he dislodged the cushion, missed his footing and fell head first, hitting his forehead on the top of the pew in front as he went down. Zoe scooped him up and rushed outside, his screams reverberating as she dashed for the open air. Zoe got as far from the church as she could before she examined the damage.

Then Scott arrived. Zoe said through gritted teeth, 'Get back in there, it's nothing to do with you. We can manage quite satisfactorily, thank you. Hush! Darling. Hush!'

She spotted a seat among the gravestones and rushed across to it. With Oscar on her lap she rocked him furiously, trying to comfort him. But he wouldn't be comforted.

'I have some sweets in my pocket. Shall I give him one?'

In desperation Zoe agreed. With the pastille in his mouth Oscar's sobs lessened. A bruise and a fair-sized swelling was coming up on his forehead. Other than that he didn't seem to be hurt.

Scott suggested a cold compress would help.

'Got one handy?'

'Well, no.'

'Then shut up.' She was so mad with him. The way he rushed out after her, everyone would think Oscar was his. Well, he was. But he wasn't. And never would be. She hugged Oscar to her and rocked him back and forth.

'He'll be sick if you rock him so fast. Slow down.'

She hadn't realized just how angry she was. Tears came,

ready for spilling over. This wasn't how it should be. All this anger against him. For Oscar's sake she swallowed back the tears and said, 'I think I'll take him straight to the George and wash his face and such, poor lamb.'

'No, wait for the photos. I've got my new digital camera, I promised Dan.'

'You're not having a photo of him. Definitely not. To look at and think of what might have been. Certainly not.' She clutched Oscar to her fiercely as though she was saving him from some terrible fate. Then the tears came, unbidden, unwanted. Nevertheless, they poured down her cheeks. She couldn't struggle with it all any more. She needed someone to take charge for her. Then Oscar started to cry again, because his dearest person in all his world was crying.

As they were inseparable, Scott decided to hug them both. So he sat beside her on the seat and hugged the two of them, speaking comfort words, caressing them with such tender care, he surprised himself.

Just as he'd succeeded in stopping the pair of them crying everyone began pouring out of the church. Everyone he knew in their best bib and tucker seeing the three of them embracing in full public view. If he'd been wearing a placard declaring Oscar was his son it couldn't have been plainer. What the hell!

'Now, dry your tears, this instant. Come on, Oscar, let go your mum and hold my hand. You can help me with my camera. Here, look, you can carry it. Careful! We'll leave her to come round, shall we? That's right, that's a good boy.'

Zoe let them go, thankful to be alone. She dried her cheeks, risked a look at herself in her compact mirror and almost died from horror. If this was what crying did to her then she'd better stop it as of now. She dried her cheeks with a tissue, patted powder on her face, re-lipsticked her mouth, put a comb through her hair and gave it that shake of the head which made it settle just right, and stood up, ready to face everyone.

To her horror, Oscar was standing beside Scott, holding the camera case as though he was photographer's assistant. The two of them together! And everyone looking at them. There'd no longer be any doubt in anyone's mind. Oh, God! Scott was busy snapping away, first one group and then another. Close by was Lloyd, buzzing about like a frantic bee, using a camcorder, determined not to miss a single moment.

Miriam and Rose were eagerly signalling to her to come to be photographed. It was the longest walk she'd ever taken to join the end of the group and be included. She found herself standing next to Letty, who was holding little John, and with Colin the other side of her. 'Your Oscar's lovely, Zoe, a little gem. We just hope our John will grow up just like him.'

'Thanks.'

The group was reorganized and Miriam pushed her into the middle and stood with her arm around her waist so there was no escape. 'He's a total sweetheart, isn't he, your Oscar? You must be proud.'

'I am.' Zoe glanced at Miriam to see if she was probing for confirmation, but Miriam was smiling at the camera.

Miriam murmured. 'Scott. I didn't realize.'

'Realize what?'

There was a slight hesitation, then very gently she said, 'That he was official photographer. Looks like he must have brought his son along to assist. Following in his father's footsteps, don't you know.'

'Oh, Miriam! Yes. He has.' Relief like she'd not known for more than two years flooded Zoe's whole being. At last it was out, this burden she'd carried so stubbornly all this time. If Miriam realized then everyone else would, and so what? she thought. I don't care. She squeezed Miriam's hand and they both smiled at each other. Miriam understood, others might not, but Miriam did. Anyone who didn't understand wasn't even worth considering.

Joy joined Miriam and Zoe. 'Aren't we lucky with the weather? Think if it had been like it was yesterday? All that rain.' She looked long and hard at Zoe, trying to read her thoughts. 'I must say, Zoe, I hardly recognized Oscar, it's so long since we saw him. Hasn't he grown? Well, children do, of course, they have a habit of it, don't they? I didn't realize he'd be talking though. You must be so proud of him. He looks gorgeous.' Then Joy wondered if she should have said that, when that was a word they all used in conjunction with the name of Scott Spencer. However, she'd said it now.

'Thank you. He's so easy to live with. Scott's amazed how much like him he is.'

'I expect so.' Joy was dumbfounded. What on earth was the answer to that comment? Frankly there wasn't one.

But Miriam expressed everyone's thoughts by saying, 'I'm glad Scott's come back and seen him. It must be lovely for you. And for him.' As an afterthought she added, 'And for Oscar.'

Is it? thought Zoe. I really don't know.

Chapter 14

The sensation at the christening party had been the realization that Scott was the father of Oscar. There'd been a lot of raised eyebrows and discussions taking place out of Zoe's hearing all the afternoon. Bunty had been shattered, both mute and pale with shock. She'd clung to Aubrey like a limpet and had to insist he took her home well before anyone else was ready to leave. The two Sarahs had said how glad they were that Kate wasn't able to come, because she'd have been shocked too, even more than they were. But Oscar was so delightful, charming, in fact 'gorgeous' might be a better word but that reminded them of Scott and so they acknowledged he was truly Scott's son. And Zoe, how did she feel? Upset by the looks of it. Ah! Well, it was a case of her chickens coming home to roost, wasn't it?

It was the sole topic of conversation at the reception desk on the Monday morning. Stephie said she couldn't believe it. 'Never in a million years would I have guessed. Never. We none of us knew anything at all about him going out with Zoe. I was astounded. Bunty, yes. Kate, yes. But Zoe! No wonder she hasn't had him in here since he was a week old. She knew we'd all realize, that's why.'

Annette said, 'I'm not surprised. Scott's gorgeous.'

'I know he is but . . . he hasn't one ounce of

commitment in him. Not one ounce. Not like my Adam. Now he is committed.' Stephie admired her engagement ring and thought about Adam. Then thought about Scott and for the thousandth time decided she couldn't cope with his overt sexual charm, day in day out. You can have too much of a good thing.

'I thought he was very committed. He spent a lot of time with little Oscar at the party.'

'Making up for lost time, I suspect.' Stephie giggled. 'I thought Zoe wasn't exactly pleased.'

'When Mungo said, "So. Is this why you came back?" I nearly died.'

Stephie confided, 'Scott didn't know you know. Not till he saw him the day after the murder.'

'Really? I thought yesterday like Mungo, that Oscar must be why he'd come back.'

Stephie whispered, 'No, she never told him.'

'No-o-o!'

Joy appeared, looking ready for battle. 'I'm quite sure that at this time in the morning you have better things to do beside gossiping. I do like to keep our private lives out of business hours, you know. It's not the thing for clients to hear about our affairs. I could hear you in my office. Please.'

After she'd left Stephie said quietly, 'She's no need to think they won't find out in quick sticks about what Zoe's been up to because they will. There's two already have mentioned it to me. Course, I pretended to know nothing about it.'

Zoe walked in from the back at this moment, asking for her list. She knew full well from their guilty faces that they'd been discussing her.

'Good morning girls, how's tricks. OK?'

'Yes, thanks. Phil Parsons needs someone to go. One of his cows has mastitis, very urgent it seemed. Blossom was almost hysterical.'

Zoe smiled. 'They're always hysterical if one of their animals is sick. You'd think it was a child taken poorly, not a cow.'

Zoe liked going to Applegate Farm. The animals were cared for with such depth of feeling. As for Blossom! She was an enigma and a half. Why on earth she'd married Phil, with his lack of hygiene and his daily wearing of a balaclava she couldn't understand. They were even more mismatched than Cecil and Francesca.

As Zoe headed for the cow byre, already in her wellingtons, because the yard had not been cleared up for years, she remembered the time when Phil's bull, Sunny Boy, pinned Scott against the wall and caved some of his ribs in and that time when Scott fell into Phil's slurry pit. She smiled to herself, just imagining how Scott would have felt, wading in cow dung right up to his chest. She wished she'd seen him.

A hurried tap-tapping of heels broke her sentimental reverie. It was Blossom coming across from the house. This morning she was dressed entirely in mauve: a sleeveless mauve top despite the cold, shiny mauve thigh-high skirt and fluffy mauve sandals, topped by her peroxided hair tied up in a bushy pony-tail with a froth of mauve and pink ribbons.

'Hi, Zoe! Phil's feeding the goats, he won't be a minute. It's Tulip. Milk yield's gone right down and this morning she's in agony. Sharp-tempered, as you can understand.'

She pushed open the byre door and led the way in. 'Be glad when they can all go outside. Here we are, look, Zoe, this is Tulip. Hello, my little Tulip, here comes Zoe, she'll make you better.' Blossom kissed Tulip's flank and then went to her head to console her.

Zoe bent to her task.

'That's a fine sight to greet a man on a morning! Your backside could win prizes!'

It was Phil coming in wearing his usual jumble of sweaters, thick shirts, old jacket and balaclava, which he was never without.

Zoe straightened up. 'That's enough of your cheek, Phil Parsons, I'm not in a show ring, thanks very much. In front of your wife too, you should be ashamed of yourself!' Phil chortled inside his balaclava, Zoe laughed and Blossom, loving the fun, joined in with, 'He's a real Romeo, is my Phil, goes after all the women. Don't you, Phil?'

He nodded his agreement but they couldn't tell if he was smiling because of his headgear. 'She's in pain and I don't like it. Hurts me right here.' He banged his chest to emphasize it.

'It's both rear quarters. Take a look. It must be agony for her. Temperature too, of course.'

Phil bent down to take a closer look, and Tulip took exception to him poking a finger at this very tenderest part of her udder. She gave an almighty kick-back with her hind leg and belted Phil on the side of his head with her hoof. He shot over backwards with the force of the kick and lay spreadeagled on the cobbled floor, stunned.

Blossom abandoned Tulip and fled to Phil's assistance. She knelt on the cobbles beside him shouting, 'Phil! Phil! Say something.' But Phil didn't answer her.

Zoe panicked. 'See what's happened to his head, go on! He copped an almighty clout.'

'He wouldn't want me to.'

'You must, his skull could be stoved in.'

'No . . . he doesn't like . . .'

Zoe, becoming increasingly agitated, pleaded forcefully with her. 'Please, Blossom, just look. He ought really to go to hospital, it could have damaged his brain.'

'I can't. I can't. He'd never forgive me.' Tears sparkled in her eyes. 'We mustn't.'

'I'll do it then.'

'No, please, I beg of you, don't take it off! You just mustn't. He won't want you to. *Please.*' When Blossom realized Zoe wasn't going to listen to her pleas, she drew in her breath with a great scream of despair.

Zoe knelt down on Phil's other side and gently lifted off his balaclava for a closer look.

It was then Zoe saw the secret Phil hid beneath the balaclava and she was horrified at what she saw. She desperately wanted to be sick, sick because she was so distressed by her almost casual removal of his balaclava, sick because his injuries appalled her. She understood now why Blossom had been so adamant.

The right-hand side of his face had been badly burned. There was no hair, no outer ear, his eye on that side had only half an eyelid and was grotesquely twisted out of place, the scars from the burn went from the side of his nose all over that side of his forehead and cheekbone and right down to his jawline. Terrible, tortuous, puckered scars, red and fiery.

Zoe was filled with compassion for him. His face was already beginning to swell from the kick.

Blossom wept.

'Phil. Phil. Answer me.' Zoe gripped his hand to shake him awake. She patted the good side of his face too, but got no response. She'd hung her jacket on a nail and she leaped up, got her mobile out and dialled 999.

'Ambulance, please. Applegate Farm. Farmer unconscious. Severe head trauma. Halfway down Short Lane on
the left-hand side, on the way to the caravan park. I'm Zoe
Savage, the vet visiting the farm. Thanks. It's urgent.'

Blossom, on her knees, begged, 'He can't go to hospital.
Please don't make him go. He doesn't want people to see
him. Please!'

'Blossom, we can't leave him like this. It's serious.'

'But think of him.'

'I am thinking of him.'

'Nobody sees him like this. I don't even. He only takes
it off in the dark. Please!'

'There's no alternative. Even if it's only concussion,
someone should see to him.'

Blossom broke down again. 'It'll kill him. It'll kill
him.'

Very quietly and at her most sympathetic, Zoe asked
how he came to be burned like this.

'Sorting out a calor gas lamp that wouldn't light and it
flared up all over his f-fa-c-e.' She covered her face with
her hands and wept again. 'Th-that's how I met him, in
the hospital, when I was n-nursing.'

'I'm so sorry, Blossom.' To give her something to do
Zoe asked her to go outside and watch for the ambulance
coming. 'They said they'd be about ten minutes.'

Before Blossom had got to her feet, Hamish appeared.
'Phil! Where's Phil?'

On seeing him, Hamish stood stock still, eyes wide with
horror, shock changing his face to grey. Even his freckles
paled. He called out in a voice full of anguish, 'Phil!'
pushed Blossom aside and knelt down in her place. 'Phil!
Phil!' It was all he could say. Time after time after time. He
touched Phil so tenderly. Stroking his arm. Patting his

254

chest. Then he bent down and kissed the damaged side of Phil's face. 'He hasn't died, has he? Say he hasn't died.'

Zoe put an arm around his shoulders. 'No, Hamish, he hasn't. Tulip kicked his head. We're waiting for the ambulance. Don't get too upset, us girls need a man in charge, you know.'

The sound of the ambulance cut through their consciousness.

'Hamish, you go with Blossom in the ambulance, she'll need someone.'

He got stiffly to his feet and, taking Blossom's arm, he moved her out of the way.

Zoe went to the ambulance men and explained about the accident, and about his ruined face. 'His wife's very upset and I think it would be a good idea if their son went with her too. That's if you wouldn't mind.'

'Course not. Poor old Phil. I've seen him with that headgear he wears and had a laugh about it. Didn't know the reason though. Nice chap, doesn't deserve that.'

After Phil had been carried away to hospital, Zoe still had poor Tulip to attend to. When she'd finished she shut the byre door behind her, went across to the house and locked up there. Then she set off back for Barleybridge, calling in at the hospital to leave the key with Blossom in Casualty.

'I've locked up for you, Blossom.'

'Bless you, there was no need. As Phil would say, we've nothing to pinch. But thanks.'

'And Phil?'

'He's beginning to come round. But they're going to give him a scan to be on the safe side.'

'Where's Hamish?'

'Locked in the lav, retching. He's so upset. I'd no idea

he relied on Phil so much, always thought it was me he needed. How wrong can you be?'

Zoe said, 'It's both of you, I expect, you know. Thank heavens he's come round. I've got to press on with my other calls. Give me a ring when there's more news, that's my mobile number.' She handed Blossom a piece of card with her number scribbled on. 'I'll let them all know at the practice. They'll be distressed. We all think a lot of Phil, you know.'

'Thank you. I will. Oh! Here's Hamish. Now, love, feeling any better?'

Hamish nodded. 'Yes, thanks.' He turned his ashen face to Zoe. 'He'll be all right, won't he?'

'Sounds like it. He's getting well looked after. You take care of Blossom. She needs you to be strong, and there's all the animals to see to. But then you're good at that, aren't you?'

Hamish nodded.

Blossom said as Zoe left, 'No one's to come to see him. Right? Understood? Definitely not. No one. They mustn't.'

Zoe raised a finger in acknowledgement of Blossom's anxiety and left, too full of emotion to speak.

Her nerves in shreds and her insides churning, halfway through the morning she rang Scott. 'Where are you?'

'Chess Gorge Farm. Why?'

'I'm just leaving Tattersall's Cop. See you in Wootton for lunch?'

'OK, then. Zoe, what's the matter?'

'Can't tell you over the phone. See you in the teashop. Half an hour?'

Zoe was there first. She sat huddled in a corner, sipping a glass of water, waiting for him. She should never have rung him. He'd begin to think she was relying on him. But she needed to speak to someone who would understand how she felt about Phil. Coming on top of everything else it had knocked her sideways. To think Phil had always been a laughing stock all the years she'd known him. If only they'd realized his reasons. If only!

While she waited for Scott she drew comfort from the lovely lace cloths on the tables, from the small delicate flower displays on each table, from the wood panelling and the beautiful blue and white chargers ranged along the top of it, the pretty original leaded windows with their soft lace draperies, and the cosy looking teapots and the delicate china in a glass display cabinet. Such a lovely old-fashioned place brought a welcome healing balm to her spirits. But the moment she heard Scott's Land Rover screeching to a halt outside, all her turmoil returned.

Scott burst into the teashop, making the doorbell not just jingle but jangle too.

He spotted her straight away, which wasn't difficult as there were only six tables. He flung himself down, breathless, and asked, 'Well, what's the matter?'

Before she knew what was happening she was crying. Instantly he was sympathetic.

'Come on, Zo, it's not like you to cry. What's happened? Is it Oscar?'

This question brought her head up with a start. She wiped her eyes and said, 'No, it is not. I do have other things in my life besides Oscar and you.'

'Right then. I'll be off.' Scott stood up. He'd had enough of her fighting him off.

'Why are you going?'

'Because you snapped at me.'

'Sorry. Don't go. I'll have tea and a poached egg on toast.'

'Not lost your appetite, then.' He went to tap on the door to the kitchen to bring out the old ladies who ran the teashop.

They were like two little hedgerow sparrows, brown, bright-eyed and perky, but very ancient.

'Oh, Mr Spencer, it's you. How nice. What can we do for you?'

They looked at him and smiled and the older one patted his arm. He explained what they wanted and the two of them peered round the curtain that shielded the kitchen door from view. 'Oh, not by yourself? We didn't realize it was you she was waiting for. She looks charming. A very wise choice. We shan't be long. Tea for two, poached eggs on toast and a slice each of flapjack? Freshly baked this morning. And the eggs were laid this morning too.' They both smiled indulgently at him, which wasn't lost on Zoe.

When he sat down again she clutched at his hand. 'Scott, hold my hand.'

'With pleasure.' He secured her hand in his and rubbed the back of hers with his thumb.

Zoe looked down at his thumb gently moving back and forth and thought how much she enjoyed him touching her, and she remembered when he was here before and they'd got carried away with their feelings for each other and Oscar had been the result. It wasn't just his strength she'd found so enthralling, it was the combination of that and his tender delicacy when he was making love which had won the day for him. That same tenderness was what she had treasured all this time. A lifetime of that would be very tempting. She'd think about it another day. Phil Parsons was more immediate.

'Well?'

'It's Phil Parsons. I went to see Tulip with mastitis and

Phil came in to see how things were progressing and he bent down to have a look and she lashed out and caught the side of his head with an almighty crack. Blossom wouldn't let me take his balaclava off but I had to insist, because he was unconscious, we had to see. Oh, God! Scott, have you ever seen him without it on? No, I don't suppose you have.'

Scott shook his head.

'I nearly died. I feel dreadful about it.'

She fell silent and Scott quietly waited, taking the chance to admire her face while she wasn't aware of him. He couldn't think why he hadn't noticed before how good-looking she was in a thoroughly wholesome kind of way. She swallowed hard and blew her nose. 'I go on about my problems and I don't know the half. At least I can walk about the world without feeling people are repulsed by my looks. Well, maybe they are but no one turns away in horror.' Before she continued she sat lost in thought, looking at Scott, trying to imagine similar scars to Phil's on his face and how she'd feel and she half reached out with her free hand to caress his face, but drew back just in time.

'Well?'

Zoe braced herself to tell him what she'd seen.

He was visibly shaken by her description. 'Poor old Phil. The times we've laughed about his balaclava.' He shook his head in disbelief. 'The times! Strewth! It makes you feel all kinds of a heel, doesn't it?'

They sat holding hands across the table, coming to terms with how they felt about Phil's face. Zoe said eventually, 'It seems to me he must have refused cosmetic surgery at the time, I'm sure they could have done something for him. It can't be right for someone to look like he does, not nowadays.'

Out of the corner of his eye Scott could see the two old ladies emerging from the kitchen. He took Zoe's hand to his lips and kissed it before he released her.

Then she looked up at Scott. If only she could rely on him. Tomorrow it could be someone else sitting here, not her, he was like that, and he'd be just as charming as he was being to her today. Her gaze fastened on his shirt, plaid, bold and colourful. She recollected the suit he'd worn at the hotel and how splendid he'd looked in his dinner jacket the night of the ball. She looked down at her two poached eggs sitting on the golden brown toast. This had been her favourite choice when her dad and she were breakfasting together. Just the two of them. They reminded her of a safe childhood and happiness, and her dad, of how much she'd loved and admired him, and of how Oscar didn't know anything at all about what it was like having a dad.

'I'm serious, you know.'

She jerked back from her reverie. 'About what?'

'You.'

She plunged a square of toast into the yolk of her egg and watched the glorious golden liquid flood her plate. 'Me?'

'You.'

'This one's double-yolked. Look.'

'Did you hear what I said? I'm serious about you. Will you give the two of us, you and me, a chance?'

'Scott, how am I going to see Phil Parsons when I know he knows I know what his face is really like? I shall be so embarrassed.'

'Think how he's feeling, which will be much worse than you, then you'll be all right.'

'Of course, yes. You can be unexpectedly wise. I'm so

distressed about laughing at him. I can't eat any more, I'm too upset. Must go. Thanks for being so kind. Here's some money to cover the bill.' She pushed away her plate. One slice of her toast and one egg untouched. Scott pushed her twenty-pound note back across the table to her.

'Please, Scott, it was me asked you to come.'

More angry than he could remember he said loudly, 'Put your bloody money away, will you? Have you heard a word of what I've been saying?'

Zoe's dark blue eyes looked straight into his. 'Take heart from the fact that you were the one I called when I was in need. More than that I cannot say.'

'Right. I'm talking about settling down here and buying a house.'

Both astounded and appalled at the idea Zoe said, 'You are?'

'Yes. With you.'

'With me!' Zoe couldn't take it in. 'You! In England?'

'Yes.'

'With me?'

Scott nodded. 'Married to you.'

She'd thought of a way out. With nothing short of relief she asked, 'But . . . what about your pa?'

'Last time I spoke to him, my sister's husband was thinking of going into partnership with him, so that's good news. He's a great chap, just needs a guiding hand now and again to stop his flights of fantasy. He's got a smaller spread about thirty miles away. He'd sell that and buy a share in Pa's.'

'So if he does, you're free?'

Scott nodded. 'Give us a chance, then?'

Zoe answered him with, 'Scott, what's really worrying me is I'm beginning to think that Oscar witnessed the murder.'

Scott laid down his knife and fork, unable to understand how she could so positively ignore him laying his heart on the line for her, and also how she'd come up with such a ridiculous idea. 'Now, Zoe, sure you're not just imagining it?'

'I'm not a fool. If you think I am then I don't know why you're asking me for a chance for the two of us.' She picked up her car keys from the table.

'Sorry! Sorry! At least eat your flapjack. The ladies will be so disappointed if you don't.'

In a quietly angry tone of voice she replied, 'I've got something more to worry about than the fragile feelings of rejection on the part of two old crones who run a pathetic teashop.'

'Zoe!'

'Sorry. I'll put it in my pocket for later.'

Which she did and left, wondering why her emotions were see-sawing up and down every five minutes. It was true what she'd said about Oscar. He'd been playing quite happily with his toys when he suddenly began stabbing Bob the Builder with a toy knife from a picnic set someone had given him, while shouting double Dutch at the top of his voice. Then, later that same Sunday, he'd talked in high-pitched gobbledegook while ramming Bob down on a cushion he was using as a bed for his toys, and holding him there while thumping him. What really alarmed her was the viciousness he was exhibiting towards Bob, who for weeks had been his favourite toy, and whose programme he adored watching on TV. She had asked at the nursery if he was being aggressive and they'd said he was. Not massively so but definitely aggressive in a way that was not normal for him.

Of course, his father wasn't concerned, not likely. That

would be asking too much. So much for being 'serious'. He'd a lot to learn about children, had Scott. So was she going to give him the chance to learn about them? Ah! That was the million dollar question.

Zoe was just about to start the car when her mobile rang. It was Blossom, saying the scan showed Phil's skull had not been fractured but they were keeping him in for a day or two as he was still very groggy and the bruising and swelling quite severe.

'Keep in touch. I'll tell Joy the news.'

It rang again almost immediately. This time it was Joy saying could she call in at Badger's Lot next? One of their house cows had gone down and they were very worried.

Still sitting in the teashop, Scott was drinking his second cup of tea. Thinking. About Zoe and Oscar. Like he'd asked Dan, didn't you get bored with the same Sheila, day in day out? Dan hadn't seemed to think so. But then he was married to Rose, who'd been startled by Oscar being his son, but hadn't shown any disapproval at all. She'd said at Serena's christening, 'You've a lovely little boy there. For his sake and yours, don't lose sight of him.' She'd kissed his cheek to reaffirm what she'd said.

But did you marry for the sake of a son? Did he need to marry at all? They could just move in with each other. Plenty did that every day of the week, fewer complications that way. Somehow though, that didn't feel absolutely honourable towards Oscar. He deserved commitment and security. He was just debating about being free as air as he'd always been when the image of Zoe's wholesome face popped into his mind and Scott decided he couldn't not marry her. It would have to be the whole thing or catching the first bus that passed his door. Which reminded him of Mungo and how many calls he had to do before he'd

263

finished for the day. This love business was causing him more problems than it had ever done. What the hell! Usually he could have a flirtation and forget it, but Zoe would keep on coming into his mind at the most inopportune times. Was this a sign that for once he was serious about his feelings for her? Or was it Oscar and the thought of being a real live father? Or was it because he'd no woman even on the back burner, never mind the front one at the moment? Was he losing his ability to attract women? Or was it because Zoe, of all people, was the one for him? He emptied his cup, looked at the teapot trying to decide if he needed another cup, and then decided he must press on.

The two old ladies came in. Scott shot to his feet, put fifteen pounds on the table for them and made for the door. 'Thank you, that was lovely. Must go.' As he opened it, they both said in their thin, reedy voices, 'She's lovely. Just right for you.'

As he revved up he could hear the two of them calling out, 'Your change, you've forgotten your change!' But he ignored them. Their need was greater than his. In his rearview mirror he could see them standing in the teashop doorway beckoning to him. In their heyday he guessed they'd have been a very attractive pair, fair-haired and blue-eyed – the sort he'd always gone for. But now it was his heyday and he'd decisions to make.

Chapter 15

A couple of nights later Zoe was on call and had been out to a farm at the end of Kirkstall Hill, one of the most remote of the farms on their books. It was five o'clock in the morning by the time she was at last driving back home, furious that it had been a wild goose chase and could well have waited until daylight. As she thankfully turned into her drive she noticed that there was a light on in the Whitworths' cottage. Her heart almost stopped.

Her mouth went dry and she relived those dreadful moments when Oscar had been locked in their cottage. She knew the police had not released Mr Whitworth because while investigating him for the murder they had unearthed a road rage incident and various other grievous bodily harm incidents and so still had him on remand. However, they had decided that the murder could not be laid at his door. So who was in the cottage? As she sat, half asleep, willing herself to get out of the car and go to bed, the light was switched off. Gone back to bed, she assumed, whoever it was. But then curiosity got the better of her and she decided to watch for a few more minutes. Maybe it was someone turning out the light because they were leaving. She heard a door shut, but it wasn't the front door because she could see that from where she sat. Then round the corner of the cottage came . . . it looked like . . .

yes . . . it was! Mrs Whitworth! Missing since the day of the murder.

Like a fool Zoe had not yet turned off her lights so in the dark depths of a country night they shone like two beacons. She'd lost sight of Mrs Whitworth for a second and then startlingly there was a rustle right by her car and almost instantly Mrs Whitworth was at the passenger door, had opened it and was climbing in.

'Get out of my car. Now! Move!' shouted Zoe at the top of her voice. She gave Mrs Whitworth a shove and at the same time tried to reach across to lever the door open again and push her out. But Mrs Whitworth, her perceptions heightened by her weeks on the run, was too fly for such a simple solution. The knife was at Zoe's throat before her fingers had closed on the door handle.

'All you've got to do is drive. Barleybridge station. Right.'

'I won't.'

'You will.'

'I won't.' She felt the prick of the blade on her throat. 'I will not take you anywhere. Just get out of my car and I won't say a word to the police about having seen you. Not a word. Cross my heart and hope to die.'

'You will. Drive me where I want to go and I shan't use this.'

'Please no.'

'Do it!' The prick at her throat was a little more positive this time. 'Nice and steady, no speeding. Don't want the police stopping us. Just drive steady. Right.'

'There's no way I'm driving anywhere. So you might as well get out . . . right now.'

Beneath the cold forcefulness of Mrs Whitworth's voice was a hint of hysteria. 'Drive! I've waited long enough for you to come back. Saw you leave, knew you'd be back. That kid of yours won't see his mum ever again if you don't do as I say. Now! Drive!'

The only way to get rid of her was to drive like she'd said, so Zoe turned the ignition key, backed out of the drive and set off to Barleybridge station.

'Changed my mind. I'm going to Weymouth station.

'Weymouth? I don't think I've enough petrol in the tank for Weymouth, I'll have to stop at the all night.'

'Don't lie. I can read petrol gauges.'

When that ruse hadn't worked Zoe decided to drive to Weymouth as best she could, taking into account her racing heart and the ice cold shivers running down her spine. The knife was still touching her throat too close to an artery for her liking. For Oscar's sake she had to do as she was told.

What Zoe didn't like was the alien smell of the woman. It was kind of earthy and sour. Each time she moved the smell came across in a wave. Fear, combined with the smell of a stranger she was fearful of, made Zoe feel sick. Every bump and swerve in the road appeared bigger and rougher than ever before, as though the car was searching out the most uneven places of its own accord. In fact, there were moments when Zoe felt it wasn't her driving the car at all.

'Where's your mobile?'

'Forgot it.'

'You are a very naughty girl. It's here, look. Charging.' Mrs Whitworth dragged it off the charger and hit it as hard as she could against the dashboard. But it was resilient and wouldn't break. The next moment it was flying through the open window and out onto the grass verge. She wound up the window and then stared straight ahead; the knife back at Zoe's throat once again.

There were a very few cars on the road at that time in the morning and they had a clear run. The rest of the journey to Weymouth was done in silence; Zoe concentrating on her driving and looking for any opportunity to get help. But none came. Not a single solitary police car. Nothing.

'Pull up before the station. Here, here will do.' She heaved her bag from under the dashboard and was about to leave when she said. 'That kid of yours. Was going to polish him off too but I couldn't do it. Not a kid like him. Too nice. Not a bloody word to a living soul, mind! Not a word!' There was a pleading note in her voice as she added, 'I need a chance. Just a chance to get away.'

'So it was you.'

'Yes. It was. There's limits. Bringing his tart home for me to see. Expecting for her to lodge with us. I was upstairs all the time while you were screaming and your mother crying. Got away through the back just as the police arrived. Come back for some clothes. I never meant for your kid to see her. He just walked in and it was too late.' She turned to look at Zoe and studied her face. 'Don't you ever do what I did, putting up with the kicking and the beatings. Drives yer mad, always hoping he wouldn't do it again, believing his promises. But he did. In spite of the promises. He's scum. Absolute godforsaken scum. And his tart was too.'

'Where are you going now?'

'As if I'd tell you.' The knife she stored away in her holdall. She opened the door and sat with her feet out on the road, the bag clutched to her chest. Mrs Whitworth appeared almost reluctant to leave the security of Zoe's car. She hesitated again. 'Should have been him I knifed, shouldn't it? Nice to talk to you. Thanks.'

Zoe watched her walk away. She didn't go into the station entrance but disappeared into the dark shadows beyond the building. Her screams of relief welled up inside but wouldn't come out. Then she began hyperventilating till her head felt to be bursting with the pressure and the sweat was pouring off her. Her phone. Her phone. She reversed by swinging the car round in the widest part of the road and set off back hell for leather down the empty roads till she came to where she thought the phone had been thrown out. She felt the same as Mrs Whitworth; dare she leave the safety of the car? She must. Right now. Torch.

Zoe's powerful torch, despite the shaking hand that guided it, sought out every blade of grass, every sweet wrapper, every cigarette end, each and every piece of the detritus of modern litter and there was the phone! It had landed on a fish and chip shop wrapper and showed up easily against the whiteness of it. She hugged it to her and raced back to the car. She locked all the doors and without even giving it a second thought she rang Scott.

He was a while before he answered. When he spoke his voice was husky with sleep.

'Scott Spencer speaking.'

'Scott!'

'Zoe?'

'It's me. Scott!'

'What you ringing me at this hour for? What time is it?'

'Six.'

'Six! It's my day off. What's the matter?' His voice was more alert now.

'Scott! I came back from a call, and she got in before I could stop her. I've just driven Mrs Whitworth to the station in Weymouth.' Her voice rose in a panic-stricken crescendo.

'Mrs Whit . . . That was a damned stupid thing to do. You should have called the police. She's a murderer.'

'She . . . held a knife to my throat. I couldn't do any other.' Zoe began sobbing.

'Zo! Oh, God! Are you at home?'

'No. I'm just outside Weymouth.'

'Just let me pull myself together and think what to do.'

'Shall I ring the police?'

'Let me *think*.'

'I'm so frightened.'

'You've driven off? She can't change her mind and get back in the car?'

'No, I'm about two miles away from the station on the Weymouth Road. Scott, I tried so hard, but what can you do with a knife at your throat?'

He heard her shriek. 'Zoe! What's up? What's happening?'

'I-I-I j-just put my hand to my throat and there's b-blood!'

'Calm down, it can't be too bad because you can speak, so she definitely hasn't actually cut your throat.'

'It's all right for you, safe at home in bed.'

'Don't try to drive, the state you're in. Ring the police and explain to them where you are. I'm coming as soon as I can. Can't come buck naked as I am. Hold tight, love, Scott will soon be there.'

Zoe said, 'Be quick.'

'Don't tell the police Oscar saw what he saw at their house. They'll rake up psychologists and the like and question him, pretending it's therapy, and make matters worse. Right?'

She clicked off her phone, took a few deep breaths and dialled 999.

Incoherent though she was, the police quickly picked up on what she was trying to tell them. 'Stay where you are, someone will be with you. Stay calm. Keep your doors locked.'

'Do you understand where I am?'

'Exactly. Flash your lights as soon as you see us coming. A blue Citroën? Right.'

It was the longest twenty minutes she'd ever spent. Oscar and Mum! She rang to reassure herself.

The first to arrive was Scott, screeching to a halt and swinging round in the road to line up behind her. They both leaped out of their vehicles and she rushed into his arms.

Scott held her tight, feeling the pounding of her heart, sensing her fear. 'Zoe! Zoe! You're safe now. Have you rung the police?' He felt her nod. 'Good. They'll be here soon and you can tell them all about it. There. There. Your mother and Oscar, are they all right?'

'I've rung. They're OK. Thank God.'

They stood another moment with Scott holding her close, then once her heart had stopped pounding quite so frantically she let go of him. Her face was streaked with her tears, and she most certainly wasn't looking her best, but he thought the look in her eyes was the very best he'd ever seen in any woman's eyes, so he held her close again and rocked her a little. 'Here, let me see your neck. Oh! It's not too bad. Hardly a scratch even.'

They heard the police siren from afar off. 'Don't let go of me.'

'I won't. Promise.'

So they stood, side by side, his arm around her shoulders.

The police listened to her story and immediately called in for reinforcements.

'It'll be the docks she'll be heading for. Or she might have doubled back to the station.'

'She said Barleybridge station to begin with then changed her mind and wanted to go to Weymouth.'

'Did you see what she was wearing?'

'It was dark and I was too frightened. But I do know she had a navy blue woolly hat on, like a fisherman wears. No pompom, all her hair tucked in. And I think a black anorak, but other than that . . . or a jacket of some kind and trousers, yes definitely dark trousers.'

Scott squeezed her shoulders to give her encouragement.

'How did she get into your car at that time in the morning?'

'I'd just come back from a call, about five and I pulled into my drive and noticed there was a light on in their cottage so I waited a minute and saw the light go off. But for whatever reason I decided to watch and see who came out, if anyone did. I thought perhaps you might have let Mr Whitworth go. Then before I knew it she came and was in the car before I could lock the doors to stop her. I couldn't do any other than drive her because she held a knife to my throat and I know, positively know, she would have used it.' Zoe shuddered.

Scott said, 'Can Miss Savage go home now? There's her little boy at home and her mother. They'll be frantic.'

'We need the car for forensics. Can you take her home?'

'Certainly. Now?'

'Yes. We'll be in touch for a statement, Miss Savage.'

Scott tightened his grip. 'I'll do your calls today. You must have the day off.'

'No calls till lunchtime with being on call all night.'

'Of course. Feeling better?'

Zoe nodded. They were passing through Barleybridge town, which was just coming back to life after the night. Zoe couldn't believe how normal everything appeared. Ordinary, everyday Barleybridge. How could it be so relaxed when she felt nothing would be the same ever again?

They pulled into the drive. Scott got out and so did she, but found her legs giving way and that she needed a hand to get into the house. Then the reality of what was about to happen struck her with such force she felt on the verge of collapse. This time her mother would realize about Scott and Oscar. She was in the kitchen getting Oscar his breakfast.

Joan shouted, 'At last you're back.' She appeared in the kitchen doorway, still in her dressing gown but showered and hair combed and looking a much younger woman than she had before she met Ivan.

'Mum, this is Scott. He's driven me home.'

'Why, hello, Scott. Do you know I haven't had a chance to thank you for saving Oscar from next door. We're for ever in your debt. I wasn't expecting visitors, you'll have to excuse me.' She gestured at her dressing gown and tightened the belt.

Zoe bent over to kiss Oscar and in her relief that he was unharmed she hugged him very tightly and didn't let him go.

'Let him eat his breakfast, dear, or he'll be late for nursery. Zoe! There's something wrong, isn't there? What's the matter? What is it? What's that blood on your neck? What have you been doing?'

'Scott will explain, but not in front of Oscar, please. He mustn't know.'

Scott guided Joan into the sitting room and sat her down to explain. He'd reached the point where Zoe had rung him when Joan's face changed first to puzzlement and then to illumination. 'Why! Oscar is the spitting image of you. Did you realize? You're . . . yes, aren't you? *Oscar's father.* Yes, you are. She's never said. Well, would you believe it.'

Scott acknowledged she was right.

'You shameless, totally shameless, male chauvinist pig. Going off to Australia as fast as your legs could carry you, leaving her, deserting her, when she was carrying your child.' Without any warning at all, Joan picked up a cushion from the sofa where she sat, stood up and beat him over the head with it. It happened to be a particularly well-stuffed one, hard and sausage-shaped, and she was putting all her strength and anger into beating him.

He tried defending himself, saying, when he had the chance, 'Honestly, I didn't know. I honestly didn't know. She never said. Never.'

But she wasn't listening. It was only when Joan's strength gave out that she sat down and cried, 'How could you? How could you? My poor Zoe. Going through all that on her own.'

Zoe came to the doorway at this moment and said, 'I never told him, Mum. He'd no idea. Don't blame Scott.'

'Don't blame him? It wasn't a virgin birth, now was it? He's to blame and he's a—'

Oscar walked in at this moment and stood looking at the three of them. There was a smear of egg yolk on his chin, and a moustache of milk on his top lip. His hair needed brushing and his pyjama trousers were beginning to slide down his legs. He appeared so small and so vulnerable with those great blue eyes of his on the brink of tears, that they all three looked at him and smiled to reassure him.

'Scott! Breakfast, Scott? Eggie and soldiers?'

'Thanks. Yes, I'd like that, if it's all right with your mummy.'

Zoe hesitated, concerned about the intimacy this would bring about. Breakfasting in a hotel was something quite different from breakfasting in her kitchen. 'Yes, of course. Mum?'

Joan was still sitting on the sofa, overcome by her realization and furious to boot. 'Me? Breakfast! Absolutely not. I'm not eating at the same table as him. How could you?'

'It isn't his fault, Mum, I never told him. He's only found out because he happened to come back to England, otherwise he would never have known. Now, I don't want it discussing in front of you-know-who. So we'll let the matter drop. Scott, you're more than welcome to stay for breakfast but we'd better phone the practice and let them know what's happened.'

While the three of them were eating breakfast together, Joan appeared and, taking a tissue from a box on the kitchen worktop, she wet it slightly under the tap and leaning over Zoe she dabbed her neck where the blood had dried, wiped it clean and then kissed her cheek. 'My dear Zoe. What you've been through. I don't know how you've coped,' she glared at Scott, 'all on your own. You should have told me, you know. And now all this, this morning. What a terrible shock. I just wish she'd killed Mr Whitworth as well, she'd have done us all a good turn.'

'Well, she didn't, Mum.' Zoe patted her hand where it lay on her shoulder.

Joan left her hand there while she said, 'Well, seeing as it appears to be a morning for revelations, now's as good a time as any to say that,' she drew in a huge breath, 'Ivan has proposed.'

Zoe got to her feet, looking completely shell-shocked. This was something she hadn't seriously anticipated. 'Mum! Honestly! Well I never. A bit sudden, don't you think?'

'At my age there isn't time for waiting and pondering, you've to make up your mind and get on with it or it'll all be too late. We're both widowed, so what's to stop us?'

Zoe drew back. 'You've accepted?'

Joan nodded. 'Yes. I have. We've not fixed a date, I said I wouldn't until I'd told you. Do you think I'm doing right?'

Scott cleared his throat and said, 'Why not? You should grab happiness while you can, that's my philosophy.'

Joan looked at him with surprise. 'How very true. You're quite right. I've not forgiven you but if Zoe says she didn't tell you then how could you know? He's a beautiful boy, the joy of my heart he is, and I shall miss him every day.'

The full impact of her mother's news hit Zoe like an avalanche. In her bewilderment she asked, 'Why, where are you going?'

Quite tenderly for her, Joan replied, 'Well, of course, dear, I shall live with Ivan in his house in Weymouth. It's lovely, just on the outskirts and very pretty. His first wife had such good taste, there'll be very few things to change, except . . . well . . . we'll see. I know it's going to be a wrench for you and quite what you'll do about his little lordship, I don't really know. But I've got to do it, darling. I really have.'

Scott looked at Zoe, realizing full well what it was going to mean to her. He could see from her face that the

ramifications of her mother's news were only just beginning to hit home.

'But what about me, eh? What about me?'

Oscar slid down from his chair and put his arms around
his mother's waist. 'Mummy! Mummy!'

Everything had happened all in one morning. Fear.
Shock. Terror. Despair. And now abandonment. She'd
kept a tight rein on herself over the murder and Oscar's
reaction to it but now, today, was more than she could
endure.

But Zoe didn't cry. She was so shattered that she was
beyond tears. Oscar cried. Joan began to cry, having
expected that her news would be met with joy, and Scott
came very close to it.

He was the first to pull himself together. 'Now, look
here, this won't do.' But his words fell on deaf ears. Joan
showed more emotion on Zoe's behalf than she'd done in
years. 'My dear, I can't help it. I can't really. I've got to do
it. I really have. I've had twenty years of loneliness and
bitterness and I can't take any more. Please understand.'

Oscar lost the will to cry any more and he sat exhausted
on Scott's lap. Scott wiped his face of tears, and offered
him his beaker. 'Here, finish your milk off. Let's cuddle
mummy, shall we?' He shifted his chair round so that
Oscar could reach her and he could put an arm around
her shoulders. 'Zoe, sweet, come on now. We'll solve it
somehow. You should be pleased for Joan to have found
someone to make her happy. Come on, now, give us a
smile.'

Zoe didn't even turn to look at them both. She stared
straight ahead. All the sweetest persuasion and assurance
in the world couldn't put a stop to her despair. This was
one thing too far for her to cope with. She'd lost all her

resilience, all her toughness and all her survival instincts.

Joan said, 'It's the shock, having to drive like that with a knife at her throat. I'm going to ring the doctor. Perhaps he'll give her a sedative. After all, she's been up half the night on top of everything else.'

Scott nodded.

'I just wish I could get my hands on her, they'd be round that woman's throat strangling the life out of her. That dreadful witch, frightening my Zoe like that. But I'm doing it, Scott, I'm marrying him. It may sound selfish, I know, but I do love him. If I was forty years younger everybody would be saying, "How wonderful for you," but because I'm older they'll think I should be the one to make the sacrifices and forgo my chance of happiness, but I won't. I'm marrying him a.s.a.p. I've always been selfish, I admit that, but that's how I am, and I see no reason to change that.' She patted Zoe's head, kissed Oscar, almost kissed Scott, but just in time recollected how she felt about him, and hurried into the hall to get the phone.

Scott heard her ask the doctor to call, then she made a further call, apparently to Ivan, and went off into the sitting room, shutting the door behind her.

'Zoe! Listen to me.' He gave her a slight shake to make her pay attention. 'Listen to me! Go to bed, the doctor's coming to give you something to make you sleep. Go upstairs to bed, please.'

But Zoe was too distraught to listen. Her hands were held to her face, and she gulped in a great breath of air every now and again. She looked totally crushed.

'Oscar and I, we're going to help you upstairs. Come on.' He stood Oscar on the floor, put a firm hand under Zoe's elbow and heaved her to her feet. 'You lead the way, Oscar, show me where Mummy sleeps.'

They climbed the narrow stairs, Oscar leading the way and Scott pushing her up step by step. Every footfall was an effort, and she clung to the handrail as though about to roll back down the stairs if she didn't.

Scott went into the bathroom to get her a drink of water while she undressed. He could hear Oscar saying, 'Mummy! Shoes off. Mummy! Please.'

But it was Scott who removed her shoes, Scott who undressed her with Oscar's help, Scott who tidied the bed for her and Scott who persuaded her to lie down. He pulled up the duvet, lifted Oscar up so he could give her a kiss and couldn't help smiling thinking of Zoe's words when the two of them kissed in front of Samson lying in pieces on the operating table. And now he'd undressed her, something he would have loved to do in the right circumstances, but it couldn't have been less romantic, their own son giving a hand. Would they never get things right?

'Doctor's on his way, Zo. Leave everything to me. I'll sort out things at the practice, don't fret.'

In acknowledgement of his generosity her hand came out from under the duvet and caressed his cheek, then she pulled the duvet right over her head to shut out the world. He thought to himself that she couldn't have looked more unattractive, tear-streaked and exhausted as she was, but the touch of her hand on his cheek was sheer bliss.

Chapter 16

A week passed with Zoe still unable to 'pull herself together', as her mother kept urging her to do. It was all she could manage to get Oscar his breakfast and ready for nursery each morning, then she retired to bed and stayed there, not eating unless her mother climbed the stairs with an attractive snack to tempt her.

'I've brought you some of the sherry trifle from yesterday. Now, now! No protesting, it's only a small portion. Ivan and I ate the rest. Sit up. And that's an order. Come along, dear. Sit up. It's not much to ask when I've trailed all the way upstairs with it. That's a good girl.'

Zoe propped herself against the bed head, spooned down the trifle as fast as she could, handed the empty dish to her mother, then slid down under the duvet again.

'What can I do to make matters better for you? If you're not careful it won't be a clean nightie you're putting on it'll be a shroud.'

'Good.'

'Right. This is it. The wedding's only three weeks away and you're going to be looking like a wraith and we don't want that, do we? It's not fair on Oscar, you know, you being like this. The poor lamb. I'm ringing the doctor again.'

'I shan't speak to him if you do.'

'No problem, as they say. I'll do the talking.' Slyly she commented, 'I can't imagine what Scott must think of you.'

'Don't tell him. I don't want him to know.'

Joan cleared her throat. 'Matter of fact, he does know. He rings every day asking.'

Zoe shot up from under the covers. 'How dare you defy my wishes! I said not to tell *anyone* what I was like.'

'Bit difficult to say you're hale and hearty, bounding with health, when you're not even going to work. He knows differently.'

'What does he want?'

'To come to see you.'

'I said I don't want anyone to see me and I don't.'

'To be honest, I feel sorry for him.'

'You? I thought you didn't like him.'

'I didn't, but I do now.'

'Oh, I see. He's won you over.'

'No, he's been *honest* with me.'

Curiosity got the better of her and Zoe asked, 'In what way?'

'He's told me all about when he was here last, and how differently he feels now than he did before.'

'If you mean he's fancying marrying me you can forget it. One marriage in the family is more than enough.' But this time Zoe didn't go back under the duvet, she stayed sitting up.

Joan sat on the edge of the bed. 'Look, Zoe, I've got a chance of happiness, why don't you see it like that with Scott? Why struggle on alone? I know he's a naughty boy for the girls, but I feel, from what he says, well . . . I'm convinced since he came back he's a changed man. It's you he wants. He says since he returned to England he's never looked at another woman, he doesn't find them interesting at all. He swears it's not because of Oscar, it's because of you. Just listen to him, Zoe, and do what I've done – grab happiness before it disappears before your very eyes and you spend the next forty years of your life full of regret. Please?'

'I'd have to love him.'

'Of course. Just like me with Ivan. One day I thought he was just OK, the very next I looked at him and thought, "Yes! Yes! He's what I've been looking for all my life. Someone like him to love and who loves me."'

'Didn't you love Dad then?'

'Not really. I thought he was a good catch and determined to marry him. I ensnared him, told him one day that if we didn't get engaged by the next weekend, I'd commit suicide. I wouldn't have done, of course, but he believed me. He was a good catch, was your dad. Money, you know, that was the key. His money and his house. And I'm doing it all over again, but this time I love him too.'

'Well!'

'Life's a gamble, Zoe. You know you're taking a risk but you take it, that's what life's about. Risk management. That's all it is. That Scott needs a lively girl, who never, ever refuses him in the bed department, one who smooths his path through life by taking charge of the nitty-gritty things, like well-ironed shirts and good meals, one who listens when he talks about his work, and one who never tells him what to do but gets her own way by making him think the decisions are all his. After all, if he's going out every blessed day to work to put a roof over your head he deserves to be taken care of. That's my philosophy. He'll be eating out of your hand inside a year, mark my words. I ought to know, I did it for years with your father.'

'Mum! Honestly!'

'Lie there and think about it. It's a good recipe, believe me.' She flounced out of the bedroom, calling over her shoulder, 'I'll pick up Oscar from nursery after Ivan and I have been ten-pin bowling. We're going this afternoon, he loves it. To my mind it's damn blasted boring and I'm no good at it and don't intend to try, but I shan't tell him that.' As an afterthought she added, 'It's a small price to pay for love.'

When her mother left the house, Zoe got out of bed and went for a shower, having decided after listening to her mother's recipe for a happy life that lying in bed day after day was doing no good at all and solving absolutely nothing. She lathered herself with her best shower gel, switched on her shower radio and listened to it, but couldn't find the energy to sing along with it like she usually did. Above the sound she heard a persistent ringing of the doorbell. Zoe knew her mother was expecting a parcel and decided to give the postman a surprise and open the door with the bath sheet wrapped around her. She switched off the shower, took hold of the bath towel and wrapped it enticingly around her sarong wise.

The postman was Scott, standing there, smiling from ear to ear, holding the parcel.

'Oops! Sorry. Didn't know if you'd be up.'

'Neither did I. I thought it was the postman.'

'It was, we met here on the doorstep. You're wet.'

'Yes. Have you time to come in?'

'Yes. Ten minutes is all I can spare.'

'OK.'

She took him into the sitting room. Scott sat on one sofa and she on the other.

His first word was, 'Well?'

'Well, what?'

'How are you?'

'Think I'm feeling better. Just a bit. Legs wobbly, though.'

'Good. Not before time. There's all kinds of rumours flying about.'

'Really?'

'Yes. Like . . . Look! Would you prefer to get dried and dressed? You're temptation personified like that, and your hair is wetting the cushions.' She watched Scott bite his bottom lip with his strong, beautiful, perfectly white teeth. Oh, God! I'm getting sentimental about him. Admiring his teeth! Whatever next. My brains must have addled.

'Tell me the rumours.'

'Is she in serious decline? Why is she taking so long to recover? There must be something more than someone holding a knife to her throat. It's not like Zoe, it isn't. She's always so tough. She isn't pregnant, is she . . . again?'

Zoe sat up. 'I do hope you scotched that idea.'

'Of course. I held up my hands and said, "Well, if she is, it's certainly not to be laid at my door." So what is it, Zo?'

'Is Dan back?'

'Doing mornings and managing quite well, though he looks knackered by lunchtime. "Come back, Zoe" is the cry on the streets.'

Zoe made a decision. 'I'll come back Monday.'

'Brilliant! Though I don't know why I'm pleased, I shall be out of a job.' Scott leaped up from his sofa and went to sit next to Zoe. He took her hand, kissed it twice and said, 'Zo, I never told you the outcome of the Goodwoods' pig poisoning episode, did I?'

'No, you didn't.' She grinned wryly. 'But I must say, you're the master of the stunning opening line.' He was uncomfortably close, however, and his thumb caressing the back of her hand like it was, back and forth, back and forth, was wonderfully soothing.

'Well, the police found evidence at Crossways, and they're being prosecuted. It's all got very nasty and the local paper's been full of it. The Farmers' Union have had their say and Mrs Goodwood has persuaded Cecil to put a lock on the feed shed. Apparently the case coming up in court has excited him so much, seeing as that was what he suspected, that he's been energized into activity. Going round boasting to all and sundry that it was him who put the police on to it.'

'I got on to it first.'

'No, you didn't, I came up with the idea first.'

'No, you didn't, I did.'

Scott pushed her hair back from her face, and kissed the wet patch it had left behind on her cheek. 'All right, then. It was you.'

'Which it was. I did the research.'

'I guessed it was poisoning first.'

'I was just too busy to get round there and prove my theory.'

'I'm going to court as a witness for the prosecution.' Scott kissed the same wet patch. 'What shower gel have you used? It smells gorgeous.'

'Keep to the subject, please.'

'Right. I really came to tell you that I've just heard on the way here, on local radio, they've caught Mrs Whitworth.'

This statement caught Zoe's attention more than his overtures to her. 'Where?'

'At Bristol airport.'

'*Bristol airport*! That poor woman. Really it was him

who killed her, though it wasn't his hand holding the knife.'

'I know. Zoe, I feel in need of a kiss.'

'I have said, keep to the point.'

'I can't, you're too tempting. Either get dressed or suffer the consequences. Can't expect a young virile chap like me to resist—'

Zoe shot to her feet, angered by his flippant remark. 'It's all very well you being irresponsible as always. I, me, have responsibilities. I'm not free to make ridiculous flirty remarks like you can. I've so much on my mind. What *is* going to happen to Oscar? My mother, married, living in Weymouth. No minder. What is going to happen to him?'

'I'm sorry. I haven't found a solution, yet.'

'No, because there isn't one.'

He glanced up at her with a speculative look on his face. 'Are you really ready to go to work on Monday? Do you want to, with the same old fire you've always had?'

Zoe stood looking down at him, thinking. 'Of course,' she said, but she didn't sound any too convincing.

Scott smiled at her and she felt dazzled by his charm. He reached out a hand. 'How about you take two weeks' holiday and take Oscar away and I could come at the weekend to see you? You've put up with a lot of late, a break would do you good.'

'Absolutely not. I'm going back, then you can find another job and things will be back to normal.'

'But they won't be, will they? There's still Oscar. All right until you're on call, but you can't expect Colin and Dan to do all the nights. In an emergency, yes, but not permanently.'

The new-found enthusiasm Zoe had briefly discovered

that morning evaporated. She slumped down on the sofa, exhausted, and stared out of the window. 'You're absolutely right. I can't go on like this, can I?'

'Could you have an au pair? Live in and such.'

'No.'

'How about the friend up the road? Would she have him? Pay her, of course.'

'No, she has a husband and three children of her own. So already the cottage is filled to bursting point without having another child staying nights. I wouldn't want that anyway, too unsettling for Oscar. He's still suffering as a result of the murder. I can't take that kind of a risk with him. I do love him, you see.'

'I know you do.'

'I didn't let myself love him like I should, not until the day of the murder and then I faced up to it, and I do, I love him.'

'You wouldn't be you if you didn't.'

'This conversation is getting mushy. For God's sake, just go and leave me alone.'

'How about a sabbatical?'

'Can't see Mungo paying for me to lounge about, can you?'

Scott got to his feet. 'Well, no, he won't. But he could pay me instead of you. Can you afford to do that?'

'I wouldn't have Mother to keep and her car to pay for so I might manage for a few weeks.'

'Just to give you a breather, mmm?'

'Sometimes you do have bright ideas.'

'Shall I broach it to Mungo for you?'

'There you are, you see, taking over as if I'm a congenital idiot. It won't do. Just go. Go on. Go.' Zoe pushed him towards the door. 'Go on.'

'OK. OK. But think about it. I won't mention a word. Not a word. Leave it to you.'

In one marvellous overwhelming flash, Zoe knew, but wouldn't for the world admit it to him, that she'd fallen in love with him, just like her mother had said. *One day I thought he was just OK, the very next I looked at him and thought 'yes!'* . . . Wham! I'm in love! So it had happened just when she least expected it. She'd test this new feeling straight away. 'I'll let you give me that kiss, that's if you want.'

Scott stopped her from saying any more by kissing her full on the mouth and she responded enthusiastically, gripping hold of him as if she'd never let him go. When they pulled away from each other, Scott groaned. 'Jeez, God Almighty! That was spectacular! "T'would ring the bells of heaven, The wildest peal for years." Where does that come from?'

Zoe laughed. 'I think you made it up! You'd better go. Right now, before it goes to your head and you make up something even more ghastly.'

'I think so too. Time I went. I want to do things right, Zo! I mean what I say. I want marriage and all the trimmings.'

'Too early for that, Scott. Come for supper tonight?'

Scott nodded and rushed away. He was driving Mungo's car at the moment as Dan was using the old Land Rover again, and he revved the engine far, far too much, roaring away down the lane giving victory salutes on the horn till he almost overshot the junction and came in for a lot of cursing from an irate driver.

Zoe winced, closed the door and then spun herself round and round till she went dizzy and had to flop on the sofa with her eyes closed till the spinning stopped.

She'd have to take the gamble like her mother had said. But it would be worth the price. Now she'd admitted she loved him, a great fountain of love roared up inside her. It took in Oscar and Scott and everyone in the whole wide world. The fountain invaded every part of her brain, her arms, her legs, her body, her very heart, till it filled her with power like she'd never known before. All her thinking of the last two years appeared muddled and confused compared to the thoughts she was having now. Clarity, that was it, clarity in her mind at last. She could think straight and she could see plain as day what she should do. All that deception and covering up about Oscar and his origins, which had so dominated her every waking moment, had gone. She'd never liked deceit and now it was gone she realized just how much her life had been dominated by it. Before, that one time with Scott, had been lust for a fantastic, sexy man, this time it was love for that man but also for the considerate man he was, the joker which was him, the sparkling effervescence of him and the tender lover she knew he could be.

Zoe jumped up, clenched her fists, raised them above her head and shouted, 'Yes!'

Several times. This was living life as it should be lived. No more keeping secrets, no more deception in defence of Oscar. She raced up the stairs, clutching the towel in her hand, turned on the shower again and standing under it, revelled in the washing away of her tangled past life to face, free as air, the years to come.

When she'd dressed she set to and converted Oscar's cot into a child's bed. Something she should have done weeks ago and couldn't. But now she could face him growing up and she was going to give him the father he should have had from the very beginning, and one day, she'd have the absolute delight of telling him who his father really was.

The father in question was balancing on his right leg, putting on his left wellington boot. He was at Applegate Farm, having received an emergency request from Blossom Parsons to attend their cows.

Both boots firmly in place, he set off across the yard. Blossom came out from the house to speak to him.

'Hi, Scott. Thanks for coming so quickly. Lovely to see you. Just like old times, isn't it? Seeing you marching across the yard. Remember the time you fell in the slurry pit? Hell! But Phil and I have laughed about that! It's another serious case of mastitis, I'm sorry to say. Zoe got Tulip better, but now Zinnia and Petunia have got it just as bad if not worse.'

'That doesn't sound any too good. How's Phil? Home yet?'

Blossom didn't answer for a moment. 'I'll tell you later. Here they are.'

Scott didn't need to do much in the way of examination, he could tell from where he stood. 'You know, Blossom, the hygiene in this cow shed is not of the best. That is one of the prime reasons for this happening.' He bent down and felt Zinnia's udder with gentle fingers, careful to avoid being kicked as Phil had been. 'It's always more prevalent when they're inside in the winter. I'll attend to these two first and then I'm going to come back either later today or tomorrow morning and have a word with Hamish about hygiene. Everywhere could be a lot cleaner, you know.' He shook his head at Blossom and then smiled at her to let her know she wasn't entirely out of his favour. But this was maddening.

When he'd finished Blossom said, 'Sorry. You know Phil, he'd rather sit talking to them than cleaning them out. Thinks that's more important. Will you come in the house?'

He was about to say no as he had done all the time he'd known the Parsons, but Scott, feeling so full of love for the human race this particular morning, readily agreed, though he did enquire as to the whereabouts of Hamish.

'He'll be in shortly for his breakfast. He won't eat till all the animals have been fed. Funny lad, but he's like that.'

Relieved, Scott answered, 'Right. Managing OK, then?'

'Yes, we are.'

The kitchen appeared not to have been touched since he was there last time. Still the chaos that was Blossom's, everywhere heaped with belongings of one kind or another, but he did notice with relief a certain air of cleanliness about the work surfaces where Blossom prepared their food. She sat herself down at the kitchen table, pushed a pile of magazines to one side to make room for her elbows and said, 'Phil's having plastic surgery. On his face. Well, his eye to begin with. Had the op yesterday afternoon, so Hamish and I are going in this afternoon to see him. He'll be all bandages so there'll be nothing to see. Zoe told you, I expect.'

'Yes, she did. She was deeply upset about it. So was I. I'd no idea.'

'You've no idea what Phil was like about it. Scared to death of anyone seeing how he looked. Daren't have the surgery done at the time. Too frightened. But he's decided now that for Hamish's sake he must. He's gone private.'

'Wow! That'll cost a packet and then some.'

Blossom patted his hand where it lay on the magazines.

She tapped the side of her nose with her index finger and said, 'Don't say a word to anyone, but we own the caravan park, you know. We never let on to anyone, ever. But we do own it. Phil bought those two fields years ago, for the land to begin with, then he realized what good access it had, so he decided he could earn more by putting caravans on it than by farming it and it's paid off. We've built toilet and shower blocks, a shop, you name it. We've a manager in and she keeps it immaculate. We're always busy with punters because the facilities are so good. So he can afford the surgery. When they've done the eye he's having the rest sorted as best they can. Wonderful surgeon, so sensitive to how Phil feels about himself.' Blossom dashed away a tear. 'He's an absolute love, he is. That's Phil I mean, not the surgeon. I'm hoping it's the start of a whole new life for him.'

'And for you. I expect Hamish is pleased.'

'Well, that's the other thing. Hamish. You remember he couldn't speak when he first came, but we never knew why? Well, we came home the night Phil got kicked and sat down here, like we are, drinking our hot chocolate before we went to bed when Hamish suddenly said, "He won't die, will he?" I said of course he won't, take more than a kick in the head to polish Phil Parsons off. Then Hamish let out such a howl of grief, like an animal it was, terrible. I managed to calm him down and asked point blank, what the matter was. I said, "You tell me right now all about how you ended up in care." Then he began telling me his story.'

Blossom leaned forward and rested her forearms on the table.

'Apparently the reason he stopped speaking was because of his stepfather. Well, I say stepfather, he'd had a succession of fathers since his own dad died but this one was a brute. Hamish's mum had a baby to him and for Hamish the baby was the most beautiful thing in the world. He could love it and care for it with no strings attached. Just pure love. He adored her. His stepfather realized this and used the baby to torture Hamish. "I'll do this, I'll do that to the baby if you don't . . ." Hamish was terrified that one day he would do what he threatened. So his stepfather's threats grew more and more outlandish and Hamish more and more terrified. Till one day the stepfather made a sexual approach to Hamish saying if he didn't do what he wanted he would kill the baby. So, Hamish scared out of his wits, agreed for the baby's sake, and then when he'd done with him the stepfather killed the baby just the same.'

Blossom's voice broke as she was speaking. She took in a deep breath and added, 'That's how Hamish ended up in care, unable to speak.' Blossom rubbed her eyes vigorously as though trying to blot out the memory.

Shocked, Scott murmured, 'We don't know the half, do we?'

'No, we don't. Still, he's told me and he's better for it, but that was why he stopped talking.'

'Poor chap. But you've sorted that for him, Mrs Parsons, it must be all the love and confidence you've given him that's helping him to heal.'

'Hope so. He appeared such an idiot at first. But he's not, you know, he has a good brain that kind of got snuffed out by fear till he almost couldn't function like a human being. Enough of me and my problems, how about you? I hear Dan's back. Will you not be staying?'

'Dodgy question that. Might. Might not. Got to wait and see.'

'I'm always surprised you're not married. Fine, up-standing man that you are. Still, there's no harm in playing the field. What's life if it isn't fun?' She grinned with something of the old Blossom he remembered.

'Exactly. Must go.' Scott stood up, wished her good morning and left.

What's life if it isn't fun? Scott repeated Blossom's words to himself and thought, Yes! She's absolutely right. Zoe and me, we'd have fun between us and with Oscar, fun every day. Life would be all sorts of brilliant colours. When Ma died everything was grey and bleak but since Zoe . . . He remembered her kiss as he left. If she wouldn't have him he'd go home to the sheep station and bury himself there for ever. A living death. What was life if it wasn't for living? Zoe took possession of his mind again. That kiss of hers. He remembered the passion in it and felt sure she'd fallen in love with him. He'd go back there in his lunch hour and ask her, no tell her, she must marry him.

Scott glanced at his watch, five minutes past twelve. Damn and blast it, he'd go back there now for another one. But . . . Yes, he would. Hang his calls. They'd have to wait.

He rang the doorbell and went straight in. He found her in the kitchen rolling pastry. The spring sun was shining through the window right on to her and her floury hands and the floury table. He was shocked to realize how thin she'd become. She looked up surprised. The dark circles round her eyes were still there.

'You're early for supper, it's only lunchtime.'

'Just popped back for another kiss like the last one. Could you manage it, do you think?'

She gripped hold of the rolling pin, and for a nano-second he thought she was going to hit him with it. Then she put it down very, very slowly and turned towards him. 'If I try really hard I *might* manage another one. Would you like that?'

Scott didn't answer.

'Well?'

'Zoe Savage. Would you marry me, please?'

'Certainly.'

'I know it's a bit sudden but I mean every word I say . . . so if you could possibly find your way to—'

'Certainly.'

'The last thing in the world I want to do is go bury myself at home in Australia, it would be like a living death, but I'm going to do that if you won't have me. But what I most want is to marry you because I love you, and I want to begin being a father to Oscar and perhaps in time—'

'Certainly.'

'You see I love you so very much. Would you like to think about it?'

'I've said "certainly" three times, Scott.'

The realization that she actually wanted to marry him dawned on Scott and he stood open-mouthed, gazing at her.

'But not until after my mother's wedding. We'll get that over first and then—'

'Zo!'

'When we're married I shall stop working and stay at home, making a life for you and looking after Oscar like I've never had the chance to do before. Right at this moment he needs me more than he ever has.'

'You will?'

'Yes. I shall rely on you to keep the roof over our heads. Bring in the money, you know.'

'Of course. Of course. That suits me absolutely.'

'And Scott Spencer, if you take one single look at another woman from today, you can say your prayers.'

'What?'

'I mean it. When I marry you it's for *ever*. One single look and it's . . .' She drew her finger across her throat. 'And I'm not joking.'

'Ouch! But Zo, it's the same for me. For ever. That's how I feel. That's what I came back to tell you.' Scott looked at his watch. 'God almighty! I should be at Lord Askew's.' He set off for the front door, came back in, kissed her with gutsy fervour, went out, returned for his mobile, dusted the flour off it, kissed her again and left.

Zoe shuddered, as the door swung shut behind him. She cringed as he started up Mungo's car and sent up a prayer as he raced away. There was one thing about it: life would never be boring with Scott.